The Sunrise Girl

Dragonfly Publishing

LISA WOLSTENHOLME

Third Edition published by Dragonfly Publishing, December 2021

Copyright © 2021 Lisa Wolstenholme

This is a work of fiction. Names, characters, businesses, places, events and incidents are either the products of the author's imagination or used in a fictitious manner. Any resemblance to actual persons, living or dead, or actual events is purely coincidental.

Because of the dynamic nature of the Internet, any web addresses or links contained in this book may have changed since publication and may no longer be valid. The views expressed in this work are solely those of the authors and do not necessarily reflect the views of the publisher and the publisher hereby disclaims any responsibility for them.

National Library of Australia
Cataloguing-in-Publication data:
> The Sunrise Girl/Dragonfly Publishing

ISBN: (sc) 978-0-6453505-0-0
general – fiction

Dragonfly Publishing books may be ordered through online booksellers or by contacting:
> info@dragonflypublishing.com.au
> www.dragonflypublishing.com.au

DEDICATIONS

For Mark, Annabel, Yvette, Shannon, Tabetha, Helen and Glen.
This book wouldn't have existed without you x

CHAPTER 1 – BEFORE SUNRISE

'Say something, Joe. Please.' I can barely look at him.

We are at an impasse, the last few hours spent shouting, swearing and slinging insults and accusations at each other, culminating in the argument to end them all.

'Say what, Lucy? That it's okay; I forgive you; don't worry about it? *You've got to be fucking joking!*'

Joe's tall, proud stature shrivels before me. I edge towards him and with trembling fingers lightly touch his shoulder, desperate to build a bridge between us, but he shrugs me away.

'Is this what you want?' he says, swinging around, his swollen, bloodshot eyes and tear-stained face presented for my inspection. 'You want my forgiveness because you're *bored*?'

'I... I'm sorry,' I reply.

'*Sorry?* You're *sorry*? Christ, Lucy, *sorry* doesn't even begin to make up for what you're putting me through!' His face contorts as crimson anger spreads over it. Round eight or nine of this trial of my making begins.

Joe, well versed in matters relating to law, is my victim *and* my prosecutor, accusing me of a heinous crime against him. This nightmare will not come to a satisfactory end, though. I am guilty as charged, and we both know it. What can I say or do to appease him or justify what I've done? My hard-working, loyal husband of almost eight years has discovered I am a fraud. One who in his words is, 'self-obsessed and behaving like an irresponsible, insatiable eighteen-year-old.' There is no happy comeback from this.

'You selfish, heartless bitch,' he says, fists and jaw clenched. 'You and that slut of a friend of yours! I bet she put you up to this!'

'*What?* What the f— How *dare* you!' I reply, seething from head to toe. 'For your information, *she* was the one who encouraged me to stay with you... against my better judgement!'

'What did you say?'

'You know damn well what I said!' I hiss, poised to strike.

'I can't believe I put up with this shit for so long. I mean... the last seven years of my life... they've been a fucking joke! *Seven years, Lucy*! I thought you'd change once we settled down, but I should've known. You and that whore. The only thing you two can commit to is partying. You and Emma, you—' Joe spins around and punches the wall hard, roaring with fury and pain as plaster and fist collide. '*Happy now?*'

The punch winds me too. The air between us thickens with rage and despair.

'Your hand... it's bleeding,' I point at his wounded fist. His handsome face, blotchy and damp from tears of frustration and anguish, is hard and stony.

'I'm done here,' Joe says growling, striding past me and out of our sparse bedroom. The whole house shakes as he slams the spare room door. I should go after him and convince him to talk it through, only, he's an impenetrable cave when he's like this. And I'm reeling from his vicious attack on Em.

He emerges moments later and moves towards the top of the

staircase. He's wiped away his tears and grief, replaced them with pursed lips and fiery eyes.

'Joe, I—' I reach for him.

'Fuck off!'

He swings around, but instead of deflecting my outstretched arm, his hand slaps hard against my face.

Time stops.

Joe stands frozen before me, eyes wide, jaw gaping. My cheek prickles as the sting sets in and hot salty tears tumble uncensored down them.

He *hit* me.

My mind whirs.

'You bastard! Get the fuck out! I hate you! I hate you!' I push against him raining blow upon blow against his chest as my venom pours out.

CHAPTER 2 – TWO YEARS LATER

Sunlight seeps through wafer-thin curtains, kissing my cheek with a warm caress as distant knocking calls me from slumber.

'Joe,' I groan rolling over towards him, eyes still closed. 'Someone's at the door.'

He doesn't answer.

'Joe!' I reach over to shove him, but my hand falls flat on the duvet.

'Joe?'

A thousand buffalos stampede over my chest and I bolt upright, gasping for air. Beads of sweat pool and trickle from my temples like tributaries, and I can't—I can't breathe.

Moments feel like hours until the veil between reality and nightmare finally lifts. Pulling the covers over my head, I curl up foetal-like, cocooning myself in blankets and guilt.

And so begins another shitty day. Forever engrained in my psyche and punishing me daily ever since the fifteenth of May 2009, the day I killed my husband.

'You *have* to come tonight!' Em says, her high-pitched tone creating the perfect whine down the phone. 'You can't keep shutting yourself off like this. It's been over two years now.'

It's pointless protesting. Em will not miss an opportunity to go out and dance the night away, and her 34th birthday is as good an excuse as any, only it's just not my scene anymore. I'm better off in my cave. Safe. Leashed. Watching mindless TV with only my wayward thoughts for company.

Em, has been my best friend since high school. Outgoing, popular and an absolute man-magnet, she was, still is, the life and soul of the party, and I was her wing woman.

'Two peas in a pod,' my mum used to say. At least, that's how it used to be.

'Luce!' Em barks, bringing me back. 'You are still coming, aren't you?'

'Yes,' I sigh, resigning myself to being conquered by the Queen of Party.

'Good. I'll be round yours at six-thirty to get ready, and we'll get a taxi to the city from your place. It's still okay for me to sleep over, isn't it?'

'Sure... like I have a choice.' My sarcasm goes unnoticed.

'Great. I'll see you later. Oh, and don't forget my present.'

She ends the call on a high, but expectant note. Good job she can't see my eyes rolling.

Em tuts as she picks up my jeans.

'Seriously?' Her glare speaks volumes. 'We're going clubbing later!' She throws them on the bed, scowling.

'I never said anything about clubbing,' I protest.

'We'll see about that,' she says, lips pursed.

Sighing, I rummage through my wardrobe and pick out a red knee-length skirt and hold it to my hips. 'This?'

Her expression softens. She strides over, and without a word wraps her arms around me and the skirt. A wisp of glossy black straightened hair tickles the side of my cheek, the heady mix of Calvin Klein perfume and hair lacquer drifting up my nostrils.

'It won't be the same if you're not there. You know that, right?'

She strokes the back of my head with French polished nails.

'Besides, you haven't had a good night out since—' Drawing in a breath, she corrects herself and whispers, 'Sorry Luce'.

'It's okay. Honestly.' I give her a squeeze, needing to move on from the discomfort of two-year-old hurts threatening to seep through the cracks in my already thinned armour.

Em releases me, planting a soft, reassuring kiss on my cheek.

'I know you said it's still early days, but it really is time to put yourself out there again. Two years is a long time to be grieving.'

'I know,' I say, acknowledging words spoken many times, offering up a faux smile. It does the trick and her flawlessly made-up, smoky-brown eyes light up.

'So, you'll come clubbing?'

'Fine,' I say with a groan. 'But I'll wear what I want to,' and turn my back so she can't see the tears welling.

'At least put something sassier on. For me?'

I spin around to face her about to plead my case, but she's one step ahead, searching through my clothes and eventually pulling out a relic from the old days.

'This'll do,' she says, chucking a strappy yellow dress my way.

Em, as always, looks gorgeous in a short purple number with matching stilettos. My statuesque mocha-skinned bestie looks every bit the trendy girl about town. I'm lucky if I'd make it through the door at a kids' party.

Our waiting taxi honks its horn as I put final touches of mascara on.

Em scans me up and down, nodding her approval, but I can guess what she's thinking: C+ for effort. I still look unkempt, lucky if I pass for forty-three and not my actual thirty-three years. My face shows signs of decay like a once-favoured necklace tarnished from neglect: sallow skin; blue eyes dimmed from lack of sleep and too much thinking; and hair, once my crowning glory of sleek shoulder-length brown tendrils, now hanging twig-like around skinny shoulders. You'd never guess I was Em's partner-in-crime.

Thankfully, my fluttering nerves have been quelled by several glasses of cheap SSB, courtesy of Em. But it does little to stop the sense of foreboding rattling within as I lock the front door and get into the taxi.

The downtown city beckons us with illuminated streets buzzing with boozed-up revellers. We meet up with friends and work colleagues at The Wallow, a wine bar in the fashionable Eastern part of the city. Most are Em's workmates, but there's a couple of girls from school and college who we both know, so luckily, I'm not short of people to talk to. But the fluttering in my gut returns with a vengeance as we head towards the crowded bar.

In the distant days before Joe and married life, this would have been a regular hangout for me. But the bars and clubs of downtown Norwich are only an occasional sight for my tired eyes to behold these days.

After sorting out drinks we seat ourselves around the largest table we can find, its black wooden chairs not designed for the long-haul. Such a pretentious little bar: gleaming glass racks lined with bottles of overpriced wines, spirits and liqueurs; clientele who dress in racier versions of their Sunday best, flashing credit cards and cash around like their coat of arms, voices always raised. Its saving grace is the sleek black Grand Piano housed in the far corner, a pianist tinkling erratically on the keys creating a jazz-like ambience. I'm out-of-place here, my discomfort surely obvious for all to see.

After meeting and greeting her fellow partygoers, Em plops herself down beside me, but the cool, calm exterior I've been faking quickly fades, giving way to fidgeting and clammy hands.

Glancing around the table, I catch one of our old college friends throwing me the 'pity look'. I pretend not to notice, taking a huge swig of wine to bury any errant feelings that may threaten to pop out.

'I need to pee,' I whisper to Em, heading off to seek solace in the ladies' toilets.

When I return, our table is surrounded by a pack of post-pubescent males, and Em's revelling in the attention. It's only been a few weeks since she split from her last boyfriend, but Em's not a keeper. As soon as commitment is on the cards, the 'current' swiftly becomes the 'ex', left choking on dust as she hot-foots it out of the relationship.

To my annoyance, my seat has been taken by a grown-up version of Dennis the Menace, sporting a blue Ralph Lauren polo shirt instead of Dennis's trademark red and black jumper. Em is oblivious, engrossed in a Greek Demi-god to her right. My cheeks heat up like a halogen hob as I edge towards Dennis.

'Erm... sorry, you seem to have taken my seat,' I say, stammering.

Smiling, he looks up at me.

'I know.'

He eyes me up and down, a brazen act, but I just stand there open-mouthed, stuck for a clever response.

'Matt,' he says in a thick Northern accent, breaking the silence and extending his hand towards me, throwing me further off guard.

'Lucy,' I reply, politely shaking his hand and inwardly chastising myself for telling him my real name. 'So... err, my seat?'

'Oh, sure.'

He stands and gestures for me to sit.

'Nice to meet you, Lucy. Can I get you a drink?'

'Yeah. Umm... thanks,' I reply, 'Bacardi Breezer, please,' and gulp down the remainder of my wine in readiness.

'Be right back!' He smiles like the cat who just got the cream.

I *know* that look.

As Matt heads over to the bar, Em jabs me in the side.

'I think he likes you. He's been eyeing you up since we got here!'

'I'm not interested,' I fire back.

'Oh, for God's sake, Luce! Have a bit of fun for once!' she scoffs. 'They're from out of town, so we won't see them again after tonight.' Her eyes light up and she giggles, gearing herself up for a playful night.

Em's guy grabs her arm, pulling her back towards him. She winks and turns to face him. I know *that* look too. Queen Party is on the pull.

Waiting for Matt's return, I contemplate how to give him the flick without being too obvious. Before I've had a chance to concoct a cunning plan, he's back by my side, Breezer and Corona in hand.

'Cheers,' I say, raising a salute, and take a swig, gulping down the cold fizzy liquid hoping it will soon get me tipsy enough to not give a shit.

'Cheers.' He says, tilting his beer towards me, and perches on the edge of the table. 'So, whose party is it?'

'Em's,' I gesture towards her with my bottle. 'Her 34th birthday.'

No reaction.

He's definitely on the pull, and clearly not fussed about who he ends up with, let alone how old they are.

'Me and the lads are out on a stag do. Pete over there is getting married next week.' Matt points his bottle at a guy opposite who already has his arm draped across the shoulders of one of Em's work colleagues.

Lucky bride-to-be.

Matt slinks down onto the edge of my seat.

'Congratulations to Pete,' I reply sarcastically, raising my bottle again and shuffling across to the other side of my seat to recover personal space. It fails. He moves across with me.

'To Pete and his last few days of freedom,' Matt chuckles.

He clinks his bottle next to mine.

We stay in the bar for several hours. Matt has kept the drinks flowing and we're both tipsy, him slurring slightly and me smiling far too much, realising I'm enjoying all the attention. He's much younger than guys I'd normally go for, but he's showing the tell-tale signs of wanting to get into my knickers. The possibility is starting to appeal...

Chairs scrape against the wooden floor as our group, plus Pete's Posse, get up *en masse* to leave. Nowadays, this is my time to flee and return unscathed to the safety of my cave. But I promised Em I would see the night out. Besides, Matt gives me no chance to escape as he pulls me up from my chair and guides me, hand-held, out of the door to stampede with the rest of the herd. I am pissed enough not to care, allowing myself to be swept along.

We arrive at Mojo's, one of the City's many 'hip' nightclubs. Matt is still by my side, voice raised and chatting against my ear as if we've known each other for years. I know it's the alcohol at play, but even so, his hand is warm and firm, and the sensations starting to bubble inside me are not unpleasant. He's not bad looking either.

Once inside, Em and Liam, the Greek Demi-god, head to the street-level dance floor and get it on to the loud, rhythmic sounds of Swedish House Mafia's *Save the World*. Matt instructs me to stay put as he makes his way to the bar, shoving his way through a wall of people. Already lightheaded, I stand in a free spot near the edge of the crowded dancefloor, adjusting my eyes and squinting as if seeing this place for the very first time. Lights flicker and flash intermittently, alternating the room from dark to light and giving tantalising glimpses of body outlines. The thumping beat vibrating up from the floor, through my body and into my eardrums is inescapable. I close my eyes, absorbing it all.

In times gone by, Em and I would be here dancing our stiletto-clad feet off with some guys we'd met earlier. Memories of those freer times flood back, yet it all seems like an eternity ago. Em is still at home here, but I might as well be on Mars.

Matt returns and places a bottle of God knows what into my hand, grinning and jigging around as if keen to dance. Grabbing my free hand, he pulls me towards the dance floor. I pull back, shaking my head, hands held up, but he's far stronger and wins our feeble tug-of-war.

We're both uncoordinated and out of time, but any awkwardness or feelings of self-consciousness fall by the wayside as the music, the energy, penetrate every part of my being. I loosen, pulled into a state of total abandonment, my body now moving of its own accord. Closing my eyes, I am transported into a surreal labyrinth of lights and sounds, distanced from reality.

Matt's warm hands slide around my waist pulling me out of my semi-lucid state. His hot breath brushes my cheek. Hints of musk and beer waft, and for a split second a voice in my head shouts, 'pull away *now!*' But alcohol has loosened some of the bricks in my dam wall and I ignore its scornful tones, giving in to once-familiar sensations now consuming me.

Matt's lips tease my neck, flickering dormant flames into action. Firm hands glide down my spine, pulling me closer, so close I feel his heat. I melt into him, drunkenly opening my eyes and tilting my chin in readiness. His open mouth presses against mine and a lithe tongue invades, sealing our lips and fate tonight.

Our mating dance continues for some time until Matt groans and pulls back from yet another lingering kiss, nuzzling my ear, his voice rasping.

'Come back to my hotel?'

My heart pounds. I've heard this line, or versions of it, so many times before, yet it seems to have come out of leftfield.

My mind whirs and I stiffen, trying to edge away to put some space between us, but he's holding me so damn tight resisting seems pointless.

'I... I... don't—' But before I can get the rest of the words out, his mouth is on mine again.

What the hell am I doing?

Fright and flight kicks in and I yank myself back, looking around for Em, my safety net, only to see her and Liam in the throes of an intense game of tonsil tennis.

'So, do you?' Matt says, brows furrowed.

Frozen, I stare at him. And in that moment, I remember something Em said to me while we were getting ready. After hearing my whines about not wanting to go clubbing she said, 'Luce, you can't keep yourself locked up forever. You'll just shrivel up and that would be such a waste to humankind, especially for all those hot blokes out there wanting to get into your knickers. Just let go and enjoy yourself, like you used to do.'

Her 'advice' was unwanted at the time. How can *she* judge if I am ready to let go or not? She hasn't been through what I have these past few years. But Em does know because she knows me, and regardless of what's happened over the last twenty-four-or-so months, I still trust her judgement. Somewhere in the deep, dark, depths of my psyche there is still a part of me that yearns to let go; aided and abetted by pumping music, alcohol, and Matt's tongue in my mouth.

'Okay,' I say, 'but I need to let Em know,' and I untwine myself from his slackened grip and head over to Em and Liam, trembling slightly, contemplating.

Em twists around, mouthing, 'You okay?' after I tap her on the shoulder. So, I tell in a hushed shout that Matt and I are leaving the club and going to a hotel. His hotel. The cocktail of shock and jubilance on her face is priceless. She squeals and hugs me bear-like as if I've just won the Lottery.

'Be careful,' she says, squeezing me like it's our last ever embrace. 'But enjoy yourself, Luce. It's long overdue.' She pulls back, her smile fading, eyebrows narrowing. 'Have you got... you know—

protection?'

'Oh! Err... no.' An amateur move on my part, but in my defence, this wasn't on my agenda. 'I'll be sure to get some.'

She kisses my cheek and whispers in my ear, 'Don't forget the rules, our code. Well... you know.'

We do the door key check, although I suspect it's not needed, and I give her a final hug goodbye. She winks, grinning from ear-to-ear, then turns her attentions back to Liam. I expect he will be hoping for a similar outcome tonight.

My heart is pumping so fast it feels like it's going to jump out of my chest and start a conga on the dancefloor as Matt and I leave the club hand-in-hand and join the short taxi line for a ride to wherever it is we're going.

The cool night air has a sobering effect and I suddenly feel awkward and self-conscious now the safety of the crowded club has been left behind. Matt too seems lost for words, pacing in front of me with a faux grin plastered on his face.

'Where's the hotel?' I break the silence, sounding more like I'm talking to a work colleague about a business meeting than a hook up.

'Between the river and castle,' Matt replies, shuffling from one foot to the other.

He seems to pick up on my unease and continues.

'Don't worry, I'm not a serial killer or owt. Well... not yet anyway.'

He winks, softening the fragile air between us. We both giggle and he grabs my hand, bridging the gap. I take a deep breath and relax a little as we wait, enjoying the warmth of his body next to mine on this chilly May evening.

In the back of the taxi we kiss, fondle and fumble for most of the journey, avoiding small talk. My 'lust' switch has been flicked on, but not without inner dialogue casting doubts.

Can I really go through with this? Do I really want this?

And yet the outcome seems so inevitable.

Our taxi pulls up outside the lobby of the Riverside Plaza Hotel. Matt pays the driver and leads me into the sixties-style concrete three-star-looking hotel. Silence descends. An awkward, queasy feeling festers deep down as we reach his room and he fumbles in his jeans pocket for the key card. With a click, the door opens. Matt enters first, switching on lights and ushering me in. Almost too politely, he offers me a drink, perhaps he's also feeling uneasy about what's to come. I nod, glancing around the sparse room with its king-sized bed dressed in white linen. It hits home why I'm here, only I don't remember times like these ever being so... *clinical.*

'Do you do this a lot?' I ask, swaying, hoping to calm my nerves and over-analysing mind while contemplating sitting down on the bed.

'What? Ask pretty women back to my hotel?'

'I guess.'

'Sometimes,' he replies, a cheeky grin spreading across his mouth. 'Don't you?' He plonks himself down on the edge of the bed.

'No. Pretty men maybe, but not for a while.' I manage a nervous titter.

He pats the bed, inviting me to join as if reassuring he knows what he's doing. Yet the Sandra-Dee part of me is screaming, *get out of here,* only Rizzo on my other shoulder says, *fuck it. Enjoy yourself. It'll be fine.* But I don't know if I can. I don't know if I'm ready yet.

'Just let go!' Em's voice yells in my head, hushing all the doubters.

I sit down next to Matt and turn to face him. 'I'm a bit older than you, you know.' *Why the hell am I telling him this?* Maybe I'm hoping he'll decide that he doesn't want to join the Cougar-club tonight and call it quits.

'You don't look it,' he replies, his brown eyes loaded with desire. 'Besides, what does it matter. We both want the same thing, don't we?'

As if in slow motion, I nod, transfixed. He pulls me in, claiming my mouth and starting a chain of events that will inevitably lead to us being under those crisp, white hotel sheets.

My breath rasps as a stream of errant thoughts race through my mind. He's showing a lot of promise for a younger guy. Every inch of my skin feels magnetised as desire takes over.

Matt releases my hands and slides the straps of my dress from my shoulders. Loose-fitting, it drops to the floor. He kisses me hard, groaning as his fingers slide beneath the rim of my bra, pushing it up over my breasts.

'You have great tits,' he says, moaning, rubbing my nipples with his thumbs.

Common sense and reason disappear as I give in to the exquisite sensations sweeping over me. We yank clothes and shoes off in a haphazard fashion until we are naked and lying face to face on the oversized bed.

I glance across his torso, resting my eyes just for a second on his manhood standing tall and proud. With a sense of urgency, I clamber on him, rhythmically moving my hand up and down his erection as I position myself ready to receive him. Drunk and lightheaded, I'm aching for what he can give me.

He clasps my head with both hands, leaning up to kiss me, eyes pleading. Obliging, I lean down and hungrily engulf his mouth with mine.

But before the kiss deepens, he jerks back up. 'I need to get a condom,' he says. I slide off, shamefully aware of the risky situation I've just put myself in. But the ache building between my legs extinguishes all morals, the need for relief all-consuming.

'Hurry up,' I call, squeezing my thighs together.

He returns moments later, grinning and plopping down on the bed beside me, beckoning me back on top.

Straddling, I ease myself down onto him. He gasps as I clamp down, and I wince as his length fills me. I stick a finger in his open mouth. He licks and sucks and bites at it, increasing my desire a billion times over.

'God, you're tight,' he rasps.

My onslaught begins. I throw my head back and close my eyes, rocking back and forth, matching his upwards thrusts and building the tension between us. Uncensored moans seep out as the exquisite ache builds deep within my groin, and a stray hand reaches up, tugging at my exposed breasts.

Without warning, he yells out, jerking upwards as he thrusts deep into me, filling me with the full force of his orgasm.

What the hell?

'Don't stop!' I growl.

He groans, pausing, questioning me with narrowed eyes as I glare down at him. In a moment of realisation, he picks up the pace again even though he's spent. My desire has been dampened, but with the aid of two fingers, I reach the peak causing the sweetest of explosions and cry out as my orgasm consumes me.

Matt slumps into the pillow, panting and sleepy-eyed. Lying on top of him, I'm breathless and satiated, and drop my head against his almost hair-free chest. We lie motionless for a time, but the slick of sweat developing between us serves as an uncomfortable reality check. I ease myself up while Matt holds the condom in place and clamber off to the side. He rolls over and takes off to the bathroom leaving me exposed, so I sneak under the oversized duvet, tucking it tightly around me.

Matt returns and jumps into bed, tugging at the sheets. Post-coital awkwardness rears its ugly head as we lie side-by-side with nothing to say. What is the etiquette these days for one-nighters? Have they always been like this: alcohol and lust-fuelled, fast-paced sex followed by sweat and clumsy small talk?

'That was nice,' I say, breaking the silence hanging like smog in the room.

'Yeah, it was.'

He turns to face me, but at arms-length.

I feign a smile, racking my brain for what to say next. 'So, um... when's your mate getting married?'

'Pete? Next week.' Matt stifles a yawn. 'Tonight was his stag do.'

'Are you his best man?' God, this is awkward.

'No, Liam's his best man. I'm one of his workmates. Didn't Liam hook up with your mate?'

'I think so. She'll have him tied up for the rest of the night, that's for sure.' He has no idea what Em will have in store for Lucky Liam.

'He'll like the tying up bit, he's a right kinky sod,' Matt replies, chuckling.

'Probably will then.' I say, echoing his chuckle.

'Are you local then?' he asks.

It's off-topic, but he's trying to keep the conversation going, I guess.

'Yeah. You're not?' I reply, hoping it's a definite 'not'.

'No. We're all from Sheffield. Here for the weekend. Pete grew up around Norwich so wanted to have his stag do down here. You know, round his old stomping ground.'

'Oh, right. Yeah... it's a great stomping ground, but I am biased.' This is drivel. I really need to get reacquainted with the post-sex small talk manual AKA Em.

'I guess you would be.' He smiles, wriggles between the sheets pulling them more towards him, and yawns again.

He turns over, clicking off the side light. 'Night then.'

'Night,' I reply, rearranging the quilt and cocooning myself like a caterpillar, and lie there stock-still for what seems like an eternity.

Not long after, low rumbling snorts emanate from Matt, but tiredness evades me. I'm insanely alert, replaying the events of tonight over and over again in my mind.

What have I just done?

But in amongst the chaos there's a strange feeling within. Conflicting, yet familiar and *powerful*. One I haven't had for a very long time.

Time drifts, and eventually sleep gets the better of me.

CHAPTER 3

Beads of light flicker through the blinds casting flecks around the room, illuminating the scene of the crime. As I stretch out cat-like, the realisation hits that I am not in my own bed... and I am not alone.

A naked Matt lies beside me, fast asleep, snuffling and murmuring like a suckling baby pig. A quick look under the duvet confirms my fears: I am completely naked, and judging by the soreness between my legs, had sex with the near stranger lying next to me. I pull the quilt up, tucking it under my chin and plot my escape, praying I don't wake him.

I really don't want to stumble through the fake pleasantries and awkwardness of 'the morning after the night before'. I ease myself over to the far side of the bed, slink out from under the covers and tiptoe towards the bathroom, scanning for my clothes and shoes.

Mine and Matt's clothes are strewn across the floor, the tell-tale signs of drunken desire at play. After gathering them up, I flee into the bathroom, pushing the door to as quietly as I can, and sit on the toilet.

Breathe, Lucy. Just breathe.

My 'morning after' look is a wakeup call, resembling an overgrown trick-or-treater rather than a sex goddess.

Shaking my head, I hold my up bra as if it can impart a wisdom

I'm missing in this moment. Fumbling to fasten it, my thoughts race, trying to make sense of what has happened here. But, by contrast, a triumphant feeling wells inside, as if I've just found the key to unlock my emotional shackles.

I freshen up as best I can and finish dressing, hoping to mask my obvious 'just had sex with a random but slightly hot bloke' look. My breath hitches as I creak open the bathroom door, sneaking a glimpse before I scuttle mouse-like out of the hotel room and flee to the nearby lift. I deflate like a balloon as the elevator door closes.

The hotel receptionist smirks as I make my way to the desk, tossing me an 'I know what you've been doing' look, but I glance away, pretending not to notice.

'Can you order a taxi for me please?' I ask politely, smoothing down unkempt tendrils of hair in a vain attempt to look respectable. She obliges, still smirking, as she lifts the receiver and dials a taxi firm.

A few minutes later, a taxi pulls up outside the foyer and the receptionist points me towards it. After telling the driver my address, I slump into the back seat knowing my getaway is almost complete.

My thoughts drift, wondering what kind of night Em's had. She might even be in the same hotel with Liam, or, worse still, with him back at my place. Goose bumps prickle my flesh at the thought. But Em wouldn't let me down, would she? She knows the rules, the code we have to keep each other safe and out of strife. And one thing's clear in my mind, I'm not interested in seeing Matt again. He was nice enough, and the sex was passable, but it was just a bit of much-needed fun, wasn't it? And what will Em make of it all?

The taxi arrives at my place. After paying the driver, I get out of the cab and bolt for the safety of home.

'Thank God!' I say aloud, diffusing stifled nerves as the door shuts behind me. And for the first time since waking, my breathing finds its natural rhythm again, like the steady thumping on a frame drum. Kicking my shoes off, I race upstairs, checking the spare room en route to mine. Sure enough, Em's fast asleep in bed, and to my relief, she's alone.

Security restored and tensions released. My comfy bed beckons.

Em jolts me awake. Dishevelled and hungover, the sweet stench of stale wine oozing from her pores, she lies down next to me on the bed, shoving me over to make room. She props her head on her hand and grins. 'Well?'

'Well, what?' I look away, yanking the covers from under her. My pounding head signals the need for water and more sleep.

'You know very well what! You and Matt. Last night! Spill Morris!'

'Oh, you know... sat and talked,' I reply, yawning.

'As if!' Her eyes widen.

A wry smile forms across my lips. 'Actually, we had mind-blowing sex and then I left.'

Em's mouth drops. 'Are you kidding me?'

She sees my grin and tuts.

'So, how was it *really*?'

'Well... you know. It was okay,' I say, flushing. *Have I really become such a prude?*

'Was he any good? Did you... ya know?' she asks, giggling like a teenager who's just taken her first drag on a spliff.

'Em!'

'It's never stopped you in the past!'

22

She has a point. We used to spend hours poring over the intimate details of our one-night stands. Things have certainly changed since then.

'Okay, okay. It was fine, and yes, I did. What more do you need?'

'Are you going to see him again?'

'Are you kidding me?' I gawp in disbelief. 'Not a chance. It was a one-nighter.' I can't believe she thought I'd even consider it. Irritated, I bounce back her inquisition. 'What about you? What did you and Liam get up to?'

'Same as you, pretty much, although he wanted my number, so I gave him a fake one.' Em examines her nails like it's a well-practiced routine. 'It was pretty awkward when I left, though 'cos I think he realised it was a one-time only deal.'

'Yeah, same. Someone should come up with 101 topics of conversation to avoid post-sex awkwardness.'

Em and I titter as we remember all too well what it's like.

'I woke up at the usual time, though, and legged it as soon as I could. He was still snoring his head off when I left.' I smile, inwardly congratulating myself on an expert getaway.

'Shag 'em and leave 'em, eh!'

'Always!' I reply, laughing.

Em's expression changes, a frown crinkling her forehead.

'What's the matter?'

She doesn't respond as if struggling to find the right words.

'Em?'

'Well... it's just that last night was a lot of fun. Kind of reminds me of how things used to be before... well, you know. But, Luce, was it too much too soon?'

'It was fine, Em. Honest.' I cup her hands. 'I've been cooped up for so long I think I'd forgotten how to have fun. If nothing else, last night proves that I've still got it in me. Maybe I just needed a good, old-fashioned shag!' I feign a laugh, but who am I trying to convince?

She throws her arms around me, sighing.

'As long as you're okay, Luce,' she whispers. 'I'd never forgive myself if I let any more crap happen to you.'

She strokes my hair and I'm touched by her concern, catching a much-needed glimpse of what our friendship used to be like and could be again.

The previous night's escapades fuel several hours of chatting, reminiscing and analysing, just like old times. It's all so surreal, and it surprises Em as much as it does me. Still, I feel like I've turned a corner, and Em and I are having a proper catch up for the first time in ages.

Eventually, our party for two finishes and Em packs up, calls a taxi, and heads back home to her bachelorette pad. We agree to meet for lunch the following Monday. Only, after she leaves, I feel like I'm on the Space Shuttle Endeavour's return voyage with my mind racing for the Olympics. My dirty deeds play out like a movie, only Matt's face is obscured.

But despite all of this, something inside me has ignited. The music, the alcohol, the sex, they all conspired to bring back a part of me I'd forgotten existed… and I like it.

CHAPTER 4

As I approach my desk, Anna, a work colleague at Slater, Forter & Aveling, pops her head up from her booth.

'Morning Lucy.' Her tone is chirpy. 'Good weekend, was it?'

'Yes,' I smile back. 'Actually, it was.'

'Sounds intriguing. What did you get up to?'

'Clubbing. You know.' She tosses me an approving smirk as I rummage through my bag.

My job as a paralegal attending to the needs of Corporate Lawyers has always kept me busy. Today, though, I seem to glide from task to task like a bee collecting pollen. Errant thoughts have quietened as though I've brushed away some of the dark dank cobwebs of the past two years. I feel more alive and alert than I have for such a long time.

Em and I meet for lunch in a cute little café a few blocks from my workplace. Our Saturday night escapades are still the topic of choice, and Em is still buzzing from discovering that Lucy the hermit has finally left the mountain and re-joined humankind.

'Tell me more about Matt. What did he look like in the light?' Em asks, stirring her coffee and gazing at me all glassy-eyed.

'What's to tell? He was tall-ish, thin-ish, looked good and was okay in bed,' I say sarcastically, knowing full well it will get her hackles up.

'That's it? That's all there is?'

'Em, he was a one-nighter. What else is there to say? I'm not going to sit here going gaga over him!'

'At least we're on the same page with that. I wouldn't want to think that you'd go all 'Joe' on me again!'

'What's that supposed to mean?' I say, banging my coffee mug onto the table.

'We had a good routine for years until Joe came along and you tried to be all Stepford Wife-y,' she says, glaring. 'And after he died, you changed again. Became a recluse. I just hope Saturday night wasn't a one-off, and you go back to being the Lucy I used to know and love.'

Em has never said anything like this before. Gobsmacked, I clench my fists under the table. 'Where the hell has this come from? You never had a problem before.'

'I wasn't exactly Joe's biggest fan, though, was I? And he definitely wasn't mine.' She rolls her eyes. 'He was a right prick to you on more than one occasion, even though you were trying hard to be all-in.'

Words escape me. This truth really hurts.

'Face it, Luce, you were born a party girl and you'll die a party girl,' Em continues. 'It's the only way to stay true to yourself, and once you realise this, maybe we can get back to being the friends we used to be.'

Her sword-edged words bring the realisation she has spent the last few years *pretending* our friendship hasn't changed.

'All this time you've *supposedly* been there for me, and it's all been a lie?'

'No!'

Her eyes widen as if her words have suddenly taken shape in front on her in big bold letters.

'Shit! Luce... I'm sorry. That came out all wrong.' She frowns, bowing her head. 'What I mean is that our friendship changed because we didn't get to do what we loved doing anymore, but that was more down to Joe than us going pear-shaped. I'm so sorry, Luce.'

Puppy-like eyes plead for forgiveness.

'Please don't think for a minute that you aren't the most important person in the world to me, because you are.'

I cave in and nod. She has a point about Joe, though. I cut myself off from our nights out—from Em—because I felt Joe expected me to. I wanted to be his demure and dutiful wife, but maybe I was just living a lie.

I sip my coffee and wipe away tears.

Em reaches over and squeezes my hand.

'Bestie,' she says, welling up.

We sit quietly for a moment as if this gush of realities needs to finish spilling over.

Eventually, her expression softens, and she pipes up, 'So do you want to hear more about Liam?'

And that's my Em, trying to lighten the mood in the best way she knows how.

'Of course,' I reply, feigning interest while deep down, still reeling from her comments about me and Joe.

'Well, he was really nice to look at, dull to talk to and just average in the bedroom.'

Em wrinkles her nose and tuts as though somehow cheated out of what should've been a far better present on her birthday.

Em never stopped clubbing, even when I went into hiatus. It seems like an addiction for her. She knows what she's doing, and her expectations are high. Mine, not so much. I'm just happy the arid landscape that was my sex-life for many years has had a much-needed drink from the fountain of fornication.

I leave work just after five and catch the bus home, unaware of the raindrops plopping down from a blackened sky. I'm still preoccupied with recent events, replaying them over and over in my mind only, the reruns have changed and are no longer about Matt. He's just a faceless actor. I'm the lead, the one in complete control steering scenes like a director on a movie set. Question is, would I want to do it again? Do I want to return to the old ways, to the younger, carefree, *reckless* Lucy? Or have I changed too much to go back to her completely? Yet I can't ignore the longing growing inside like a recently germinated seed, sown with anticipation of exciting times ahead.

CHAPTER 5

Stella, a close work mate, has been promoted. After work, a group of us go to a nearby pub to celebrate with her.

I haven't eaten, and after sculling two glasses of House Shiraz, am feeling relaxed yet restless, like a dog circling to find a comfy spot.

'What do you reckon, Lucy?' A voice carries over the hum.

'Huh?' I reply, flustered, realising I've been paying them all lip service, tossing snippets of conversation in here and there only when I've actually been paying attention. 'Oh, yeah, sorry... I can't hear properly over the racket in here!' I say, making a trumpet shape next to my ear. But the moment has gone and Rachel, the voice's owner, has moved on to the next topic.

I'm too preoccupied, looking around the darkened, musty room and focusing on a guy over there who looks like David Beckham, or another walking through the door wearing a snazzy suit. Scanning. Searching for something... someone to ignite the stirrings deep within.

My eyes come to rest on a guy sitting on a stool by the bar tapping away on his phone. Dark-haired and clean shaven, he's wearing a black pinstripe suit giving him a professional air like a lawyer or banker, maybe. I've always had a thing for men in pinstripes, for the power they seem to exude.

Zoned out from the group, I plot my assault. Gulping down the last dregs of wine, I call in a round and take the orders, then walk over to the bar feigning confidence.

Phone guy taps away, oblivious to my presence.

'I'll have a glass of house red, two pints of draught, and three bottles of Becks, please,' I tell the barman, casting a glance over at phone guy.

One by one, the barman lines the filled glasses and bottles on the bar. As I fish around in my purse to pay, coins spill out onto the counter, clattering and pinging off the mirror-like brass. Several land in phone guy's lap. I gasp, staring at him like a rabbit caught in car headlights.

He looks down at his lap then back to me, a smirk spreading across his face.

'Shall I get them, or do you want to?'

Heat engulfs my cheeks. He picks up the coins from his lap and hands them to me, his smirk replaced by a wide grin as he blatantly checks me out.

'You could've just asked me to buy you a drink.'

'I'm so sorry,' I reply, cupping my face.

'It's fine, honestly,' he says, and points to my wine. 'How about I buy you that drink?'

'Um... you don't need to do that. I should buy you one for disturbing you.'

'Nice disturbance, though,' comes his reply. 'Well, okay. I'll have a scotch on the rocks, thanks.' He extends his hand towards me. 'I'm Jeremy, by the way.'

'Lucy,' I reply, shaking his hand.

'Nice to meet you Lucy. So, what's a clumsy girl like you doing in a pub like this on a school night?'

Cheesy.

I offer up a smile, casting a flirtatious glance over his face and down to his chest.

CHAPTER 6

Work is dragging. I'm tired, my head is banging as if it's been hit by a wrecking ball, and again, I'm preoccupied with running the movie of my latest exploits through an already overactive mind. I'd get an A+ for embracing my rediscovered siren. Em will burst when she hears about this.

After what seems like an eternity, my working day draws to a close and I can finally head home. Food, sleep and more painkillers are high on my list of priorities. I'm such a lightweight nowadays, and last night tested my endurance to the limit.

Arriving home, I rummage through the post then ring Em with a sense of urgency. My confess-all cannot wait any longer.

'Oh my God!' Em squeals. 'She's back! She's really back.'

I can picture her doing a victory dance around her living room, whooping and slapping her thigh like a cowboy who's just lassoed a bull. And of course, she wants to know *all* the details.

'Was he a looker?' Em asks, her pitch higher than the Eiffel Tower.

'Not too shabby,' I say, chuckling.

'C'mon Luce, details please!'

And Em's persistence pays off as I give her the lowdown,

including gory bits.

'I reckon he's married, though, or at least has a partner.'

'Why do you say that?' she says.

'Second toothbrush, pictures, you know. And the place was spotless!'

'Cheating bastard,' Em retorts.

Her comment stings, but she will never know why.

'I guess...' I reply, my mood taking a downward slide. 'But I was too pissed to care.'

As I'm divulging the intimate details of last night's deeds in a surprisingly blasé fashion, an official-looking letter on the kitchen table catches my eye. I pick it up and a sense of foreboding twists in my gut.

I tear at the seal, oblivious to what Em is now saying. 'I'll have to call you back,' I murmur, dropping the phone.

Pulling out the letter, I stare down at the words willing them to say anything other than what I suspect they do. Instead, in black and white letters on crisp, white paper, I now hold the Deeds to the house. Joe's life and mortgage insurance payments have been paid out in full.

Instead of Joe, I now have a fully paid for house. The life I took away has a total value of £364,394.

My mind spins like a roulette wheel, periodically stopping on the words, 'It's all your fault,' erupting sobs from deep within.

I take the letter and head to the lounge, sinking into the sofa, cradling myself and pulling tissue after tissue from the box next to me. I am wallowing in the deep, dark dungeon of guilt; cursing myself and unable to stop tears flooding out.

What am I going to do?

The words go on repeat, holding me in this bleak place with no torch for guidance.

Eventually they dry up, replaced by numbness as reality hits like a shovel to the face that the past few days have been nothing more than fleeting feasts of fancy.

I am held ransom by the memories of that fateful night and the morning that followed.

A scene flashes through my mind: a policewoman tapping my shoulder and handing me a card for someone in my situation. Riddled with guilt and treading water, I trudged through each day hoping that, at some point, I'd come to terms with it all. But now my carefully caged emotions are busting out again, and I know I can't carry on like this. Tonight has been all the proof I needed.

I need to find that card.

Cushions are thrown, magazines flicked through, drawers opened and emptied, cups of tea left to go cold, and books yanked off the shelves. After hours spent searching, I find it wedged between two of the few remaining books still on the shelf. Relief washes over at the prospect of a possible lifeline, and I keep re-reading the details as if to check that they are the right:

Margaret Evans

Counsellor, specialising in guilt and grief counselling

Can she help me? Can she get rid of the scornful voice in my head that constantly reminds me of what I did to Joe?

My living room looks like a tornado has whipped through it. Yawning, I shove the card in my bag and tidy the mess up then drag my sorry butt off to bed in the hope it will all seem better in the light of a new day.

As if.

CHAPTER 7

The morning has been a blur. My throbbing head tells me I should've pulled a sickie, but I just had to get out. The house has Joe's life—his death—written in pound signs all over it.

'You okay, Luce?' Darren asks.

My boss casts a sympathetic smile I've become all too well acquainted with.

'Joe stuff,' I say, shoulders hunched as I sink deeper into my chair.

'Okay. Well, if you need anything...'

His reply seems automatic, obligatory. He leaves me be.

Staring at my half-eaten sandwich, I contemplate ringing Margaret Evans. Can she fix this? Is it even possible? Nerves flutter with thunderous force as I pick up the phone, noticing a missed call and two messages from Em, and dial Margaret's number. After a few rings her voicemail kicks in.

'Hello, it's Thursday, 2nd June 2011, and this is Margaret. I'm unable to take your call at the moment, so please leave a message and I'll call you back as soon as I can. Thank you.' *Beep.*

The voicemail message catches me off guard. 'Um, hello, my name's... err... Lucy Morris. I was given your number by a police officer after my husband died and I— Well, I hoped I could perhaps, if you have availability, come and see you about it. Um... my number is... I'll give you my mobile number, it's 07918 110082. Okay, thanks. Bye.'

The next few hours trudge by. I can't concentrate, and every time I'm at my desk, Joe's death replays repeatedly in my mind. I go to the loo, go outside, go anywhere, just to escape the barrage of bleak memories. And it's during times like these the urge to smoke again hits hard. If nothing else, it would give me excuse to get away from my desk, only I gave up not long after Joe and I married.

When I finally return, all I can muster is mindlessly scrolling on my laptop, and it takes a few moments to register the ringing coming from my bag. I fish out my phone and answer the call.

'Hello, Lucy speaking,' I say on autopilot.

'Hello Lucy, this is Margaret Evans. You left a message for me earlier?'

'Oh... hi. Yes, I did. Thanks for getting back to me. I was... err... I was wondering if I could come and see you, you know, talk to you about some personal stuff.' *Why am I so nervous?*

'Yes, of course,' she replies.

Her voice is soft like a towel pulled straight from of the dryer.

'Shall we make an initial appointment for you to come and see me? I can let you know what's involved, and you can give me some background as to what's going on for you.'

'Okay. That sounds good. When are you free?'

'I have an appointment available tomorrow night at eight if that suits you?'

'Friday? Eight pm? Yes, I think I can make that.' *Of course I can. I don't have a hectic social life now.*

'Good. I'll schedule you in. Do you know where to find me?'

'I think so.' I glance over her card still sitting on my desk. 'Your address is on the business card I have. I'll probably drive.'

'No problem,' she says. 'And just so you're aware, the first session is £75 and will last about fifty minutes. Each session thereafter is £50. I'll go through the format and any expectations you have when I see you. Okay, Lucy?'

'Yes... that's fine. See you tomorrow.'

'See you then. Goodbye.' The phone clicks.

Am I relieved or *worried*? I've never seen a counsellor before and not sure what to expect. Will she analyse me and tell me all my bad points, or interpret my dreams as some sordid act out for my father's love? And what if she discovers the truth?

Stashing my phone back in my bag, I scribble the details of the appointment in my diary and resolve not to tell Em what I'm doing. Her bubble will burst if she finds out and I just can't do that to her. Not now. Not since we've started getting our friendship back on track. Em's all I've got, and I just can't expect her to keep taking all this shit from me.

CHAPTER 8

Orange numbers on my dashboard clock read 7.56 pm and I'm parked outside a Georgian-style town house on the west side of the city, fiddling with the wedding ring I have only just put back on my finger. A not-so-merry little dance is going on in my stomach, so I coach myself through deep breaths to quell the fluttering. At some point, though, I must get out of this car and go to the door, but do I really want to do this? Do I want to dredge up the past and expose my inner demons to a stranger? Do I want to suffer more judgements, or worse still, *pity*? My mind lingers over these thoughts until a more practical one flits. *But what have you got to lose?*

I've already lost my self-respect and any semblance of a happy life, what else can I do to erode the last frontier of my self-worth?

Fuck it. I'm going in.

I shut off the engine, get out of the car and climb the three concrete steps leading to Margaret Evans' door. A small plaque by a round brass doorbell reads, 'Margaret Evans – Counsellor'.

My breath hitches as I press the button with a trembling finger. A few seconds later the door buzzes and clicks open, and I step into a large bright hallway, squinting at the contrast between outside and in. Lofty ceilings nod to its Georgian origins. Chequered tiles in black and white line the floor, the walls clad in a beige sponge-like wallpaper adorned with embossed swirls. A round table and two chairs sit half-way up the corridor on the left, and further along on the right is a door with an 'Occupied' sign. I take a seat by the table, noticing the lace doily underneath a vase holding artificial lilies, and the faint waft of Mr Sheen. I twist my hands on my lap as I wait for Margaret Evans to appear.

A few moments later, the door creaks open and a short, older lady steps towards me. The scent of lavender breezes past as she greets me with a broad, white smile. Streaks of brown hair give her a youthful appearance, countered only by lightly sagging skin and deep-set wrinkles around her eyes. She has the air of a sweet old grandma.

'Lucy?' she asks.

'Yes,' I reply, standing up and smoothing down my skirt.

'Hello, I'm Margaret.' She extends her hand.

'Lucy. Lucy Morris.'

'Please come through.'

I follow her into the 'Occupied' room. It seems bland, devoid of home comforts; the only furniture in the room is a square blue sofa and matching armchair facing each other, a pine coffee table in between. On the table is a jug of water, two glasses and a box of tissues.

Is she expecting me to cry?

Margaret motions towards the sofa as she settles into the armchair, and I take my seat like an obedient child.

'So, Lucy, before we start our session, I'd like to go through a few things regarding how these sessions work. Is that okay?'

'Um... sure,' I reply, picking at imaginary fluff on my skirt.

'Can I start by assuring you that what we talk about in here is confidential and won't be disclosed to anyone else without your consent.'

'Okay,' I say, discombobulated by the formalities.

'As I said on the phone, our sessions last around fifty minutes, and give you time and space to talk about whatever you feel you need to.'

She smiles across at me.

'I might ask you a few questions to clarify something you've said and to explore your thoughts and feelings further, but I won't probe you for information, tell you what to do, or ask you to justify yourself.'

I'm trying hard to absorb it all, my brain bombarded by counselling speak. *Confidential? Space?* She seems to pick up on my confusion and hands me a leaflet about her services and qualifications, and also some forms to fill in. I wish I'd looked up her credentials beforehand. I feel so vulnerable not knowing who she is and what she'll do.

'You can take that info home with you. It might help quell any worries or doubts you have about coming here.' Her eyes crinkle, and she picks up a notepad and pen. 'Do you have any questions so far, Lucy?'

'Yes, um... how long does it normally take to fix my kind of problem? You know, when someone's died?'

'Ah... okay.' She cups her hands on top of the pad. 'I think it would be helpful if we talk about your expectations now, Lucy. My role is not to *fix* you, per se. I'm here to provide you with a safe and secure space to express yourself and hopefully help you explore ways to manage or overcome any problems for yourself.'

A pang rips through me and I straighten in my seat. That's not what I was expecting. I was hoping she'd ask me a few questions and prescribe the answer.

'Oh... I see.' I sink back into the chair, mirroring my deflating hopes.

'It's a process we can't rush,' she continues, 'and for it to work, you need to trust me and feel that I respect you and am not judging you. Otherwise you may not feel comfortable or willing to talk to me about what's going on for you.'

'Well... if that's the way it is, then I guess that's what I have to do.'

Margaret nods, flashing me a smile that feels strangely comforting. And even though she hasn't given me the answer I was expecting, I realise I have to give this a go.

'Okay. Good. Let's get some more quick practicalities out of the way, then we can begin. First, please help yourself to water at any time during the session. And if you need the bathroom, it's back into the hallway, turn right and it's the next door on the right. And the fire exit is the front door.'

My head is spinning, but muster an, 'Okay.'

'And finally, I like to be called Marj. Is it okay to call you Lucy, or would you prefer something else?'

'Lucy's fine, thanks.'

Marj adjusts her position, as if a cue to us getting down to business.

'So, Lucy, how about you tell me what's been going on for you?' She flips over the notepad, her pen poised.

It's the moment I've been dreading. I stiffen, fidgeting, trying to find comfort as I search my scattered thoughts for a beginning.

'Well... my husband, Joe, died two years ago.' My throat constricts as if being crushed by a boa. I fiddle with my wedding ring again, still trying to adjust my position and finding it hard to breathe in a normal rhythm.

Marj sits in silence, waiting for me to continue.

Sifting through a barrage of conflicting thoughts, my mind comes to rest on the night of the fight.

Marj leans closer as I tell her about the worst argument Joe and I ever had. I omit the specifics and move on to the police arriving at the house at dawn.

She says nothing at first. It gnaws at my foundations, and I stutter and trip over words. And as much as my instinct tells me to not trust her, to flee to the hills, I know I have to see this through. But a foreboding, festering mass is building up in my gut as anxiety takes hold. I stare at the tissue box, averting Marj's gaze, desperately trying to hold back the full force of emotions threatening to burst through my carefully reconstructed dam walls.

I close my eyes and draw in a steadying breath, trying to figure out how to continue. 'Ever since that night, it's like I'm trapped, in limbo. I wake up at sunrise nearly every day, reliving it all like it was yesterday.'

Marj scribbles notes onto the pad.

What is she thinking? Has she figured out yet that I killed him?

'It sounds like you've been through some challenging times,' she says. 'You mentioned it was two years ago since Joe died. I'm wondering if something has happened recently to bring your feelings about Joe's death back to the surface?'

Oh god, she knows... but how? The letter. It was the letter that brought all this shit back.

I tell her about how I thought I was coping by taking each day at a time. How the settlement letter has reopened the cracks I'd papered over. How it feels like a line has been drawn under Joe's death; an end, finished, done. Only, now I realise it's not. Agony and *guilt* are still very much alive inside, plaguing me. And despite my best efforts, they're seeping out and I feel like I'm teetering on a precipice, about to lose control.

Marj's glasses drop a notch down her nose as she looks over them at me.

'I just can't cope with this anymore,' I continue, bowing my head as sobs are freed and pour out like an overflowing sink.

Marj hands me the tissue box.

Aside from my sobbing, we sit in silence for some time.

Eventually, and after many crumpled tissues, I look up at Marj and mumble an apology.

'There's no need, Lucy,' she reassures. 'This time is for you to express yourself, however you need to. I am here to listen.'

Her words give little comfort.

Depleted tears have left me raw. I twist my wedding ring again, as if twirling it back and forth around my finger can distract me from the stillness and starkness of the room. Words no longer flow, the silence becoming deafening.

Marj finally speaks. 'Lucy,' she says, her tone soothing, 'our time tonight is nearly up. I wonder how you'd feel about coming to see me again, maybe the same time next week? It might be useful for us to work through how receiving that letter has affected you. Does that sound okay?'

'Uh-huh,' I snivel into a tissue.

And just like that, my first session with Marj is over.

I pay my dues and we say our goodbyes, and I leave with

assurances from Marj that I can phone her at any time if I find I'm struggling to cope. My mind is thick with racing thoughts and crying-induced dehydration. I flee to the comfort of my car, and after popping a couple of Panadols, start the engine and continue the emotional rollercoaster as I drive home.

What the hell am I getting myself into?

CHAPTER 9

The rain is battering my living room window emulating how my head feels. When I got home last night, I opened a bottle of Shiraz to drown my sorrows. The bottle is on the floor, empty, like my heart, and I'm on the sofa wrapped in a throw.

Numb. I don't *want* to move. I don't want to do anything, least of all think about yesterday's therapy. Why in the hell did I think it was a good idea? I feel worse than before. Every inch of me wants to retreat and find shelter far, far away from anyone and anything that will remind me of what I've done and what I'm now living through again. There is only one light in all this darkness—Em.

It takes several hours for me to get my self-pitying butt off the sofa and make some effort in resuming day-to-day life. Hungover, and not in the slightest bit hungry, even the idea of a cigarette has lost its appeal.

I need Em. I haven't spoken to her since the letter arrived. There has barely been a day go by we haven't communicated, even if it is just an 'I'm okay' text. She's the only person I want to talk to right now.

'Luce! Finally! Where have you been? I've been trying to get hold of you—'

Em's voice rings out with relief as she answers my call.

I try to sound chirpy. 'Sorry Em. I've been caught up in some stuff. I meant to call you sooner.'

'What stuff? You sound... *off*? You okay?'

'I... I'm fine,' I lie, but the dam wall bursts again, and my sorrows gush out.

'Luce! Oh my God! What's wrong?'

Through sniffs and gulps I construct a reply. 'A letter from our err... my solicitor came on Wednesday.'

'Your solicitor? What did it say?'

'Joe's insurance money has been paid out. It paid for the mortgage on this place.'

'That's good, isn't it?'

I gulp back a sob. 'No.'

'Why?' she asks.

'It brought back memories. The bad ones.'

'Oh Luce, I'm so sorry. Are you okay?'

'I... I don't think I am,' I reply, weeping uncensored into a scrunched-up tissue pulled from my pocket.

'What do you mean? Tell me!' Her voice sounds urgent.

'The guil—grief, it came back.'

Em is silent for a few moments, then says, 'Right. I'm coming over.'

'No, Em... there's no need. I... I'm sorting it out. Honestly.'

'Yeah, I can tell you are. Don't go anywhere. I'll be there in forty minutes.'

Without waiting for me to respond, she hangs up the phone.

Em is on my doorstep holding me tightly as the floodgates open.

After several minutes of being squeezed and shushed, I pull away, gesturing for her to come in.

'I'll make us a cuppa,' she says, heading for the kitchen.

I have no words, only tears, and take a seat at the kitchen table, mentally preparing for what I'll say to her.

'Here you go,' she says, plonking a cup of tea in front of me, then sits at my side.

'Em, I—' but no words follow, only more heaving sobs.

'Come here.'

She reaches out to me, pulling me to safety, wrapping loving arms around me as I shatter.

During the evening, Em quietly strokes my hair and hands me tissue after tissue as the guilt and grief I've been holding onto for far too long gush out in incoherent spurts.

After several cups of tea and many soothing words from Em, my rationale returns, and I finally pluck up the courage to tell her about Marj.

'Wow. I never thought you'd do it,' she says.

'I didn't think I needed it,' I reply, snivelling, after I've given her the gory details of my counselling session.

'I know it's probably not what you want to hear right now, but you need this. You've needed it for a long time.'

'But I feel worse than before!' I say, knotting my hands under the table, pulling at strands of soggy tissue.

'I don't know what to say. I guess it's not meant to be easy.'

'I know, but… it's just so much harder than I thought it would be.' A sigh escapes, and I continue, 'I don't know if I can go through it all again.'

'Maybe you need to try a different counsellor. There's bound to be loads out there.'

Em is trying so hard to be helpful, but it's just not helping me right now to hear it. I shrug, and she reaches across as I put my hands up on the table. I guess it's her way of reassuring me I'm not alone in this.

Em sleeps over for the night, which involves the two of us huddled on the sofa with a blanket and several bottles of wine. She may not be the most empathetic person in the world, but Em knows exactly what to do to get me out of my head only, it often involves running in the opposite direction.

CHAPTER 10

As Friday's session with Marj looms, and despite Em's much-needed visit over the weekend, I've become like an itch that has been scratched raw.

As I was listening to the radio on the drive to work on Tuesday morning, Coldplay's *Every Teardrop is a Waterfall* came on and I was blubbering by the end of the track. Lucky I went in the car and didn't catch the bus as usual. I spent nearly an hour in the loos splashing my face and redoing my trace amount of makeup. And just as I sat down at my desk, Darren came over and asked me into his office.

Perched on the corner of his desk, his hands resting on his thighs, he says, 'I know there's been a lot going on for you lately, Lucy, but it's affecting your work again.'

Darren sighs, shaking his head as though struggling to say what he needs to.

'I hate to point this out, but it's the fourth time you've been late in the past two weeks, and you're barely speaking again.'

I struggle to look at him. 'I'm sorry, Darren. It won't happen again.'

'What's going on, Lucy?' He purses his lips, his face stern.

'I... I can't talk about it,' I reply, my pulse accelerating as if the fight-or-flight button is about to be pressed.

He runs his hand through his hair, sighing. 'Lucy... HR have contacted me about your absences again,' he says, but then his voice softens. 'Give me a good reason to go back to them with, otherwise you're headed for a verbal, and I don't want that to happen.' His voice cracks, as if battling with the words.

But before I can say anything, tears win the race and tumble down my cheeks. Darren rushes over and wraps me up in blue-shirted arms.

'I'm sorry, Lucy. I know it must be difficult for you,' he says in a whisper. 'I'm just trying to look out for you.'

I believe him. He's always been fair to me and turned a blind eye to the many, many occasions when I've been struggling.

'I'm going to counselling,' I blurt out, 'and... it's just, well, it's harder than I thought.'

Darren shushes me through all the wails and sniffles and doesn't mention anything more about the absences. When I'm finally done crying and about to leave his office, he offers a faint smile.

'I'm here if you need anything.'

By Thursday, and after a run-in with my neighbour over their cat shitting in my garden, I'm ready to explode. So much so that a trip into town at lunch ends with me telling a pushy market researcher to 'fuck off' after she repeatedly wafted her clipboard in my face.

My bleeding heart is on show, wide open for all to jab.

Friday evening comes around too quickly and I'm again sitting in my car outside Marj's office, psyching myself up for the next session. Checking, double-checking I have enough money, I've filled in the forms correctly, and I have the right time and date. All the while dropping Rescue Remedy under my tongue as if it's Valium.

The car clock reads 7.57 pm. My breath hitches as the desire to vomit grips.

As I unclick the seat belt, get out of my car and head towards the building, I feel like a robot walking in slow motion. I'm glugging air with every breath to quell the queasiness. What do I say to her? Just being in there with her going over the past tips the scales in favour of a damning confession. And the paranoid part of me already worries that she's worked out that I'm to blame.

I press the bell, my finger trembling, heart racing, and shuffle from side-to-side as I wait for the door to click open. Déjà vu takes hold as I sit in the waiting area, tense and uncomfortable.

A few moments later, Marj opens the door, greeting me with a warming smile, and waves me in. It does little to quell the rolling rocks in my gut. I scuttle behind her into the tomb, taking my seat as we exchange pleasantries.

'How are you feeling tonight?' she says softly, eyes crinkling.

I want to lash out and let her know how crap I've been since I last saw her, but take a deep breath, clasp my hands together in my lap and reply, 'I'm okay.'

Marj stays quiet, scribbling something down on her notepad. I wish I could see what she's writing.

After an uncomfortable pause, she pipes up, 'I'm wondering how you felt after our last session... if anything came up for you that you want to talk about tonight?'

'I... err... don't know.' Words describing my rollercoaster emotions since last week are stuck somewhere between my belly and my throat. I cough, trying to free them. 'I guess the letter, and talking to you about it, well, it brought it all back to me. It's like I'm back there, going through it all again.' I stare down at my knotting fingers, tears welling.

'It feels like you are re-experiencing the feelings and emotions from when Joe died?'

'Like it happened yesterday,' I nod, staring at the tissue box on the table between us. As if on cue, Marj pushes it towards to me. I reach over and pluck one out.

She gives me a few moments to dab my eyes, then continues. 'Lucy, do you feel able to talk about any of those feelings?' Her head tilts to the side, her brows furrowed.

'I didn't say goodbye to him,' and I come undone.

Wiping streams of tears away, I try to continue through staggered breaths. 'I can't even remember what we were arguing about, but it got way out of hand...' I close my eyes, desperate to mask how I'm truly feeling, knowing I can't tell her the truth. If she knew...

'You and Joe had a fight, and you never got to say goodbye?' she says, summarising. 'How does that make you feel now, Lucy?'

I open my eyes, look up at her and reply, 'Guilty. If I—' But instantly regret it.

Marj sits up, as if her interest is piqued. 'You feel guilty?'

We have hit the panic button. 'Yes,' I nod, seeking signs of forgiveness on her face, my tears gushing out of nowhere, and long, pitiful sobs erupting once more.

An eternity passes.

The sobbing eventually subsides, and I heave in air hoping it will calm me just enough to make my excuses and leave.

Marj smiles. It doesn't help.

What must she be thinking of me?

'It's my fault,' I eventually whisper, hanging my head as shame consumes.

'You feel it's your fault?'

'Yes. If we hadn't argued—' I can't even look at Marj. I imagine her pen in hand, poised to strike as she waits for my confession.

Twisting my ring, my guilt slips out. 'I did something, something really bad. It was what... killed him.'

I can't breathe and look at Marj, waiting for the response I already know will be my undoing.

'You feel that Joe died because you did something bad?'

I nod in slow motion. *Guilty as charged.*

Another long pause. My palms are sweating. I feel lightheaded, and blink rapidly to shake it.

'You mentioned before that you feel you can't move on. That you are stuck. I'm wondering if not being able to say goodbye to Joe and blaming yourself for his death might be the reason why you feel stuck, Lucy?'

I nod again. 'How do I live with myself knowing that I caused my husband's death?'

She has no reply.

This is torture. After several more moments have passed, I finally sit up, dabbing stinging eyes, and prepare myself for the next onslaught. Only, it doesn't come.

Marj sits quietly, her hands folded across her notepad. She looks away as if giving me time to gather my thoughts.

I hate these silences. There's nothing else I want to say for fear of exposing more than I already have.

'Is talking about these feelings uncomfortable for you, Lucy?' Marj asks in a hushed voice.

I nod.

'Have you spoken about them before?'

'No. Not really. I haven't been able to.'

'Thank you for feeling able to share them now, with me. It may not seem like it, Lucy, but this is progress.' She tosses me a sweet smile as though pleased with herself.

'How can you say that? I feel like I'm going backwards!' I bark back. 'I wasn't even sure if I was going to come tonight!'

'It's understandable that you would want to avoid reliving those painful memories and feelings.' Her tone is strangely soothing like a sore throat lozenge, but then she scribbles on the notepad again causing my hackles to go up.

'What are you writing?' I challenge, although I don't mean to be so curt.

'Notes about what we say in our sessions. They help me keep track of where you're at, and what the key themes are for you.'

'And what are my key themes?'

'You seem to be struggling with feelings of guilt around Joe's death and cannot fully express those feelings. That's what may be stopping you from grieving,' she says calmly. 'You can see these notes at any time, Lucy. They are an *aide memoir*, nothing more.'

'Oh... I see.' I twiddle with my fingers again, feeling foolish.

'You seem uncomfortable again, Lucy. Do you want to share with me what you're thinking and feeling at the moment?'

'No!' I snap, then pull back realising I've said it aloud. 'I'm sorry. I didn't mean that.'

'It's fine.'

Fine is not how I'd describe it, but I know the time has come for me to lay my cards on the table. 'Marj, can I be honest with you?'

'Of course. Honesty is the best way forward.'

'Well, it's just that I... I can't cope with all this.' I can feel myself welling up again. 'I've been living like a recluse for the past few years, and just when I think my life is taking an upturn, all this happens, and I feel worse than ever.'

'You feel like this is making you feel worse than you did when Joe died?'

'Yes... I mean, no.' I take a deep breath to steady my thoughts. 'What I mean is that I'm not sure I can deal with the crap that's coming out. I thought I'd buried it all.'

Marj looks pensive as if formulating her next response. Finally, she looks me square in the face. 'Do you think it might be useful to go through a few things that might help when you're really struggling?'

It's not what I was hoping for. I wanted her to say, 'Okay Lucy, perhaps we need to stop this and let you crawl back into your cave.'

'What do you mean?'

'Coming up with some ways for you to cope when you leave these sessions.'

'Okay,' I reply, but am filled with trepidation.

'So, in the past when you've felt, say, really down or upset, what have you done that has helped get you through it?'

'I... I don't know.'

'What I mean is, what has got you through any bad times?'

What has got me through the bad times?

The answer comes quickly—Em. 'My best friend, Em, has got me through the rough times. She's always been there for me.'

'Do you feel you can count on her to be there during any rough times you experience because of these sessions?'

'I know she will,' and in an instant, a sense of calmness spreads over me like a warm blanket on a cold day.

'You can of course contact me during the day if you're struggling with anything we've covered in our sessions.'

'I know,' I reply, acknowledging Marj's contribution.

Marj looks at a clock on the wall. 'Our time is nearly up, Lucy. How would you feel about coming to see me next Friday, same time?'

'Okay.' I pick up my bag and fumble around for the envelope with Marj's money in it and slide it across the table towards her.

'Thank you,' she says.

After saying goodbye, I hotfoot it out of the building to my car, start the engine and turn the radio up loud to drown out errant thoughts. It's all still so hard, but Em's with me, every step of the way. I'm sure of it.

CHAPTER 11

Morning sunlight streams through my kitchen window as I flick through the Sunday paper. A lawnmower chugs and the earthy scent of mown grass wafts, igniting hopes for a warm summer. After spending most of Friday night crying, Saturday has passed by more smoothly, and yet I still feel... hollow.

My mobile pings.

'Got some news. Can I come over? X' Em's message reads.

I can't shake this empty feeling and being alone is not helping, so type my reply with fervour. 'OK.'

Em's grin widens as we sit down at the kitchen table, coffees in hand. 'You remember my folks were thinking of buying a villa in the Med?' she says, slurping.

'Uh-huh.'

'Well, they've only gone and bought one in Ibiza of all places. Clubbing central! And, we can be the first to use it!' She sits back in her chair, arms folded in triumph. 'It's available from 25th June for a couple of weeks. Can you get time off work?' She squeals, clapping her hands together as if we have just scored tickets to see Lady Ga Ga.

'Are you insane?' I reply. 'I can't go! Not now. Not with everything that's going on.'

'And that's exactly why you *should* come. You need a break, Luce. You need to get away and leave this crap behind for a while.'

Despite my whines and protestations, Em doesn't give up.

'I promise you it'll be fun, and a heck of a lot easier than counselling, that's for sure.'

'But I'm not ready for this,' I say, still whining. 'Besides, you encouraged the counselling.' She's being ridiculous. I can't just drop everything—work, life, counselling—and run off to Ibiza as if it's the sanest thing in the world to do.

Em glares, the wind pulled from her sails. I've rarely seen her angry, not at me, anyway, except when it came to Joe. She didn't like him. I could tell from her scowls and crossed arms every time he was near that she resented him. Probably resented him pulling the plug on our 'free life', as she called it.

'Em?' I search her face for a glimmer of reprise. 'EM!'

'What do you want me to say, Lucy? It's been two fucking years since he died, and you still come up with all these excuses. It's like you need to keep punishing yourself, and for what?'

Anger bubbles under my already heated flesh. My desire to wound her with hurtful words is rising, and it's all I can do to keep my mouth zipped. But then Em's expression changes. Tears well and begin to trickle down her ebony cheeks, and she suddenly seems *vulnerable*.

'I'm sorry, Luce. I'm so sorry.' She rushes to my side, wrapping herself around me like a toddler with its mum as she sobs into my shoulder. 'I just want us to be like we used to be, like you were again on my birthday.'

I calm down as her words sink in, remembering the nights with

Matt and Jeremy, and how good I felt, even if it was for a short while. There is truth in what she's saying, much as it pains me to acknowledge it.

'Okay,' I whisper.

Em pulls back and scrutinises my face.

'Okay for what?'

'Okay. I'll go to Ibiza.'

Her eyes widen. 'Really?'

'Yes, really.'

'Luce, that's awesome. You won't regret it. We'll have an amazing time. We'll go to the beach, shopping and clubbing. Yay!'

She squeals again, bear-hugging me.

'Whoa, hold on. One step at a time.' Now it's my turn to pull back. 'I'm going, but I have to take it steady. If I'm doing this, I need to know you'll be there for me, that you'll have my back.'

'Of course,' she replies, unwrapping herself from me.

'Good. Shall we plan it out then?'

Em grins wide and pulls out a notepad from her bag.

After Em leaves, I am once again left alone with my thoughts. Perhaps a holiday *is* what I need. Joe was always working; he couldn't relax if there was a case he had on the go. On the rare occasion when we got away, it was never about chilling on a beach or partying with friends. His agenda was sightseeing derelict buildings like the Luxor Temple in Egypt or the Mycenae in Greece. Or slowly trawling aviation or maritime museums being sure to read every description or account of some notable flight or voyage. It bored me, but excited him, and who doesn't want their hard-working partner to have some much-needed down-time? But now he's gone, and there are no restrictions on where I can go and what I can do. No accountability.

Maybe I *can* escape for a while and recharge my batteries in a place where no one knows me or my past. Maybe it will help clear my head so when I resume my sessions with Marj I won't turn into a blubbering wreck each time. The more I consider the 'maybe's, the more I convince myself it's a good idea, even starting to feel excited about what might happen.

Maybe Ibiza is just what I need.

CHAPTER 12

I'm convinced Marj has figured out the back-story to Joe's death and put me on the condemned list. Don't get me wrong, she's doing what she always does during our sessions: sympathetic smiles, nodding, asking me questions to clarify things. If it was me and I suspected wrongdoing, there's no way I could carry on as normal.

'Lucy, you seem lost in your thoughts,' she says.

'Oh... sorry. Got a lot on my mind, I guess,' I say, stumbling over the words as she breaks my train of thought.

'Do you want to talk about it?'

I shake my head, lips pursed, and stare at Marj.

Should I ask her what she's going to do?

But somehow her kindly smile draws me in, flicking the closed switch to open. 'It's just that... well, I told you last week about it being my fault that Joe's dead, and—'

'And you're wondering what I think about it?'

'Well... yes.'

She puts down her pen and looks me in the eye.

'I'll be honest with you, Lucy. I think there is more to this than you've told me, *but* I'm not going to push you. You will tell me, if and when you are ready.'

'Oh.' I'm puzzled. What more does she need?

Marj leans in towards me and I mirror her.

'It's about when you're ready,' she says, picking up her pen again as if poised to take down the next lot of damning notes. 'Maybe it's time for us to talk about grief a little more.'

'Grief?'

'The stages we go through when we grieve. It can be a complicated process.'

I just stare at her.

'You see sometimes we are stuck and cannot move through these stages if something else is holding us back.'

'How do you mean?'

'Well, after we've gone through the shock and anger of our loss, we can find ourselves feeling hopeless and overwhelmed by it all because we have no control over it. We end up stuck until something happens that forces us to reach out for help. Only then are we ready and able to work towards acceptance of that loss, without getting angry, and without needing to blame someone, something or ourselves.'

'But how does any of that apply to me?' Has she even been listening to a damn word I've said?

'I'm wondering if blaming yourself for Joe's death is causing you to be stuck, stopping you from going through the grieving process.'

Although her words are making sense, they surely don't apply to me, do they? Yes, I was in denial at first that Joe was gone, but I don't believe for a minute I'm stuck. I'm here because it's where I *should* be. It's my punishment.

The *kerching* moment hits like a shot in the forehead and I stare at Marj, eyes wide. She seems to sense my epiphany but stays quiet.

Moments pass. No tears come. *Huh?*

'I think I understand,' I finally tell her, and it's probably the most genuine thing I've said to her so far. 'But what now?'

'Well, we work on dealing with the guilt. Why you feel the need to blame yourself?'

Uh-oh.

'You've reached out by coming to see me, so believe it or not you're already moving forward.'

'It doesn't feel like it,' I reply glumly.

'What does it feel like?'

'Like I'm back to square one.' My curt reply reflects the anger bubbling inside as we cover old ground.

'You sound frustrated by my comment,' she says, and I instantly regret being so flippant.

'I just don't want to go away feeling like crap!' And then I realise I haven't mentioned the holiday to her yet. *Shit!* I was going to wait until the end of the session.

Marj looks into me without saying anything. I feel I owe her an explanation. 'Em's asked me to go away to Ibiza with her for a few weeks. We fly out a week tomorrow.'

'That sounds like it could be good for you, but I sense you're still feeling like you haven't moved forward?'

'I don't want to spoil it for her.'

'Or yourself?'

'I guess so.' I look to Marj for some solution that will give me a reason to look forward to rather than dread going away carrying more baggage than any airline would permit.

'I'm not sure there's anything we can do today that can help with that as we're running out of time. Will you come to the session next week?'

'I don't think so. I'll be busy packing.'

She nods. 'In that case, let me give you some information to look through in the meantime so you have a better idea of what our next steps together might be.'

'Okay,' I reply, not entirely sure what she hopes to achieve.

'Until then, perhaps you might be able to put this aside for the duration of your holiday, safe in the knowledge that you'll be coming back to it when you return. How does that sound?'

'Yeah... okay. What information?'

'An article about the stages of grief. A bit more detail than we've gone into today. It's written from a counselling perspective, so may help give you an insight into where we might go with it.'

Marj excuses herself and leaves the room to get the information.

On the one hand, I feel frustrated at still being in this impasse, but on the other, Marj's words have given me hope there is a way forward, that she's with me on this journey. That the holiday is respite until more work can be done.

Maybe I can put this on the backburner until after the holiday. And just the idea of it brings a sense of relief as if letting go of my need to find a solution right now has freed me a little.

'Here you go.'

She passes me a booklet.

'I know you don't feel it at the moment, but the fact that we're here, going through this together is progress.'

I only hope she's right.

CHAPTER 13

On a hot, hazy late afternoon as the sun arcs high against a cloudless cyan sky, Em and I drop our bags onto cool terracotta tiles and breathe in our new surroundings. Her parents' two bedroomed villa, clinging to the hillside just outside of Santa Eulalia, one of Ibiza's main resorts, is our home for the next few weeks. From the balcony we are treated to a tantalising, albeit distant strip of azure blue water lined with honey-yellow sand far below the rooftops of cascading whitewashed villas. I smile to myself.

Yes, this will do.

Our four-hour flight was bearable, with Em spending the first hour or so going through our, mostly *her*, itinerary. Occasionally, I'd nod and smile in agreement, keeping to myself my own agenda of simply relaxing and getting a tan to brighten my pasty-looking skin.

As I head back inside, Em has already grabbed the larger of the two rooms with the queen bed, relegating me to two singles. I can hear her humming as she unpacks and wander through to her room.

Her suitcase is upside down on the bed, her essentials—mostly slinky dresses, makeup bags, hair dryer, and shoes—sprawled alongside it. I spy a box of condoms next to her book stack on one of the bedside tables, which can mean only one thing...

'Looks like you've packed for two months, not two weeks!'

'You can never have enough clothes and shoes,' Em smirks, holding up a pair of deep red Louis Vuitton heels.

Tutting, I head back to the living room and grab my bag and much smaller suitcase, and cart them to my bedroom.

Marj's leaflet juts out from the front pocket. Just having it with me seems enough to quell my doubts about being here, as though I've come equipped, just in case.

Em and I reconvene in the small living room to plot our next move.

'I'm starving!' she says, wrapping arms around her taut stomach. 'The food on the flight was bloody awful. We could head into town and grab something to eat.'

The kitchenette cupboards are barren, save for a few tea and coffee provisions, so we grab our bags and a complimentary map and head down into town. Before leaving, I take my wedding ring off, stashing it in my toiletries bag.

The downhill walk, navigating lanes and main roads in shoes ill-equipped for pot-holed tarmac and uneven paths, leads us to the main street. The smell of beer-drenched fish and chips greets us and my stomach grumbles. Port Esportiu, a large marina housing everything from small fishing boats to huge luxury yachts, sits over to the left. Swanky hotels and bars line the pink paved promenade, interspersed with souvenir shops and restaurants, all open, busy and loud with tourists hell-bent on having a good time. To the right is a vast stretch of sandy beach fronted by more whitewashed lux hotels and apartments, forming a crescent round to the Punta d'en Castelló from where the second stretch of pristine beachfront emerges. This beach is littered with people, sun loungers and the odd windsurfer or canoe. A constant hum in the background from music pumping out of bars reminds me we've arrived at the start of party season. Em rubs her hands together in glee. My gut twists.

'What do you fancy eating?' I ask, turning to Em.

'Seafood, definitely,' she replies, pointing to a small eatery across the street from us.

'We can eat and walk, then hopefully find a decent bar for a few drinks,' Em says, all too eager to get going. Rest and recuperation do not seem a high priority for her.

I roll my eyes but say nothing. We are on holiday after all, and throughout our friendship, Em has always taken the lead so, like an obedient sheep, I follow her crook.

After grabbing dinner, we stroll along the narrow main street taking in the heady mix of holidaymakers, bars, restaurants and souvenir shops. We stop every now and again to check out the more popular drinking holes along the way. Thrusting a leaflet in my hand, a young woman lures us into a small bar port side. It's a typical ex-pat business, serving fish and chips and selling Boddingtons and Carling Black Label on tap.

We find a table and Em heads off to get some drinks, making no effort to disguise she's checking out men on the way. Ever the flirt, she can't help herself, flashing a smile at every attractive male within a two-metre radius.

As the night progresses and the drinks flow, many of them freebies from men making it far too obvious they are trying to get into our knickers, I relax a little, easing into my surroundings. Em is once again in her element.

So here we are on our first night in Ibiza, fresh off the plane and drinking cheap Spanish Cerveza by the sea, surrounded by men. To be fair, I'm paying them lip service. Em is the one doing all the work while I sit at the end of the table and drink the rewards. I'm still in my head far too much to let the reins slip just yet, and coupled with the travelling and an early start, am knackered and ready to hit the sack... *alone*. Edging in towards Em, I tell her I'm going back to the villa to get some sleep.

'I'll come too,' she says, tittering as my mouth drops. 'I'm pooped and want to be fresh and ready for action tomorrow night!'

We say our goodbyes to whoever they are, avoiding the requests for phone numbers and future meet ups. The looks of confusion and disappointment are evident on their overly sun-baked faces, and we make our way back up the sloping streets to our villa.

Maybe Em will go easy on me. I'm not yet sure if there's another *itch* that needs scratching, but knowing Em, this will be one head-spin of a ride. My two recent one-night stands brought me back to life, albeit for a moment in time, but am I ready to do it again?

But as I ponder the thought, a tingle of excitement builds in my gut.

CHAPTER 14

Santa Eulalia is on the eastern side of Ibiza and our villa is in prime position to catch the morning rays. I fumble on the bedside table for my phone: 6.30 am. I feel groggy and can't get back to sleep, so ease myself out of bed and head for the bathroom.

After a quick shower and dress, I head out onto the villa's balcony and sit at the small wooden table, squinting as I sip my first cup of Spanish coffee, and reminisce of mornings long-ago sat with Em, a coffee and cigarette in hand. I tingle, smiling to myself.

Staring out at the small scrap of sea visible from the balcony, my thoughts drift to the past few weeks, settling on my last conversation with Marj. Sobering thoughts for the second morning of my holiday, and ones I need to push out of my head while I'm here if there's any chance of relaxing and recharging my batteries. I only hope Em doesn't have other ideas.

Sometime later, Em *quietly* bangs around in the kitchen, eventually joining me on the balcony, tea in one hand, a plate of toast in the other. With *Amy Winehouse* hair and hot pink slippers contrasting a demure satin dressing gown half-falling from her slender shoulders, I stifle a giggle as she plonks herself down next to me.

She rubs her eyes and glugs her drink. 'Hey.'

'Hey back,' I say. 'How'd you sleep?'

'Yeah, not bad. Bed's a bit soft. You?' She slides into her seat, yawning.

'Same. Strange waking up in a new place and staying, though.'

Em raises her eyebrows as if acknowledging the irony.

I decide not to elaborate.

'What do you fancy doing today? Shall we hit the beach?' I ask, sipping my coffee as Em munches on her toast.

'Sounds good. We can beach it for most of the day, then hit the bars after dinner,' she replies between mouthfuls. 'Maybe even go to a club?'

Her sheepish grin belies the fact she knows I want to ease myself in. She smirks at my groans, knowing she'll eventually get her way.

After a late breakfast and waiting ages for Em to get ready, we head into town and onto the palm-fringed crescent beach. Platje de Santa Eulalia is a clean, family-friendly beach, leaving little room for frolics. With manicured golden sand and rows upon rows of umbrellas and sun loungers, its main purpose seems to be sunbathing and swimming. We settle on adjacent sunbeds for some serious baking, greasing each other up with sun cream.

Ibizan sunshine warms me through, and I close eyes, drifting.

Em nudges me. 'Luce wake up! You're snoring!'

She belly laughs as I bolt upright, squinting, checking to see if anyone's watching.

'How long have I been out for?'

'About fifty minutes.'

Nearby sunbathers seem oblivious to my cat nap and so-called snoring. My dignity remains intact.

Em shuffles around on her lounger then flips over. 'Right, that's me cooked enough on that side.'

I feel like a swim. The Mediterranean is always so calm, lacking the surf that bashes the tidal coastlines. I tiptoe across warm sand to the water's edge.

Seawater laps around my feet as I step further and further into its cooling depths, drawing in sharp breaths as I adjust. After trudging for several minutes, it reaches chest height, deep enough for me to lunge forward and pierce its film to submerse myself in translucent wash. I swim for ages, the cool liquid, hot sun and salty kisses reviving my travel-weary body. I feel cleansed and freed all at once, totally present. Something I haven't experienced since...

Eventually, I swim back towards shore, dragging my lead-weight body out of the water. Heading back to Em, I notice a man sitting on the sand watching me walk by. He smiles, and I flush as I take in his sculpted chest, glinting eyes and salt-water kissed skin. A tingle, working its way from my face to between my thighs, takes hold and with head bowed, I quicken my pace and hurry past.

Em's still toasting as I approach, blocking her rays.

'Enjoy your swim?'

She twists her head towards me, squinting.

'Very refreshing.' I plonk myself down on the lounger, pick up the towel and pat myself down. 'Saw some nice views as well.' I chuckle and settle onto the lounger with a copy of 'Meet Your Match' to read.

'That's me done for today.' Em sits up and glances around. 'Let's head back to the villa via the deli. Tonight's going to be a big night.' She grins and rubs her hands together.

I roll my eyes and ease myself up from the lounger, pondering why this dusky beauty needs to sunbathe anyway, her skin already glowing. We gather up our stuff and make our way back into town.

We spend the rest of the day on the balcony chatting and drinking local vino. By mid-evening we are showered, dolled-up and raring to go. Em struts around in the shortest of skin-tight dresses, with heels almost as high as her legs are long. Full face paint, double strength for maximum effect under dim lights. I sigh, knowing what this means. She is, without question, on the pull tonight.

She looks me up and down.

'You'll do.'

She nods her approval of my short denim skirt and sleeveless white top. Compared to Em, I look plain, but at least I've made an effort, gaining a good inch in height from wedge heels. And Em's seen to it I'm wearing more make-up than has been my recent norm.

She shakes her head and walks towards the door, a familiar lioness glint in her eyes.

I can't help but giggle as Em totters down the hill beside me, knowing those stilettos must be trashing her feet. We meander down more familiar lanes and dart across the Carrer Margarita Ankermann to the outer rim of town. The closer we get, the more the white and cream buildings spring up from each side of the narrowing roads, clinging together as if they could fall at any time. We follow the paved promenade to a small Tapas bar near the marina and grab some dinner, the heady mix of garlic, spice, and sea food drawing us in.

After eating a commercialised version of what should've been a traditional paella at a small wooden table in the crowded, rustic dining area, we move to the bar for drinks. The sharks soon circle.

Being with such a raven beauty has its perks. It guarantees us a cheap night, but as I watch the men vie for our attention, I can't help thinking we're just playing an elaborate game of cat and mouse. We're in our thirties, for God's sake. Shouldn't we have wised up by now?

But I'm on holiday, so who cares?

I gulp down a cheap Rioja to flush the thoughts away.

We leave the bar with Em draped over some baby-faced, bronzed Ken-doll called Ant. I am stuck with his friend, Tom, a hulk of a guy who is already incoherent. Stumbling around, he uses me for support, pawing at my arms or hands. It's irritating as hell, deepening my desire to leave so I can chill out on our peaceful balcony. For Em's sake, though, I stay. Safety in numbers and all that.

We reach a nearby beach club and stand in the queue to get in. Santa Eulalia is much quieter than Ibiza town, more family oriented. There are no clubs here with top DJ's hitting the decks and spaced-out acid heads raving until the wee hours. There are a few discotheques in the bigger hotels and joined to beach bars, with clientele ages ranging from teenage to really-should-know-better.

Tom hovers in my face, his beer-breath wafting up my nose, not at all aware of my lack of interest. I sigh. This is going to be a long night.

Once inside, Em and I wait beside a bar table and chat while Ant and Tom put heads together, discussing god-knows-what.

'Em, I... err... think I might go.' I throw her my sweetest smile.

'No! You can't leave me! Ditch what's-his-name and come dance with me!'

I can barely hear her above the thumping nineties disco beats.

But Ant breaks away from Tom and drags Em onto the dance

floor. She throws her free hand up and tosses me an 'eek' look. I shrug and watch her go, resigned to Tom's company. He mumbles something about a drink and leaves me standing by the edge of the bar watching Em and Ant getting it on. I'm pissed off but knowing it's way too early to leave Em until I know she'll be safe with this Ant guy, resign myself to an evening of bullshit with Tom.

I stand alone, debating what to do, knowing I really can't be bothered listening to Tom's incoherent shit anymore, so plan my escape to a quieter terrace overlooking the beach. But my plan is foiled as Tom returns, plonking a beer in my hand and grabbing the other to yank me towards the dance floor.

'I don't want to dance!' I pull my hand free from his sweaty grip.

'What?'

'I said, I DON'T WANT TO DANCE.'

'Suit yourself.' He shrugs, releases my hand, and staggers off towards Em and Ant.

I gulp my beer, relieved, but it is short-lived as the reality sinks in that I'm standing on my own in a nightclub I've never been to before. I feel like the fish bait in a sea of sharks and glance around, contemplating, casting my eyes over the bodies on the dance floor, watching them sway to the rhythm. Mirroring. Tessellating. Touching. It reminds me of Matt, conjuring memories of drinking, dancing, and desire at play.

Edging back to the safety of the bar, I watch the writhing dancers from afar, tapping my thigh as the beat consumes me. Everyone and everything around me float further and further away until I'm spaced-out. Not from alcohol, but from drifting to where the veil between dance and trance is so tantalisingly thin.

'What are you doing in a club if you don't want to dance?'

A soft Irish voice and warm breath brush my cheek, cutting through the din of the club and pulling me back to the present. A shiver runs through me.

I turn, drinking in the man standing beside me: tall, smartly dressed, red hair, I think, it's hard to tell in the dim lights. His eyes are soft and inviting, yet his face is etched with life and experience. I flush, a vague memory of a stranger on the beach coming to mind.

'Huh?' I cup my ear.

He stands in front of me and leans in again. 'People generally come to clubs to dance. What's here for you?'

'Oh…' Heat rises in my cheeks as uncensored words tumble out, 'the music, I guess… and to watch.'

'A voyeur, eh? *What* do you like to watch?'

His molten voice challenges me. My mouth drops. 'People escaping into another world, I guess.'

His eyes bore into mine.

'You like to escape?'

'I used to.'

'Used to? Well, it's a shame you don't dance.'

'It is?'

'Yes. I would've asked you to dance with me, but seeing as you don't, maybe I can buy you a drink instead?'

I quiver, his proximity and directness starting to crumble my protective shell.

'I'm Brian.' He grins, holding out his hand.

'Lucy.' I return the gesture, my palm now clammy.

Brian holds onto my hand just long enough for a current to charge through me. He stares intently, and in *that* voice continues.

'Very nice to meet you Lucy. So, what can I get you?'

'A beer please... um... thanks.' I tease my hand out of his as flush number two takes hold. He heads towards the bar, leaving me rooted to the spot, bewildered. It's been a long time since a man has had *that* kind of effect on me.

He returns clutching two beers. 'So, what are you doing here, Lucy? Holiday?' He hands me a San Miguel.

'Yeah. You?'

'I live here.'

'You live here? Oh...' This could be a game-changer. 'So, what is it you do?'

He pauses, as if constructing his reply. 'Hospitality mainly. How long are you here for?'

'Two weeks. We arrived yesterday.' My mind whirrs.

'We? Is that your friend over there?' He points towards Em, who is up close and personal with Ant.

'Yes, that's her,' I raise my eyebrows in feigned shock.

'She seems occupied. Who's going to entertain you tonight, Lucy?'

I'm lost for words, but against my better judgement, and as my brain screams, 'Run away NOW!' I brazenly reply, 'I guess that would be you, then.'

His wicked grin speaks volumes. He grabs my free hand and walks me towards the dance floor. I'm brimming with anticipation for what might happen next, and as we reach a clearing, he pulls me closer, and rasps in my ear.

'I guess you will be dancing after all.'

His face is so close that the smell of his spice-laden aftershave invites me further in.

'I guess so,' I slink into him, knowing full well my fate is sealed tonight.

We move in unison to the entrancing beat, the spark inside reaching inferno proportions. No longer playing kiss chase with the boys, I am with the grown-ups; the connoisseurs of teasing touches and skilful sex.

Time becomes meaningless as we move and sway to track after track, the distance between us narrowing, our intimacy increasing.

Brian shifts behind me, wrapping his arms around my waist. His torso presses against me and, running on instinct, I tilt my head to the side. He moves my hair away from my neck, his hot breath brushing my skin. Our bodies sway, seemingly in slow motion, as his lips and tongue trail my neck, the buttons from his shirt pressing into my magnetised flesh registering all the way down to my groin.

His lips leave my neck and he moves round to face me again, still holding my waist as his free hand travels to the base of my neck. His mouth covers mine, his tongue infiltrating.

Reaching up, I clasp my hands around his neck as his other hand moves from my waist and up my back, a cold beer bottle pressing against my aroused flesh. His lips, leaving an aching, tantalising trail across my cheek, stop when they reach my ear.

'Wanna get out of here?' he says, his voice low and seductive.

I pull back. 'Where?' And my heart thumps out of my chest.

'My place?' Silken tones roll provocatively from his mouth.

I nod in slow motion, driven by an unspoken need.

'Do you need to let your friend know where you're going?' He tilts his head in Em's direction.

I pry myself from his hold. 'Uh-huh. Wait here.'

Each step towards Em feels feather light. Drink-induced lust is not a stranger, but I'm not drunk. This stranger has pushed every one of my buttons, a rarity I will not relinquish. I smile as I reach her and tap her shoulder.

'You okay, Luce?' She peels herself away from Ant.

'Yeah, I'm good. Listen, Em, I... err... well, I've met a guy. I'm kind of heading off to his place.' I pause, looking at the floor to hide my sheepish grin. 'I may not be back until morning.' She looks towards Brian and turns back to me, eyes wide.

'Him?'

I nod.

'Not bad...' She nods her approval. 'Have you got your key? I may be, err... tied up for the night as well.' Her wide grin says it all.

'Sorted,' I reply and kiss her cheek. 'Stay safe.' In this moment there is no pretence between us, no hidden agendas. We both know what we will be doing for the rest of the night, it was once a well-practised routine. We say our goodbyes and I head back towards Brian as if my life depended upon it.

'Ready?' he asks.

'I think so.'

He grabs my hand, leading me through the crowd and out of the club. I'm exhilarated and terrified at the same time, a heady mix wreaking havoc with my sense of reason. The cooling night air gives a welcome respite as we make our way to the roadside to flag down a taxi. Brian's hand is firm around mine, fuelling the pretence I can trust him... for tonight.

A taxi pulls up and we get in. Brian speaks in semi-fluent Spanish to the driver. I've no idea what he's saying, it's all too quick for me to follow. Besides, I'm too distracted and aroused by his warm body against mine. Once buckled in, he turns to face me, stroking my thigh with a firm, yet gentle touch as he claims my mouth again. His hand travels further up, and I can barely compose myself as an ache builds down low.

All sense of time diminishes.

The taxi eventually slows, and Brian pulls away. I gaze out of the window to see we are outside an old, white-washed farmhouse. A gravel driveway curls around to the front of the two-storey home, the taxi's wheels crunching as it stops near the main entrance. The windowless lower floor is decrepit in contrast to the upper floor, with a freshly painted iron staircase leading up to it, matching balcony and white wooden windows. I cast my head around, taking in the view framed by the taxi's rear-view window of twinkling lights and distant sea. Shades of magnolias and light greys from an almost full moon illuminate the surrounds with a welcome glow. The outline of dark hills over to the left, rooftops and dimmed white-washed buildings hugging the hillside to the right. Much nicer than the scant view afforded to Em and me from our villa.

Brian converses with the driver. They seem friendly, as if they know each other, and he hands over a small wad of euros. He gets out and comes around to my side, offering his hand after he's opened the door. We walk across the driveway and climb the staircase. At the top, he unlocks the door and goes in, switching on a nearby light as we enter.

The interior is modern and minimal, very different from the more traditional villa I am staying in and belying the outside impression of a rustic farmhouse. We enter through the kitchen with an open plan dining and living area flowing from it. Its design is sleek and masculine: dark kitchen cupboards and glinting pale stone surfaces, a black wood-stained dining table with leather-bound chairs, and a corner couch in cream leather. White walls and timber floors, not a hint of anything traditional. Nor a sniff of a woman's touch.

'Drink?' Brian asks, smiling.

'Please,' I nod. 'A beer if you have one.' An uncontrollable shudder takes hold as I survey my surroundings. Brian stands side-on, preparing our drinks in the kitchen, giving me the opportunity to sneak a peak in full light. Smart black trousers and a crisp white shirt adorn a sleek body standing, at a guess, just over six feet. Fiery kinked hair and russet stubble pepper his face. Not my usual type. Older. More commanding. An attraction I can't fight. Lust is building.

As if sensing my desire, he walks over, hands me a beer, and grabs hold of my free hand, leading me to the sofa.

'I like your place.' I glance around hoping to distract myself from the butterflies rave dancing in my gut, absorbing minute details like the jacquard pattern of the stoned-coloured curtains hanging rail to floor in the living area. Every nerve ending has fired in unison as if performing a gun salute. I grip his hand to steady my now quivering legs.

'Thanks. It's not long been finished.'

Brian sits on the sofa, unfazed, and pats the cushion next to him. I follow, even though the rational part of my mind once again screams, 'RUN!'

'Tell me about yourself, Lucy.'

I take a large swig of beer, place the bottle on the coffee table and face him. His blue eyes ensnare me, daring me, inviting me in as I rack my brains for something smart to say. Small talk is challenging in situations like this, more so when I'm not drunk enough to give a shit.

As if sensing my dilemma, he cups his hands around my head,

pulling me towards his delicious mouth, kissing me hard. Our tongues touch and caress. Involuntary moans seep out as our kiss deepens. He knows what he's doing.

I pull back, flushing with desire, eyes fixed on my lap.

'It's okay. We can skip the entrée, if you like,' he breathes.

I gaze up into his eyes and feel myself drowning, and in a bold move, climb onto his lap and begin undoing his shirt buttons.

He moans, clasping my shoulders as deft fingers pull the straps of my top down. Every inch of me ignites as his skilful fingers glide down the backs of my arms. I work my way down his chest, tantalising wisps of hair brushing against my fingers, then pause, slipping a hand beneath his shirt to explore. He draws in a sharp breath. A wave of lust consumes me as I undo the last few buttons and push his shirt over his lean shoulders.

I gasp at the sight of his firm, defined torso as his purposeful hands move down my back and unzip my skirt.

I shuffle deeper into his lap, his erection pressing against me, and tug the shirt from his trousers, inhaling the spicy yet sweet scent imploring me to taste him. Throwing his head back, he moans as I slide back and clasp his manhood through zip and pants.

He pulls down my top exposing my white lace bra and traces a gentle, yet firm line from my waist to the backs of my shoulders.

Rasping as desire takes hold, he slips his fingers through the straps and peels down my bra, licking his lips as if he's about to taste forbidden fruit. Those eyes, as blue as the coastal waters off Ibiza, pierce every inch of my defences. My breath hitches as he leans in to taste an engorged nipple.

Eyes closed, he groans and stiffens as I move my hand rhythmically over his erection. I tighten my grip, gasping as his mouth engulfs my breast. I'm aching to taste him, to have him inside me, to conquer him. I release him and slide onto the floor, parting his legs on the way down. He leans back as I undo the zipper and release him and rhythmically run my tongue from base to tip, engulfing him.

He groans again, and I sense he's on the edge, so slow my pace, triumphant and exhilarated by my power over him. His eyes burn into me, fuelling my desire further, the dampness between my legs signalling my need.

I release him, ease myself up, and cast off my skirt, top and bra with urgency. Brian follows suit, discarding his remaining clothes until we are standing face to face, naked, willing players in a grown-up game of lust.

'You're a tease,' Brian says, lowering his gaze over my exposed flesh.

My last line of defence breaks as he bends to engulf my nipple with his mouth, licking and biting.

'So, this is how you want to play.' His mouth claims mine again as his hand travels down my side and across my stomach, leaving a tantalising tingle in its wake. Deft fingers delve through my pubic hair, probing my clitoris with masterful strokes. My body weakens, and I fumble to grab his erection and continue my onslaught as I teeter on the edge of this precipice, spurred to jump by his quickening breath.

His fingers and mouth release me.

'Please, don't stop.' Panting, aching, and throbbing from his touch, I want to explode as if it's the only thing in this world that matters right now.

'Come to bed with me, Lucy,' he growls, grabbing hold of my

hand.

I nod slowly, eyes locked on his, and he takes my hand and leads me into a bedroom.

He pushes me down onto the bed, then retrieves a condom from a bedside drawer, rolling it on with fervour. He stands at the foot of the bed eyeing me from head to toe, my whole body blazing under his gaze. I part my legs, granting the access we both so desperately need. He moves up between them, thrusting into me in one swift, measured motion. I gasp at his welcome intrusion.

My legs curl around his back as he builds an urgent pace. The ache inside me is almost too much. Too sweet. Verging on painful. Brian speeds up his onslaught, each thrust faster and deeper than before. I can't hold back and my orgasm rips through me like an untamed animal, crying out as the aftershocks ravage me again and again.

Panting and breathless, Brian yells out too, collapsing on top of me, spent.

We lie motionless for a time, suspended, revelling in the afterglow.

He was good. *Really good.* His weight on top of me, his subtle, spicy smell, the saline taste of him in my mouth, his heated skin against mine, unfamiliar, yet... *welcoming?*

He tosses a drunken, post-coital grin, then rolls off me and the bed, making his way to the bathroom. Returning a few moments later, he plops down beside me, propping his head on his elbow, his eyes narrowing as if searching for the answer to a question he hasn't yet asked.

We lay together, catching our breaths, him studying me; me drifting.

'You okay?' he asks.

I nod. 'Why do you ask?'

'You're not saying much.' He reaches over and strokes my cheek.

'This part is always... awkward.' I look away, cheeks flushing.

'Is it?' He leans over and plants a soft kiss on my lips. 'Does this feel awkward?'

'No,' although inside, jitters take hold.

'Then stop worrying about it. We can talk, or not. We can fuck, or not. No expectations.' He winks, lightening the mood.

'Okay,' I reply, already seduced by the thought of more mind-blowing sex. The part of me that wanted to flee has remained quiet, much to my relief. But I can't trust the other part. As much as Brian is pressing buttons caked under layers of dust, I must stay on my guard. Joe pressed those buttons too, and that didn't end well at all.

My mood drops like an express elevator as inner dialogue messes with all sense of reason. The only thing I'm sure of in this moment is Brian has reached me, albeit in a sexual way, and I want to revel in the afterglow for a while longer.

As though he's sensed my nosedive, Brian pipes up, 'I could really do with a smoke. Coming?' His comment throws me, but he winks again, pulling me back. I manage a smirk as I recall the moments before when he made me come in spectacular style.

'You smoke?' I hadn't smelled it on him.

'Every now and again. It's a pleasure thing.'

He gets off the bed and opens a white-shuttered wardrobe.

'Okay, I'll join you.' Another itch will get scratched tonight.

'I was hoping you would.'

Brian pulls out two hotel-style white dressing gowns, puts one over himself and slips the other over me, then grabs cigarettes from his bedside drawer. I wrap myself up and follow him through French doors out onto a balcony, the cooler air refreshing my enflamed skin as I take a seat at a small white table.

I have no idea what time it is. Tiredness has left me. I am energised and awakened.

Brian grabs two cigarettes from the packet, passing one to me. He lights his and then holds the flame for me to light mine. The acrid smoke hits the back of my throat and I cough at its harshness.

'You don't smoke?' Brian says exhaling.

'Not for a while.' The coughing passes and I take another drag. A heady rush soon kicks in.

I slink back in the chair and puff away, the oversized dressing gown slipping from my shoulder. Brian tilts his head to the side and smiles.

Does he do this often?

I gaze at the twinkling lights of the town below. 'It's a great location.'

'I know. As soon as I saw this place, I knew it was the one.'

'I can see why. Have you been here long?'

'Just over a year, and most of that time has been spent with renovations going on.' He shakes his head. 'The Ibizans are known for their laid-back approach to any kind of hard labour. If it's too hot, too cold, raining, or over three hours work, they seem to fall shy of it.'

I chuckle, imaging Brian roughing it in a dusty, barn-like building. 'Drink?'

'Yeah. Okay.' The tobacco has left a stale taste in my mouth.

'I have a drop of Can Rich Tempranillo, if you're a red wine fan.'

I have no idea what the wine is, but nod. 'Do you fancy yourself as a connoisseur?'

Brian lets out a belly laugh. 'Not at all. Can Rich is a local winery. It just sounds impressive.'

He disappears to get the drinks leaving me with the opportunity to suss out the area. Other than the lights of Santa Eulalia, the surrounds are dark, with only a few nearby buildings visible. I try to second-guess where my villa is, but Brian's place is also on a hillside, and I haven't been in Ibiza long enough to have memorised where the land lies.

Brian returns with a bottle and two glasses of red, passing one to me. I take a few gulps, the tannin in the grapes instantly drying my mouth.

'So, whereabouts are you from?' he asks, taking a swig. He pulls two more cigarettes from the packet.

'Norwich. I'm an East Anglian born and bred. You?'

'I'm from Bray in Ireland.'

He registers my blank expression.

'It's just south of Dublin.'

He lights the cigarettes and hands one over.

'Thanks,' I take a long drag without coughing this time. 'How long have you been in Ibiza for?'

'Nearly nine years.'

'A while, then. What brought you?'

'Oh, you know... this and that. Fancied a change more than anything.'

'That sounds a bit vague.'

'One for another time, I think.'

His response takes a few seconds to register, and he frowns when he sees my puzzled expression.

'You're thinking there won't be?'

'What?'

'Another time.'

I look away, searching for the right words.

'It's okay. I get it. You're on holiday and you just want to go with the flow, right?'

'I guess...'

'It's okay. It doesn't stop us enjoying tonight, though.'

'No, it doesn't.' I'm confused by something, though, and figure I can ask the question without repercussion. 'I guess you're used to this kind of thing.'

'What kind of thing?'

'This... one-nighters. What with all those willing girls to pick and choose from.'

Brian shakes his head. 'Actually, no. This is the first time in a while.'

'Oh? Then why me?' The question slips out.

'You seemed lost.'

'Lost? What do you mean?'

In the darkness, I swear his eyes glisten as much as the lights below as they bore into me. Yet, instead of disarming me, I feel steady, like it's just two people having an adult conversation.

'Well... when you were with that guy, it seemed like you didn't want to be there, but didn't know where to go.'

'So, you thought you'd come and rescue me?' I know my tone is a tad sarcastic.

'Not at all. When you brushed him off, I thought I'd offer an alternative.'

'Oh, you did, did you?'

'Are you saying you wished you'd stayed in the club?' His cheeky grin challenges.

'Well... no,' I stumble a reply. 'I just want you to know that I wasn't looking for this.' I can almost hear an inner voice mocking and laughing at my pointless attempt to salvage my dignity.

'And *this* is something you don't do?'

'Not for a while.' I mimic his earlier comment, but shame bubbles below the surface.

He smiles, reaches over and squeezes my hand. 'Don't worry. This is what it is. Let's enjoy what we have of it.' And with that, he tops up the wine glasses.

After we empty the bottle and smoke a few more cigarettes between small talk, Brian whispers, 'Come back to bed with me?'

He rises, holding out his hand, and without hesitation, I take it.

We reach the bed and he clasps my shoulders, kissing me hard and sliding my robe off. I can't help myself reciprocating as he pushes me onto the bed, his full weight bearing down as I again succumb to him. The ache inside builds rapidly as we once again explore each other's bodies, more slowly this time, and with deliberate touches.

I've no idea what the time is when we've finished. I lie with my head resting on Brian's chest listening to his slowing breath, lulling me as my eyelids get heavier and heavier.

CHAPTER 15

Blinking, I wake up, stretching out as the sun's warmth spreads across my face through the undressed window in Brian's bedroom. He's still asleep, the sheets just covering his legs and torso giving me a teasing view of his naked body.

I ease myself onto my elbows, the reality of the situation sinking in. Much as I liked the way Brian's body moulded with mine, how I drowned in the depths of seemingly mutual desire, I can't be here when he wakes up.

I slip out of bed and creep towards the bathroom, the urge to pee strengthening. The mirror throws back a bedraggled image.

Who is she, and why is she still here? The voice in my head goes on to taunt me with, 'you just can't help yourself, can you?' I wish it would shut the fuck up.

Freshening up as best I can without making a racket, I sneak out of the bedroom and into the living room to gather up my clothes. My pulse quickens as I rush to dress, but I can't resist having a final look at Brian before I leave. I tiptoe back to his room and watch him for a few moments, his chest rising and falling gently in his slumber. Memories of his lips trailing kisses on my neck flood back, reigniting my desire. I shake my head and sigh. *Shame.* A one-time trip, even though I'm tempted by the thought of a second test-drive.

Trying to push last night's dalliance far from my mind, I make my way to the door, but as I leave, the realisation hits like a punch in the face. I have no idea where I am. *Shit!* I wish I'd paid more attention to the taxi ride.

It's already warm and bright outside considering it's still early. I wish I had some sunglasses and a decent pair of walking shoes. I look around, trying to get my bearings, hoping to remember fragments of the trip up here. The driveway veers off to the right towards a road, so I walk as lightly as I can, but my wedges still crunch in the gravel.

At the road, left seems to head further up the hill, so I turn right and walk down a narrow lane barely covered by tarmac. It isn't long before my feet ache, so I take off the wedges and continue barefoot down the hill, even though the surface is already hot and uneven.

I feel like I've been walking for ages but notice the houses along the roadside are getting closer together, hopefully a sign that civilisation is nearby. The rooftops of the three- and four-storey hotels in the town span the horizon ahead, so I stop for a moment to breathe it in. The sun has risen a few centimetres above the still sea, the morning haze throwing out rose-gold hues. It's so beautiful. Of all the times I'd woken at sunrise in a panic or despair, I'd never once gone outside to sample the therapeutic effects of a new dawn. It's warmth and kaleidoscope of oranges, pale pinks, and golds might've illuminated me with the promise of a better day. And even though my dry mouth and throbbing head tell the story of a long, sex-filled night and the need for respite, this moment in time somehow feels precious. This sunrise, my eyes are open and not clouded by guilt and hopelessness.

A battered blue truck passes me from behind, tooting its horn. An old guy leans out of his window, yells something in Spanish and laughs, driving on. I can guess what he's saying. I must look ridiculous walking barefoot down a craggy road in last night's clothes. I cross several more roads in my quest to reach the town centre, wider and smoother than where I've just walked from.

'Thank God,' I breathe as town comes into view, relieved I can now find my way back to the villa.

It takes another twenty or so minutes to get back. The uphill walk seeming so much steeper than before.

When I finally arrive at the villa, I fumble around in my purse to find my keys, tiptoeing as I let myself in in case Em is still asleep.

It's cool, darkened, and quiet inside. Plopping my shoes on the floor, I head to Em's room to see if she's there. The door creaks as I open it a notch, and I hold my breath. She's fast asleep, but lying next to her, barely covered, is Ant. His naked body exposed, and his leg draped across Em's. I gasp, quickly shutting the door and scrunching my eyes to block out the image.

What the hell was she thinking?

My mood nosedives like a plane in steep descent. I don't want to have to deal with this when she wakes up. But my head is throbbing and sleep looms, so I head to the bathroom to find pain killers. The image of Ant's naked body plagues my thoughts. Splashing my face with cold water doesn't help. I'd rather reminisce over last night than have to think about this.

I pop a few Panadol and head off to my room, sinking into the too-soft mattress.

The whistle of the boiling kettle wakes me. Em's hushed voice is still shrill, intertwined with Ant's low, dulcet tones. I will myself out of bed and head for the bathroom, hoping they won't notice me, knowing I will have to talk to Em about this *situation*.

'Luce, hey!'

Em calls as my attempt to sneak to the bathroom fails.

'Hey,' I reply, rubbing eyes encrusted with last night's make-up. 'Be with you in a tick.' I shut the bathroom door, locking it behind me.

Attempts to freshen up prove futile as I splash handful upon handful of cooling water on my face, brush last night's wine stains from my teeth, and down more Panadol.

'Morning, sleepyhead,' Em chirps.

I trundle into the kitchen area. She acknowledges my grimace, pulling a face like that of a scolded child.

'Coffee?'

She avoids my glare.

'Yeah, thanks.'

Em pours me a cup, spoons in some sugar and hands it over, lowering her gaze. I think she's got the message.

'Can I talk to you for a second?' I ask, eyebrows raised.

She looks over toward Ant. 'Um... Luce, you remember Ant from last night?' she says, diverting the focus again.

Ant is slouching on one of the sofas, wearing nothing but striped blue jocks and fiddling with his phone. Hairy legs hang over the armrest and I cop an eyeful of chicken-skinned chest with contrasting arms sizzled by unshielded sunshine.

Urgh.

I put down my coffee and wrap my arms around my chest.

'Err... yeah. Hi,' I say, barely making eye contact and offering a half-smile and wave of the hand as I try to hide my distaste.

He pops his ruffled head up and grins as if we're lifelong friends, but the sloshing around in my gut tells me otherwise. Catching Em's gaze, I jerk my head towards the patio door.

Em follows me out onto the balcony as I mentally prepare to get on my soapbox and give her what for, but she gets in first.

'Before you say anything, Ant forgot his keys, and when we got back to his hotel, Tom wasn't there.'

I toss her a nod, arms folded, waiting for more.

'It won't happen again. I'll make sure.'

She proffers a hopeful smile and hugs me just as Ant peeps his head around the door.

'I need to get back, babe.' He walks over and hooks an arm around Em's shoulder, planting a kiss on her cheek. 'See you tonight?'

'Sure. Seven-thirty?' Her face flushes.

'Cool. See you at the bar, babe.'

'I'll see you out.'

She throws me a feeble smirk, shrugging her shoulders as if to say, 'I know!'

'See ya,' Ant calls over as he and Em make their way to the door. I think she believes she's placated me enough, but annoyance niggles like pawing cat.

Em comes back a few minutes later and pulls up a chair, scraping along the tiled floor of the balcony.

'So, what do you think?'

Another attempt to throw me off guard.

'He seems nice.' I play along, still reeling, twisting my fingers under the lip of the table.

Em and I have a strict code which *she* came up with after an awful relationship in her early twenties. She vowed never to let herself be hurt again, and with that, concocted a plan to ensure nights out stayed safe and uncomplicated, never allowing anyone to scratch below the surface unless it was on her terms. And like the sheep I am, I followed suit: no guys back at our places; condoms *always*; and no repeat performances, unless there's little chance of future encounters. She's broken the first, not sure about the second, but, no doubt, wants me to agree to the third.

Em believes her Mr Right won't be found amongst the drunks and desperates frequenting nightclubs. Our code makes sure liaisons are short-lived, so why break it now?

'So, you ended up back here.' My tone is flippant.

'Sorry Luce.' Her chocolate eyes plead for forgiveness.

'Well... I guess it couldn't be helped. But you're seeing him again?'

'Um... I guess so.' Her sheepish grin says it all, knowing an explanation is owing. 'He's cute, and we got on really well. And I thought, well, since we're on holiday... it couldn't hurt. Just a fling, ya know?'

She bats her eyelashes as if hoping to score an approval. Why, I've no idea; she'll do what she pleases anyway, and I'll go along with it.

I roll my eyes. 'Whatever you like, *babe!*' Although, deep down I can't blame her for wanting a bit of fun.

She giggles and throws her arms around me, planting a wet, sloppy kiss on my cheek.

'So, tell me, what did *you* get up to last night?' She says, turning the focus three-sixty.

'You know what I got up to. I went to Brian's place...'

'And?'

'We had sex... twice, and then I left.' I can't help grinning as I recount the prior night's events.

'Luce! Tell me!'

I chuckle, deliberately leaving her hanging.

'Was he any good?'

'Very.' My reply is as much a shock to me as it is her, judging by her flashy smile, wide eyes and raised brows, but it's true. Too true.

'Are you going to see him again?'

'No! I'm not you!' I spit back, instantly regretting it. He was a one-nighter, albeit a very nice one, I tell myself, quivering as I remember Brian's smell, his touches, the way he teased my body into life.

'Why can't you just let your hair down and have a bit of fun! We're only here for a short time, what harm can it do?'

She's right, if this were pre-Joe circumstances, but keeping control is my safety net. If I loosen its grip, I risk an emotional investment I'm not ready for. I just can't allow myself to fall into that trap. Not now. Having a night of passion and walking away with my dignity and emotions intact is the only option.

We chat for a while, discussing the night's arrangements, but tiredness and the need for respite has taken hold, and I don't want to meet up with the likes of Tom again. But Brian. What if there's a chance I could see Brian?

The more excited Em gets about meeting up with Ant again, the surer I feel about wanting a night on my own, chilling out. Em's stamina far outstrips mine these days, and this is the start of what promises to be a few wild weeks.

Em is glammed up and ready to go out to meet up with Ant and has sworn to keep him away from our villa. The thought of his pasty, hairy body slouching across the sofa leaves me cold.

'You'll be okay?'

She kisses my cheek as she's about to leave.

'For sure,' I smile, clasping her beautifully manicured hand in reassurance.

The door slams behind her and the balcony beckons. With a glass of local red in hand and a newly bought packet of overpriced Marlboro Lights and lighter, I pull up a chair and just breathe in the solitude, grateful for the headspace.

The evening air brushes against my skin, refreshing and cooling flesh already over-exposed to the sun's rays. I gaze out over the rooftops, my eyes following their trail to the town below and the small strip of blackening ocean. The refreshing smell of pines from the surrounding hills mixes with the meaty, smoky smell of a nearby barbeque. Laughter and chatter ring out as I light up a cigarette, put my feet up on another seat and lean back, sipping on a dry fruity Rioja.

Two glasses of wine and three cigarettes later, and with the sun already dipped behind the hills, my eyelids droop heavy like lead. I drift off into a world of strobing lights and thumping music, of dancing with a red-haired man who's trailing scorching kisses up my neck...

A slamming door wakes me.

Moments later Em is standing at my side, glaring. Her face crimson and blotched by tears.

'Em?' I blink, bolting upright.

'That fucking prick!' She shakes her head, pacing back and forth, wiping her nose with the back of her hand.

'Who? What's happened?' A chill takes hold, as if a cold front has suddenly moved over.

'I can't believe that arsehole! Men are such useless pricks!' She says, spitting feathers. 'I should never have agreed to meet up with him, especially with all his mates there. What is it about blokes being total dicks when their mates are around?' She carries on pacing, fists and teeth clenched, her eyes glistening from tears still being shed.

'What happened? Em?' My heart thumps as panic grips. *What have they done to Em?*

'Ant. That's what happened. He was already tanked up when I met him, been drinking practically all day. It went downhill from there.'

'What do you mean?' I stand up, grabbing her arms, staring into eyes wide with a fear I've never seen before in them.

'Showing off in front of his mates. Groping me. Making lewd comments about us fucking like it was a big joke.' Her voice jellifies. 'It was like I... I was his trophy.'

'What the—' My stomach knots.

'By the time we got to the club he was full-on doing my nut in, and it was pretty obvious he wasn't going to be able to perform! Fucking men!'

She can't keep still, rubbing her eyes, tugging her hair, barely looking at me.

'What happened at the club?' I ask, trying to reach her.

'Him and his mates, they...'

I gasp. 'They what?'

Em shakes her head as if trying to rid her mind of the awful memories.

'Em. Tell me. They what?' Panic rises from the twist in my guts, and I fear the worst.

'They all wanted a piece of me,' she says, glaring. 'Ant was goading them, telling them that I was his and they'd have to wait their turn… It was like I was being paraded around a meat market.'

'Oh my God! Em.' I wrap my arms around her, bringing her into me, hoping to soothe.

'I felt sick… humiliated, so went to leave, but he came after me.'

She wriggles from me and grabs my wine glass, gulping down the remainder as if burying the unsavoury feelings.

'He called me a slag, a whore, or something. I told him to fuck off and then ran for it.' Tears flow from eyes that speak of a hurt long since buried.

'He said what? I'll fucking kill him.' Every part of me shakes as anger bubbles from within. And like a wolf protecting her cubs, the urge to defend my beautiful friend takes hold as my fists clench.

'I told him he was a limp dick in front of his precious mates who'd gathered round like a pack of hyenas to watch the performance.'

Em's emotions are on show—a rarity—as I pull her back to me. She snivels into my hair. 'I'll get some more wine. You sit down.'

She snorts, but like an obedient puppy, does as she's told as I head indoors to get the wine.

She downs the first glass like her life depended on it, then after several more gulps, sighs, as if finally accepting this unsavoury turn of events. All the while I listen, holding her hand, hoping to calm us both.

She sighs again, shaking her head. 'I should know better, shouldn't I?'

She throws me a weak smile and goes in for another glug.

'We both should.'

'Maybe when we're old and grey, eh?'

She wipes her face and faux smiles again, but I can see the frown, the hurt on show.

'At least my mascara's waterproof.'

We both giggle, lightening the fragile air surrounding us. Em shivers, pulling her hand away.

'I'm going to get a blanket.'

I'm not used to seeing her like this. She's usually the one in control, the one who knows what she wants. But when she returns and pours more wine, she changes tack, as if wanting to erase what has happened. She chats about other things like excursions and beach visits, ignoring the unspoken thoughts of what might have come to pass if she had stayed in the club. The hurt brushed over with alcohol and, in my case, cigarettes.

All traces of tears now wiped away, Em says, 'That Brian guy was at the club. He came over and asked where you were.'

'What did you tell him?' I try to mask the panic vying with excitement rising in my voice.

'I told him you were sick.'

Her eyebrows rise arch as if to check she'd said the right thing.

'He said that might explain why you didn't stay after you'd, you know.'

She chucks me a knowing glance.

'He asked for your number, so I lied and said I didn't have my mobile on me.'

'Nice one, Em. Thanks.' A breath escapes, but the pang still grips, and my pulse quickens. Do I feel relief, or *regret*?

'He looked gutted but gave me this to give to you.'

She hands me a crumpled business card retrieved from her pocket. I offer it a chaste glance: 'Brian Phillips – Proprietor' ignoring the logo, then toss it on the table and reach for my cigarettes.

After lighting up and taking a long drag, I reply, 'Trouble is, we've got two blokes to avoid for the rest of the holiday now! Three if you include Tom.'

Em chuckles, cocking her eyebrow. 'There're so many bars and clubs here, especially in Ibiza Town, I'm sure we'll manage it.'

She may have had one strike, but she's not down and out.

'So, smoking again?' She says, eyeing the fag packet on the table.

'I guess so,' I reply, taking another drag.

She tuts.

I ignore her.

We chat for a while longer, the earlier drama becoming locked away in the vault of unfortunate incidents, then head off to bed.

Before leaving the balcony, I cast a quick glance at the card lying on the table. I should throw it away, but I just leave it there. *But I should know better, shouldn't I?*

CHAPTER 16

My time in the sun has helped me bloom like a tulip in spring pushing through once frozen ground and opening its petals for the first time. The berating voice in my head has quietened. The late nights, alcohol and lingering kisses from strangers have played a part, but I feel refreshed and ready only, I'm not sure what it is I'm ready for.

Em and I jostle over bathroom space as we apply the finishing touches to our hair and make-up. I glance at her as she applies mascara with poise and precision to eyelashes already full and stunning. It's as though this final layer will make the difference between passable and drop-dead gorgeous. But she has no problem getting interest from guys, what with legs that go on forever, pert little breasts and smouldering dark eyes. Only, something feels different today. Em's shine has dimmed. Any bricks dislodged from her carefully constructed walls have been sealed back in and plastered over thicker than ever. Every now and again she sighs, as though her reflection is not what she expected, and reapplies make-up where it's not needed, adding yet more layers.

I run the brush through my hair one last time and give Em a quick twirl.

'You'll do,' she says with a low titter.

She knows full well I'm making much more of an effort to look as good as I'm feeling. My dresses are shorter, shoes higher, mind open to the possibilities.

'Just remember what we said.' I wag my finger and throw Em a fake stern glare, even though this is no joking matter. It's all we have to keep us safe and ensure maximum fun with minimum fallout. And given what happened to Em with Ant, we've tightened the rules of our game, almost padlocked them.

We leave the little villa that is now our home from home and totter into town, ready for a fresh night of clubbing. We set our routine: food, bar, taxi to a club in Ibiza Town, and home, *alone*. I haven't indulged in any one-nighters again, and neither has Em. We've both raised the stakes. Brian was a cut above the usual pub and club boys; more mature, sure of himself, and enigmatic in an understated kind of way. And as for Ant, well, once bitten, twice shy springs to mind.

I'll be honest, I've daydreamed about my night with Brian on many occasions, but encounters such as these must stay just that, encounters. I want to make the most of the freedom and anonymity this place has to offer. To nourish my soul while I have the opportunity. No ties. No risks.

We arrive at what has become our favourite eatery, a gorgeous, traditional little café bar next to the harbour selling delicious Tapas, cheap Spanish wines and my new favourite beer: Cruzcampo Cerveza. Filled with old men sitting alongside the rustic wood as if they are part of the decor, they chat to each other and bartenders like old friends. The plinking of traditional guitar music plays softly in the background as freshly cooked seafood and chorizo wafts. There are few tourists in here, maybe that's why we like it. I'm certain the likes of Ant and Tom wouldn't dream of cramping their style in a low-key place such as this. We can eat without distraction, even though the old guys occasionally flirt with us, and spend quality time together before the serious drinking and clubbing starts.

'Can I try some of your potatoes?' Em asks through a mouthful of seared octopus.

I push one of my dishes towards her. 'Potato Bravas. Nice and spicy, too.'

'Yum.' Her eyes widen as she presses her fork into what's left.

While her mouth is full, I take the opportunity to find out how she's doing.

She drops her fork to the dish and glares across at me.

'I'm fine. Really. You've no need to worry.'

'But I do worry. We've done some stupid shit in the past, but the other night—' I look away, hoping the image of what might have been will not materialise.

'Look... it was just one of those things. We're old enough and wise enough to figure out that boys and booze aren't necessarily a good mix. I've learnt my lesson. Only grandpas for me now.' She smirks, her eyes glinting as she flicks ebony locks away from her face and eyes up the old codgers lining the bar.

I feign a titter, wishing I had as much faith in her statement as she did when truthfully, how we've avoided getting ourselves into worse situations is beyond me.

'You're such a worrier, Luce. Always have been.' She gobbles down some more potato and giggles. 'Do you remember when we met those guys in your local in Trowse? They must've been fifty-odd!'

I shake my head, grimacing, as I recount the story.

Two eighteen-year-olds already pissed on Lambrusco, propping up the bar near closing time in the Red Lion, approached by two 'old enough to know better' guys, one wearing a wedding ring. The wedded guy thrusted his business card into Em's hands, and in the cheesiest of tones asked, 'Can we buy you two lovely young ladies a drink?' Needless to say, we both jumped at the chance of free drinks, with another bottle of wine soon appearing on the bar top.

'We were so naïve then, weren't we?' Em states, shaking her head in disgust. 'I didn't think we'd ever get rid of them.'

I sip my beer. 'Yeah. They seemed even more excited when we pretended to be lesbians!'

Em belly laughs, but her face quickly sours. 'Those things they were suggesting—'

'Ew,' I reply, taking another glug. 'Just as well the barman rescued us. He must've known.'

'But the funny thing about it all was *you* the next day going incognito in case they spotted you in the village.'

She points at me, leans back and roars.

'That wig!'

It'd taken me ages to get over that incident. Weeks of parading around in a short blonde wig and Jackie O sunglasses until I felt safe enough to let my guard down and be me again.

Could that be when my fuck-em and leave-em attitude started?

Em and I spend a good hour or so finishing up eating, drinking and chatting, revving ourselves up before moving on to a trendier bar in town where the stakes are higher. This precious time has been enlightening. It's helped our friendship flower again and reaffirmed we are, and need to be, there for each other because no one else will.

We eventually leave the safety of the café and head to a

beachfront bar. We meet guys in these bars who are keen to pay us attention and buy us drinks. They take us to clubs in the hope drinks will lead to dancing, and then possibly something more. But Em and I are playing it cool, ditching would-be suiters when it's clear they're pissed enough to not notice we've done a runner.

It's not long before two twenty-somethings, whose eyes fell on us the minute we walked in, break away from a larger pack and head our way. I'm grateful Em and I must still look young enough to be of interest, either that or they're too drunk to care.

One of the guys smiles at me. 'Hi, how's it going?'

I glance over at Em, bemused, replying, 'It's going good, thanks. How's it going for you?'

He beams and nods at me.

'Yeah, good too. Err... can we get you ladies a drink?'

Bingo!

'That'd be great,' Em says, butting in, 'we'll both have beers, thanks.'

'Cool.'

I spy his trembling hands as he turns to the other guy, mumbles something, then heads off to the bar.

The other guy smiles, his expression somewhere between terror and excitement. 'So, what are you ladies doing in a bar like this?'

His blatant cheesiness makes me chuckle.

'We're waiting for some cute guys to buy us drinks. And well, what d'ya know, here you are!'

Em's sarcasm falls on inexperienced ears.

'How fortunate because we were looking for some lovely ladies to buy drinks for,' he says, feigning confidence. Either that or he's trying out crap chat-up lines in the hope one will work.

'That *is* fortunate.' Em flashes him a beaming fake smile.

The other guy returns with four bottles of beer and hands them round. He introduces himself and his friend as 'Steve' and 'Michael', best friends from Winchester. It's all very polite, as if we're at a business expo. Steve is an Export Manager and Michael is at University in Leeds. Why this is important is beyond me, but they seem happy to part with their cash, which *is* fortunate because I'm going to need a lot of drinks to get through these next few hours.

Surprisingly, though, time passes smoothly, and my initial harsh judgements have waned. Steve is... *nice*. Entertaining and cute, although too young for my tastes. At this stage, we might just make it to a club with them. Em is doing her best to feign interest in Michael, although I can see she's struggling. He's the better looking of the two, but has an arrogance that, judging by Em's clipped responses, is getting annoying. Her arms are folded. Her guard is definitely up.

Many, many drinks later, both Steve and Michael are well on their way to being trashed, wanting to leave the bar and head to a club in Ibiza Town. At this stage, I'm not sure if I want to go with them. I'm not interested in hooking up with either of them, and by the looks of things, neither is Em. We excuse ourselves and visit the Ladies for a regroup.

'I'm not sure about this,' I tell Em as I coat my lips with gloss.

'I know what you mean, but, bugger it, we're getting free drinks out of them, and we can accidentally *lose* them once we're in the club,' Em replies, touching up her lipstick.

It wouldn't be the first time we've used this strategy to good effect.

'Are you sure you want to do this, Em?'

'Yeah,' she replies, nonchalant.

I'm sure she knows why I've asked, though.

'Fine, but let's not string them along, eh? No more messiness.' My mind is made up.

We re-join the guys and agree to go to a club with them. Steve is getting way too familiar with me, putting his arm around my waist as he stumbles alongside.

Michael leads the way, oblivious to the distance Em has put between them. But it's clear these guys haven't been on the island for long because Michael doesn't have a clue where he's going. Em tuts and takes the lead, frog-marching us to the nearest taxi rank.

The ride to Eivissa (Ibiza Town) takes around fifteen minutes along the back roads, passing terraced fields and pasture and the odd spatter of farm buildings, winding through the countryside like a snake through grass. The landscape is rugged, stark, yet beautiful, even more so with the sun setting and throwing golden hues across the crisped fields and craggy hillsides dotted with trees. Steve has taken up the middle spot between Em and me, much to Em's disgust, as Michael sits in silence beside the driver trying to impress us with his use of broken Spanish. The driver seems well-accustomed to tanked up clubbers, nodding and tossing the occasional smile, and seems to know where we're headed without Michael's lame instruction.

He drops us outside Hedonista. The boys clamber out leaving Em to foot the €22 bill. So much for chivalry! A sizeable crowd lingers in the queue, faces brimming with excitement as tall, tanned, bouncers with dark eyes scrutinise each party goer trying to enter.

Once inside, the boys redeem themselves by heading straight for the bar, giving Em and I a chance to plot our escape. After they return and handover yet more beers, Em and I exchange the 'times up' glance, ready to make our getaway. But Michael spies the look passing between us and grabs Em's hand, coaxing her to the dance floor. His grip is firm, and she gives up trying to resist, tossing me a wave as he drags her into the sea of writhing, blissed-out bodies.

Standing next to Steve, who seems too drunk to even attempt to dance, I suddenly feel alone and exposed again. Only, Steve doesn't share my opinion and tries to drag me towards the dancefloor.

'I'm not ready to dance yet,' I shout to him above the blasting beat, standing my ground. 'You go. I'll join you in a bit.' Deja Vu.

He cups his ear, feigning ignorance, mouthing, 'huh?' then grabs hold of my free hand, pulling me forwards.

'I've told you I don't want to dance yet!' I yank my hand free.

'What's your problem?'

He butts up against me so close his beer-breath makes me wince.

I smile a sweet truce to avoid making a scene. 'I just need a while to get warmed up.'

'I'll warm you up, baby.'

He awkwardly grabs my arm and pulls me closer, his enormous, open mouth sloshing down over mine.

'No!' I garble, pushing him away.

'Huh?' He looks shocked. 'Isn't this what girls like you want?'

'What?'

'All that flirting and shit to get us to buy you drinks and you're not gonna put out!' he half-yells, half-slurs.

'I don't believe I'm hearing this!' The urge to slap him takes hold, but as I raise my arm to give him a deserved whack, it's grabbed from behind and held firm.

'What the hell!' I yelp, as Steve shouts, 'What the fuck are you doing?'

I spin around to see who has grabbed me. Brian. *Shit!*

'Hey posh boy, do yourself a huge favour and fuck off before you get into any more trouble.' His voice is loud and stern.

I quiver, eyes widening with shock.

Looking outraged, Steve mouths off a string of incoherent drivel dressed up as insults, but a bouncer clamps down on his shoulder and yanks him back.

'What the fuck are you doing?' Steve's still cursing and shouting. 'You stupid bitch!' he says, hissing at me.

The bouncer drags him away, tossing a nod to Brian. I don't know whether I'm seething or grateful.

'Do you make a habit of coming to clubs with dickheads?' Brian says, leaning in against my ear.

'What?' I jolt around to look at him, trying to ignore the butterflies now dive-bombing in my gut as anger and anticipation dance the Samba.

'This is the second time I've found you in a club standing by the dance floor with some guy who's trying to get into your knickers.' A smirk crosses his face. 'They don't know what they're missing.'

'Brian!' I glare at him, my whole body igniting as shame, disgust and a huge jolt of excitement collide.

He's not fazed in the slightest, catches my hand and pulls me towards the back of the main dance area as I make a pathetic attempt to struggle free.

'Dance with me,' he commands.

I know I can't resist as thoughts of his lips on my skin and his body pressed against mine resurface, desire flowing like a swollen river.

We find a clearing and he pulls me close, wrapping an arm around my waist.

One by one my defences drop. I give in, leaning into him, inhaling him, warming myself with the heat from his body. Closing my eyes as the music thumps and swirls, our bodies moving in unison.

'Are you feeling better now?'

His breath is hot against my ear.

'Huh?' I reply, pulled from my reverie.

'Your friend. She told me you were sick when I asked where you were the other night.'

'You spoke to Em?' Then it dawns on me. 'Oh... yes, that. Hangover,' I reply. It's not a total lie.

'I see.'

His voice rasps against my aroused cheeks when he adds more words in a low, slow tone loaded with lust.

'You seemed fine when we were fucking.'

Oh God.

'I was, but... err... it was during the day, you know, at a bar by the beach.' Thank goodness he can't see my face, the crimson flaming over my cheeks. I don't know why I can't just tell him the truth. What does it matter where I was? I made no arrangements to see him again. I close my eyes again, trying to compose myself, but my body is wanton and betrays me. I curl an arm up around his shoulder and press myself closer.

Pulling his head away just a touch, he releases my hand and tips my chin upwards with his thumb. Blue eyes pierce mine in a loaded gaze I struggle to hold, fearing he can see I am falling under his spell. He looks down at my mouth and drops his head, pressing his lips against mine. My other arm circles his neck as our lips and tongues dance, and I know I've crossed that line again, ablaze with a desire only he can satiate.

We dance, kiss and touch for I don't know how long, until he whispers those magic words in my ear, 'Come to my place.'

I am about to give myself to him when a voice—my voice—pops into my head. 'What about Em?'

Reality bites. I pull away, my panic rising.

'What's the matter?'

'I don't think we should do this again.' I look away, not wanting to be drawn into those eyes.

'What? Why?' he asks, confusion caressing his voice.

'I don't do this.'

'You were fine to do this the other night.'

'That was different. You were a—' And he cuts me off.

'A one-night stand?'

I nod, shamed. His expression changes, his mouth taut, pursed. I wish the floor would swallow me up.

He glares at me for what seems like ages. I want to run, flee from this place and escape this parasitic guilt.

Finally, he breaks the stand-off. 'Is this what you do?'

'No, it's just—' I reply, head down like a naughty little girl who's just been caught with her hands in the lolly jar again. 'Em and I, we...'

'I see. Well, we're done here then.'

He releases me from his grasp, turns and walks away.

I can't move. I should feel relieved, but I'm *confused*.

What the hell is going on?

As I watch his tall, lean body stride away my thoughts race. And it hits me from out of leftfield: *I don't want him to go.* I'm not sure if I'm thinking it or saying it out loud, but I hear myself calling, 'Brian...

wait!'

He stops dead. Slowly pivots around to face me. I don't know what to say next. He's staring, eyebrows raised as if poised.

'Maybe... I can make an exception?' He stands still, studying me, saying nothing. 'Brian?'

He smirks.

I crumple with relief as he walks back to me. When he's a few inches away he cocks his head to one side.

'I get it, you don't want anything heavy. Neither do I, Lucy, but you've got to admit the other night is worth repeating. Besides, you won't be here for much longer, so why don't we make the most of it?'

I nod. What harm can it do? When I get home, he will be nothing more than a pleasant memory.

'I guess so.'

His expression softens, and he extends his hand to me.

'My place then?'

I nod again, taking his hand, giving all control and my resolve over to him. 'Wait. Em—' I gasp, remembering my beautiful friend still somewhere in this vast ocean with a man she wants to jump ship from. 'I can't leave without her.'

Brian looks puzzled and drops my hand.

'Lucy, I don't do threesomes.'

'No, that's not what I mean.' My eyes dart around searching for her, settling on a couple several metres away. 'I need to talk to her. Wait here.' And I leave him hanging as I seek out my friend.

'Em.' I tap her on the shoulder. She swings round, eyebrows raised as if expecting me sooner. 'I need to talk to you.' Michael seems oblivious to me being there, dancing in his own little world and busting moves that remind me of a crap version of the Blues

Brothers performing *Everybody*.

'Finally! I was wondering when we were going to make our escape.' She closes in on Michael. 'Sorry mate, I've gotta go.'

'What?' he shouts back, his face souring.

'I've got to go,' Em yells. 'Lucy's sick.'

Michael grimaces, then shrugs. 'Oh, okay. Can I get your number?'

'I don't have my mobile. Just meet me here tomorrow night,' and she bolts, grabbing my hand, leaving Michael standing in her wake.

He calls after her, but neither of us can make out or even care what he's saying.

'You're not going to meet him again?' I ask, frowning.

Em shakes her head and throws out a belly laugh. 'Christ no. I just needed to get rid of him without any fuss.' She squeezes my hand, smiling.

'I need to get back to Brian,' I say, yelling.

'Brian? I thought you were with Steve?'

'Long story. Anyway, he wants me to go to his place.'

'Well, why don't you then?'

'Because I'm not leaving you here on your own.'

'I'll be fine. Besides, you know I don't do sharing.'

She flashes me her pearly whites as if to reassure me all will be well, but I can't trust it will, not after Monday.

'That's not what I meant. I'm not leaving you here. I'll tell Brian we'll go via the villa.'

'And risk him seeing where we're staying?'

Trust Em to go all security conscious now, of all times.

'I'll ask him to drop you at the end of the street,' I reply, my tone stern, insistent.

She nods, and I walk her to where I've left Brian.

As we reach him, she shouts in my ear, 'He's easy on the eye, isn't he?'

I roll my eyes, hoping he hasn't seen her blatant gossiping, and let go of her hand.

'Um... Brian, is there any chance that we could drop Em home on our way to yours?'

'Sure. Hello again, Em.'

She nods her acknowledgement.

'I'm parked round the back of the club.'

'We're not taking a taxi?'

'Not tonight,' he replies, leading us through the strobing room, with its sweaty stench of dancing bodies and mind-bending duff-duff music. But we don't go out through the main exit. He takes us to a stairwell around the side of the bar, leading down to a fire exit. It seems odd. Surely someone would object. But the bar staff don't even acknowledge us. As he opens the door, the cooling night brings welcome relief from the stifling interior. I breathe it in, inflating my lungs with untainted air.

'This way,' he says, grabbing my hand and leading us around the back of the club. Em smirks, but between us we say nothing.

We reach a bay of parked cars and Brian pulls a key from his pocket and blips. The indicator lights flash on a dark-coloured BMW, sleek and shiny under the waning moon's light.

A moment of awkwardness grips as Em and I contemplate where to sit. Brian tilts his head to the back seat, smiling, sensing our discomfort.

'You don't need to do this, you know,' Em says as she manoeuvres herself into the tan leathered back seat of the low-profile car. I walk to the other side of the car and get in.

'I know,' comes Brian's reply as he gets in and revs the car into life. He turns to us both and winks as we buckle up, flicking on the car's stereo which then booms out Seal's *Amazing*.

I lean over the centre console towards Brian. 'I didn't peg you for a Seal fan.'

'What did you peg me for?' he asks, his voice low and seductive.

All at once the car seems to shrink around me as though he and I are alone, his tone spiking my hard-to-reach places.

'Techno, dance… something like that,' I stumble a reply, my hand and face heating a degree or several.

'I like a lot of different genres, but there are certain ones that keep me interested.' The statement feels loaded. 'Would you like me to put on something else?'

'No. I like Seal too,' I reply, flushed.

'Get a room, you two,' Em cackles, dissolving into fits of giggles.

The room in the car expands again and I feel Em nudge me in the side as Brian releases the handbrake and we speed away.

Brian stays quiet for most of the journey, not an uncomfortable silence, but I'm guessing he's just concentrating on his driving. Em and I don't say much, either, both lost in our own thoughts as the blackened countryside whizzes by. Every now and again we lock eyes, smiling and clasping hands as if to reassure each other all is right in our world. And a part of me feels a newfound contentment that, for once, we are leaving a club together.

When we reach the end of the street where our villa is on, Em's head is on my shoulder, her eyes closed. I give her a gentle nudge as Brian parks up.

'Em. We're home.'

She opens her eyes, yawns and stretches. 'I must've dozed off.'

She unbuckles and goes for the door handle. I do the same.

'You're not going to Brian's?' she says in a hush.

'Oh... yes, I am. I was just getting out to sit in the front.'

'Okay. Well, don't do anything I wouldn't do.'

She walks round the back of the car and gives me a hug, whispering, 'stay safe,' and planting a kiss on my cheek.

'Bye Brian. And thanks for the ride.'

'No problem,' he replies from out of the driver window, tossing a wave.

I watch Em totter along the street, fumbling for her keys, and don't move until I see her go into the villa and a light comes on. I know Brian will have sussed which villa is ours, but I'm passed caring, intent on making sure that Em is safe.

As I get into the front passenger seat, Brian turns to me, eyes glistening under the overhead car light. 'Ready?'

'Uh-huh. And thanks for doing this.'

'Happy to help,' he says, winking. 'Besides, you've just made my night a hell of a lot better.'

And with that, he releases the handbrake and presses his foot to the accelerator making the car roar into life. He zooms off, the car racing, pacing with my heartbeat.

CHAPTER 17

I am bathing in the afterglow of another night of unbridled passion, my body still tingling from Brian's skilful touch.

A lazy morning spent sipping coffee, chatting with Em, and smoking cigarettes has recharged my batteries. It's as though the universe has finally let up and afforded me the much-needed escapism I've been seeking.

Em seems content too, although I sense it has more to do with her shifting down a few gears than answering the call to escape. Unfortunately for Em, her encounter with Ant has left her with an unsavoury reminder.

'What do you mean, it's not open until Monday? What, are we in a third-world country?'

Em tuts and paces around me, her sandals clopping and echoing against the tiled floor of the villa.

'It's Ibiza. There's probably not much open on a weekend except tourist stuff.'

'Medical emergencies can be a tourist thing too,' Em whines, scrunching her face in disgust.

Ant's parting gift needs to be sorted. Only, the Centro de Salud medical centre is closed on the weekends.

'At least you used protection. You *did* use protection, didn't you?

Christ knows what else he might be dishing out.'

Em shudders and throws me an indignant glare.

'What am I, eighteen? I need to get this sorted. They're driving me insane.' She scratches down-below as if to emphasise her plight.

'You could always shave,' I say, restraining a giggle.

Em scoffs at me in response.

I pick up a tourist street map from the wooden buffet in the dining area, place it on the table and flip it over, scanning through the list of businesses and facilities.

'Farmacia Rodriguez Cavaller,' I read aloud. 'On the main street, and it's open 'til one-thirty.'

Em fist pumps. 'Let's go. Shit, it's three minutes past one now! We'd better hurry.'

Wearing our beach shoes, the only sensible footwear we packed, we dart off, heading down the hill and meandering through tourist-filled streets and lanes until, with a mere three minutes to spare, we arrive at the pharmacy.

'Thank God,' Em puffs, not used to this kind of exercise.

Em barges through the glass door and strides to the service desk at the back of the store. A plump older lady scowls at us over her glasses from across the high counter. She taps away at a punch till, printing off receipts as though she's cashing up.

Em pulls out her Spanish phrase book and coughs, 'err... ¿hablas englés?'

'Sí,' comes the lady's clipped reply, glaring at us as if we're inconveniencing her.

'Great.' Em lets out a huge sigh and in a hushed tone asks, 'Do you have any cream for, err... lice?'

'Lice?' The lady repeats, raising her voice a notch.

Em winces, her eyes darting around the room. She mumbles something as she turns to me.

'Thank God there's no one else in here.'

She quickly turns back to the lady. 'Yes. You know...' and she mock scratches her pubis, her face flushing.

'¿usted tiene piojos?' the woman replies. 'Err... itches?'

'Yes, I mean, Sí.'

'Moment.' The woman nods, tutting, and walks over to a shelf stack, scanning it for a few seconds. 'Ah-ha!' She pulls out a small box and walks back to the counter, a wry smile on her face.

'This. Twice day.'

She throws Em a 'twos-up' and slides the box across the counter. Em grabs it, shoving it in her bag, and pulls her purse open.

'How much? Err... ¿cuanto?'

'Twenty-one Euro,' the woman replies with precision as the digits appear on the cash register.

Em hands over the money and the woman chucks her change across the counter while shaking her head.

'Muchas gracias,' Em says, her tone sarcastic. And as we're leaving, whispers, 'stupid old witch.'

Once outside, we burst into a fit of giggles.

'Your face!' Even with mocha skin, I still know when Em's flushed.

'I know! That was so embarrassing. I thought the old witch would lecture me on safe sex. Like *we* need that lecture!'

I pause, the idea of being lectured on our sexual habits creating a nauseous feeling. It reminds me of our younger days when protection meant being on the pill, a rape alarm in your bag, and a 'fingers crossed' approach to sex.

'Maybe she's got a point. We're not naive teenagers anymore.'

Em rolls her eyes. 'As long as we're safe...'

And then as if on cue, she scratches down below, throwing me a, 'yes, I know' look.

'Just steer clear from the likes of Ant from now on, eh?'

'You can be sure of that,' she replies, rolling her eyes again.

We stroll back to the villa, arms linked and chatting. Em has decided to lay low for a few more days and give her 'pussy some pampering' as she puts it. It's an opportunity for me to do some exploring, take a few hikes, even in unsuitable footwear, and catch a few rays. Things I once loved to do... alone.

CHAPTER 18

As a teenager, if I was in trouble or had some drama to deal with, I'd go to my thinking spot. It was a special place near my parents' home where a small stone bridge arched over a tributary from the River Yare. I'd sit on the grassy bank just under the bridge and imagine I was flowing with the water, sometimes turbulent, but mostly calm.

Having a thinking spot had been vital to my sanity. It didn't matter where I went or what I did, I always found a peaceful place to adopt for my musings.

As my life fell into a pattern of working to have enough cash to go out clubbing, nights spent poring over guys or recounting stories with Em of past exploits, the need waned. Even after Joe's death I didn't seek one out, feeling like safety came from being indoors, not sharing my troubles with the world in beautiful surrounds.

Yet as I sit on a concrete step in front of the Ermita de 'Sa Creu d'en Ribes', breathless from the fifteen-minute hike up here, and wearing a newly purchased pair of runners, I'm drawn to this place, feeling compelled to adopt it. Surrounded by pines swishing in the salty breeze and looking down over Santa Eulalia, this tiny place of worship, with its whitewashed stone and echoing chapel, has called to me offering distance and perspective. The surrounding evergreens wrapping themselves around this place in a supportive embrace, taking me into their arms.

My mind whirs as thoughts of the weeks before the holiday resurface from their hiding places. Marj's face appears, teleporting in to check up on me, yet instead of shame, I feel comforted as though she's become my guardian angel. But then Joe appears, his reddened cheeks and tear-stained face a bleak reminder of those final hours of his life. A life I took away. A life I'm on an island in the Mediterranean trying to forget.

Guilt gnaws.

My thoughts drift to the day of his funeral. Of the gentle words spoken, the tears shed I didn't hear or see because I was wrapped up in my own self-loathing. Joe's parents, his sisters, his friends, and work colleagues all hugging and supporting me.

'Always part of this family, Lucy,' Joe's Mum had said as she cupped my face in her hands. She'd loved me then. She wouldn't now.

I haven't visited Joe's parents since.

'What the fuck am I doing?' I ask aloud, hoping the universe will come back with an answer as I pick up the take-out coffee cup I brought with me and gulp down the last of the bitter dregs.

A sudden swish of air ruffles nearby trees, catching my attention and pulling me into the present. I sit up, breath held, and head cocked to the side waiting for the pearls of wisdom I hope will come, but none avail themselves to me. Instead, a crow caws in the distance as I gaze down at the marina.

From up here, Santa Eulalia is breathtaking, set against the darkened hillside contrasting with the golden sands and topaz sea.

And then suddenly, I feel like that crow swooping overhead, filling my lungs with salty air and finding safety on a nearby branch.

The world as I know it at a distance.

The realisation comes like a bolt of lightning. I feel *safe* here. I can go where I choose. Land on any branch. I can be that crow flying from place-to-place, unseen and unheard unless I want to be. No one knows me here. No one knows what I've done, who I've been.

These thoughts are calming, as though the universe has presented me with a path that is no longer uphill.

My hands clasp the cup as I stare into it like a crystal ball, searching for something, and then suddenly finding it. Hope.

The leaves dance as sunlight streaks between them, warming me from the outside in.

'Thank you,' I whisper, tipping my face to the sunlight.

CHAPTER 19

Em's awful encounter with Ant has left a bitterness in both our mouths even whiskey can't wash away. It's a jolting reminder to us both we are not invincible. We have danced our butts off, but with a dash of cautiousness thrown in.

Only, I have found myself on this island where no one knows me. The old, fun-loving me has broken through Houdini's chains, and my friendship with Em has been given the kiss of life, once again strong and safe.

All thoughts of Joe, the letter, guilt, pushed out of mind, left swishing amid the pines near Ermita de 'Sa Creu d'en Ribes'. But I'd be lying if I didn't confess a part of me is still hoping for a final night with Brian. In quiet moments, away from the clubs and bars of Ibiza, my thoughts drift to him—the way he effortlessly teased my body and mind into submission, as though somehow knowing we tessellated. After our previous night together, he tapped his number into my phone. I haven't deleted it.

We leave the noisy, vinegar-smelling bar we've spent the past few hours in and make our way through the heaving evening crowds into a taxi bound for Ibiza Town (Eivissa). It's still well before core clubbing hours when we arrive. Only a handful of people are inside lining the bar, waiting for the night to ramp-up after more bottles of cerveza or wine have been drunk, or something else consumed.

Sitting ourselves on stools at the bar, our elbows leaning on its cold shiny surface, we order drinks, glad we can be heard before the music thumps any coherent sounds away.

'Holiday?' the pretty blond barmaid asks.

We both nod. 'Only a few days left, though,' I reply, shoulders slumping.

'I need to pee,' Em says close to my ear and slinks off to the loos.

'First time in Ibiza?' the barmaid asks.

'Yep.' I grin.

'Like it?'

'Amazing,' I say. 'Think I'm in love with this place.'

'Know what you mean. It had that effect on me, too. I was only meant to be here for a few weeks, and it's been five months now,' she says with raised brows and plonks two bottles on the bar. 'I'm Tara, by the way.' She slides over our drinks, smiling as if we're old friends.

'Lucy,' I say half-waving. 'So, how'd that come about?' Her story piques my interest.

'Came here with one of my girlfriends for a holiday pit-stop before heading to Barcelona, but just kinda fell for this place. It's just so... free,' she gushes.

'You must really like it here.'

Tara grins. 'I'm hoping to stay 'til the end of the season, then might just make it to the mainland.'

I glance around at the other bartenders cracking open bottles and sliding them across the counter to would-be ravers. 'Is it easy to get work here?'

'Piece of cake. I just asked around the bars and clubs to see if I could get a job for a few months.'

She stares at me square in the face.

'I know that look of longing. I can see it written all over your face.' She leans across. 'There're jobs going here if you're interested.'

I laugh off her comment, shaking my head. 'I don't know what you mean.' I'm not sure I'm fooling her, though, but try to keep the conversation going. 'So what did you do about living arrangements, money, stuff like that?'

'I asked the holiday reps and other people working in bars and clubs and got a cheap room in an apartment share with my mate. She left a few weeks ago, so I'm looking for a new roommate.' She winks, as though sharing a secret.

My mind whirs. It seems so *easy*.

Out of leftfield, an idea pops into my mind. *Could I do this?*

Em returns and sits herself down next to me.

My mind is buzzing, ideas sparking here, there and everywhere like a firework display. I worked in a bar when I was a student, so kind of know the ropes, and I'm not struggling for money. Not now, anyway. Shapes start to form out of the fog.

We continue drinking and chatting until the booming beat and strobing lights call us to the dancefloor, silencing all thoughts. I spend the next few hours losing myself in the trippy beats and rhythms flooding through my body.

I *love* this feeling. Love being in a world where no one knows me, no one judges me, no one cares.

And in those moments, those wayward ideas solidify.

I don't want to leave.

CHAPTER 20

We arrive back at the villa in the early hours of the morning, physically exhausted from our marathon dancing and drinking session only, I'm buzzing like a bee in a swarm. Instead of going to bed, I go to the kitchen, grab wine and glasses and head out onto the balcony, beckoning Em to follow.

Em pours the wine while I light up a cigarette.

'It's been a great holiday, Em. Thanks for dragging me out here.' A lump forms in my throat as reality hits. The end of the holiday is fast approaching, and we will soon return home.

'Hasn't it? Just what we both needed,' she grins, then sips her wine.

I follow suit, needing some Dutch courage.

'Em... you know that barmaid we were talking to, Tara?'

Em nods.

'Well, she was telling me about some bar jobs going at the club...' I try to sound blasé but hold my breath as I wait for Em's reply.

'Huh?' Her face scrunches, and then it dawns on her, confusion turning to wide-eyed horror. 'You're not thinking of staying, are you?'

'Um... kinda.' I avoid eye contact.

'What? You're not serious? What about your job? Your house?

ME?'

Oh shit, I knew this would happen.

Feigning calmness and taking a long drag on my cig, I reply, 'I'm not saying I'm going to do it. It's just an idea, that's all.'

Her glare could set concrete.

'Em, I need a change. I feel like I've been treading water for so long, and this place has kind of, well... it's brought me out my head.'

Em's lips purse.

'The house is sorted, and my job is shit, so I just thought, you know, I could have a bit of a longer break, just over the summer...' I silently plead for her approval.

'Is this about Brian?'

'*What?* No!'

'It is, isn't it? You're falling for him.'

She glares, challenging me with poised eyebrows.

'I've had a really good time too, but I'm not about to jack my life in for a bloke I hardly know. It's just a holiday!' She fidgets, turning to stare out at the twinkling lights below.

'I'm not falling for Brian,' I spit back.

She rolls her eyes.

'You're the one who keeps telling me I need to move on and let go of the past. Maybe I can do that here for a while, at least until I'm ready to go back to normality.' I'm not sure who I'm trying to convince, her or me. 'Besides, I might not even get a job, but I think I want to at least try.' I reach over and grab Em's hand. 'It'll only be short term, I promise.'

She tuts, pulling her hand back. 'Have you thought this through? You know it won't be the same, and where will you stay, for Christ's sake?'

'I haven't thought it through. It's crazy, I know, but this is what I think I want right now. And Tara was saying there's a spare room in the apartment she rents, so I might be able to stay there.'

Em sighs, resting her head on her hands and staring up at me through thick lashes.

'What about your counselling? All that stuff you've been talking to what's-her-name about. Isn't it worth seeing through?'

I know she's only trying to convince me it's a bad idea because she cares so much.

'I'll postpone it for a while. I mean… I've spent several years carrying all that shit, a few extra months won't make much difference. It'll give me a bit of badly needed head space.'

'You're out of your fucking mind!'

She takes a long glug of her wine, then turns back to face me.

'But… if you really believe it'll do you good, then who am I to stop you? It just seems such a big decision to make in such a short time.' Her eyes glisten from tears pooling. 'I worry about you… and I'll miss you.'

Maybe it's the wine talking, but I need to give this a go. I'm not ready to go back to my crap life yet.

And it's not about Erian, *is it?*

We've slept most of the day and it's just after 9.00 pm when Em and I are ready for the next round of clubbing. I'm anxious to get to the club and find out more about the job.

We arrive there just as the music starts pumping and the crowds flood through the doors. Luckily, I spy Tara at the bar and hurry over. Em slouches along beside me. After exchanging hellos, I dive in.

'I'm interested,' I tell Tara.

'Wait here. I'll fetch Juan,' she says, grinning, and disappears through a door at the back of the bar as Em tuts, making no attempt to cage her disapproval.

Tara returns a few moments later with a short, scruffy-looking guy whose thick grey and black hair flops over his eyes, and introduces him as Juan, the Bar Manager.

'Hello,' he says in a thick Spanish accent, smiling and extending his hand across the bar. 'Tara tells me you are interested in working here.'

'Hi. Um… yes, I am,' I reply, nerves fluttering, 'but I don't have a copy of my resume on me.'

'No problem,' he says. 'I have a form to fill in.'

He studies me for a few seconds as if sussing me out.

'And if you have time later, we can go to my office and have a chat. I need to get positions filled quickly. The season has already started.'

'Okay. I guess I can do that.' I shoot puppy-dog eyes at Em.

Reluctantly, she nods.

Juan hands me an application form and a pen and asks if I will be available in about an hour to go through it.

'Sure,' I reply, my pulse quickening.

He smiles and disappears behind the bar as I set to work filling out the form.

Em orders some drinks and waits beside me, tutting and fidgeting on her stool as I complete the form and hand it back to Tara. Tara seems delighted I'm applying, assuring me it's a great place to work and I'll love being here. Em is not impressed, sulking like a teenager whose phone has been confiscated as she sips on her drink.

We drink up and head for the dance floor, passing time until my chat with Juan, butterflies now taking off, engines at full throttle. Em seems to be just going through the motions and pretending to be having a good time, but her light has dimmed again, her smile absent.

Patience is not my strong suit and I check my watch every few minutes. When the hour is up, I tap Em's arm.

'It's time for my chat with Juan,' I shout against her ear as the beats drown out all chance of an audible conversation. 'Shall we go to the bar?'

'You go. I'll carry on dancing,' comes her blunt reply.

I nod and head over. Casting a gaze over the staff, I spy Tara at the other end and walk her way. She looks up and smiles, directing me to the side of the bar.

She opens the hatch to let me through and, on cue, Juan appears and strides over.

He greets me with a warm smile.

'Hello again. Follow me.'

With the raving going on in my gut you'd think I was being interviewed for PM.

Juan leads me through the back of the bar and a narrow passageway, then down a short flight of vinyl-clad steps into a compact office at the bottom. The room is dark when we enter. Juan flicks on the light and beckons me to sit on a leather swivel chair in front of a large melamine table. He sits opposite, my completed form in front of him.

Juan goes through some basic contact details and tells me what the bar work entails, how many shifts are expected and what the pay will be, before asking what about my experience.

'I worked in a bar when I was a college student,' I offer, fearing I sound like a novice.

'How long?' Juan asks, scribbling on the form.

'About fourteen months. Mainly night shift,' I reply.

'You have experience of rowdy customers? Drunk customers?'

'Yes, unfortunately.'

'And how you handle them?' He glances up, flicking a flop of hair from his face.

'I tried to keep my cool and be polite, but if things got out of hand, I'd call in the manager and security.' Juan nods.

'And what if they insult you or try to get err... physical?'

'The same, I guess. Is it a big problem over here?'

'It can be. Lots of young people come here, you know, students, young workers. They party hard. Drink too much, take *other* things, and get upset when someone tries to stop their fun.'

He's being honest. I like that.

'What do the staff do here?'

'We get the bouncers. We ban them, but it's a big club. Hundreds of people coming through every night. Hard to know who's banned and who's not. People go to other clubs in town if they don't like it.'

I tell Juan about my current job, emphasising how thorough and organised I am at work.

Juan nods like a bobble-head, jotting down notes as I talk. When we're more or less done, he signs the bottom of the form, dotting the paper hard with his pen.

'When can you start?' he asks.

Wow! As easy as that? 'Well, err... I'm heading home tomorrow, and I'll need some time to sort things out. Maybe in a couple of weeks?' My heart is pounding.

He lets out a breathy, 'Hmmm,' and rubs his chin.

I'm on the edge of my seat, hands clasped in my lap.

After what feels like an eternity, he nods. 'Okay. I put you down to start your training on Monday 25th July. Okay?'

Okay? It's bloody fantastic. I only hope I can get everything sorted back home without any major hiccups.

I grin from ear to ear, shaking his outstretched hand. 'Yes, yes, that's fine. Thank you!'

Juan hands me his business card and tells me to call him if there are any problems. We say our goodbyes and I head back up to the bar, jumping two steps at a time. This is going to be so good. I don't know why; I just know it is.

I spot Tara and she cocks her head to the side like a dog, as if to say, 'Did you get it?'

'I got it!'

'Fantastic! That's great news. So, do you want to rent the room at my place?' she asks.

'Um… yeah, probably,' I reply, my head spinning. 'Oh, fuck it… yes, that would be great. Give me your address, email and contact number, and I'll let you know when I'll be arriving.'

She scribbles some details on a nearby napkin and thrusts it into my hand. I can't believe I'm doing this, taking a job in a place I've been in for only two weeks, shacking up with a girl I only met the night before, and putting my life back home on hold. Em's right, I *am* losing my mind. But my God it's exhilarating!

'I'll get on to the landlord and email you the lease agreement. I can't wait!'

Tara squeals in delight, picking me up and twirling me.

'Juan wants me to start my training on 25th July, so I guess I'll be arriving the weekend before.' I am so excited, but it's slashed as soon as I see Em's face as she walks towards me.

'You're doing it then?' she says, her shoulders slumped and tone sullen.

I nod, proffering a half-smile as if trying to soften the blow. 'I need to be back here in a couple of weeks.'

'Congratulations, I guess.'

'Em, it's only for a few months. I'll be back before you know it. You know I can't stay away from you for too long.'

She fakes a grin as I try to lighten the mood. 'Drink?'

We spend a little more time at the club, drinking and dancing, but Em is not in the mood for an all-nighter, or celebrating my new job, and suggests we head back. Her excuse is we've got packing and last-minute shopping to do in the morning before flying home Saturday evening. Her smile seems tarnished, like an injured dog still wagging its tail, and I realise she wants to spend the last night with just the two of us.

But as we're leaving the bar, a pang rises. I won't get to see Brian again. The whole job thing has distracted me, and this was the last possible night to hook up with him again. I rummage around my purse for my phone, but realise I've left it at the villa. *Shit.*

'Damn!' I say aloud without realising.

'What's up?' Em asks as we head out of the club into the cooler air.

'Nothing.' I don't want to share my errant thoughts about Brian, it would only hurt Em more. But then an idea hits, perking me up.

'Hey Em, why don't we go back to the first club we went to? It'll be like we've come full circle.' Devious thoughts create bubbles of guilt within.

She screws up her face. 'Why?'

'Dunno. Just thought the two of us could round off the holiday where we started.'

She looks at me, puzzled. Then her brows crease as a lightbulb flashes on.

'Didn't you meet Brian in that club?' It's too dark for Em to see my heated cheeks.

'Yes, but—' I feign innocence. 'I just liked that club. Come on Em, for me?'

She tuts, shaking her head. 'Fine. Let's go.'

CHAPTER 21

My heart is thumping as loud as the disco beats as we get out of our taxi, enter the club and make our way towards the bar through crowds of sweating, spaced-out dancers. Will he be here? And will Em be annoyed if we hook up again?

Em orders drinks, giving me a clandestine moment to scan the club. On first glances, there's no sign of Brian. He could be on the dance floor. But what if he is and he's hooked up with someone else? A sickly feeling rises from my stomach, and when Em thrusts a bottle in my hand, I knock back several gulps in quick succession.

I glance over at Em, who's also scrutinising the bodies on the dance floor. It dawns on me she might be checking to see if Ant and his mates are here, and in that moment, I realise how self-absorbed I'm being.

I down the rest of my drink and motion towards the dance floor.

'You alright, Luce?' Em asks, cupping my ear.

'Fine,' I say too quickly. 'Are you?'

She ignores my question. 'You're looking for him, aren't you?'

'No!' I look away from her penetrating stare. 'Okay, maybe... Just seeing if he's around, that's all.' Guilty on all levels.

'You like him. Admit it!'

I shake my head. 'He's good in bed,' I say, hoping to placate. She's not buying it, turns and strides towards the bar.

'Where are you going?' I call after her, rushing to catch up.

'To the bar.' She beelines one of the staff.

Em leans across towards him, says something, gestures around her head, then glances back at me.

I can't breathe.

The barman shakes his head and mouths something back. Em shrugs and makes her way back.

'He was here earlier, but left a while ago. You're lucky the barman knew which red-haired Irish guy you were talking about.'

My cheeks enflame. 'Who... Brian?' My heart is thumping so hard I'm afraid it'll burst out of my chest, alien-like.

'Yes, *Brian*,' Em says, 'who else?'

An unwanted thought flashes through my mind, then pops uncensored out of my mouth. 'Alone?'

Em rolls her eyes, thrusts her finger up and shouts, 'Wait.' She goes back over to the barman and beckons him over, once again leaning over the bar to talk to him.

I watch, breath hitched, as they exchange words. The barman shakes his head again and I deflate.

Em walks back over. 'He left alone,' she says. 'Happy now?'

'What? Really?'

'Yes, *really*. He didn't come in with anyone and he didn't leave with anyone. Maybe he was hoping to see you,' she says, a sarcastic edge to her tone. She glugs on her beer.

Relief pours out, but my shoulders slouch as disappointment bites.

'Why did you do that?' I ask, surprised.

'Because I love you,' she says. 'Come on, let's go home.'

She drapes a reassuring arm around me. I glance around one final time as I walk arm in arm with my best friend in the world out of the club.

Even though we're both dog-tired, my mind is whirring as we arrive back at the villa. I'm gutted about not seeing Brian but puzzled as to why Em would sacrifice our last Ibizan night together.

'Em, can I ask you something?'

'Sure,' she replies, yawning and kicking off her stilettos, clacking them across the cold tiled floor.

'Well... I know you're not happy about me coming back here, so why help me look for Brian?'

Em pauses, eyes glazed in contemplation.

'Dunno. Guess I felt like you needed it.'

Em grabs a bottle of red and two glasses from the kitchen and we head out to the balcony, my thoughts still spinning like a Catherine Wheel. 'Needed what?'

'To see him again. He's brought you back to life.'

I titter. 'It's not him who's done that, it's you!'

Em shakes her head. 'I haven't done anything.'

'YOU brought me here and coerced me into going out and enjoying myself.' I tell her, eyes wide and eyebrows arched. 'And it was you who found me again.'

Em laughs, leaning back into her chair. 'Nah. You just needed a prod, that's all. You're still the Lucy I knew before, you just needed to find her.'

Is that what it was,' I jest, lighting up a cig. 'A prod?'

Em beams, but once again I spy a tinge of sadness.

'You alright?'

'Uh-huh,' she replies, glancing down at her nails.

'Em? What is it? Are you still pissed off at me?'

'For what?'

'For getting a job here.'

'No, it's not that.'

'Then what?'

'I dunno... I guess something's different. I *feel* different.'

'How do you mean?' I frown, my gut fluttering as worry pangs. And then it dawns on me. *Ant.* I reach over and grab her hand. 'It's that awful night with Ant, isn't it?'

Em nods, and I notice the tears pricking the corners of her eyes.

'It wasn't your fault, you know,' I say, squeezing her hand.

'I know. It's just... well... it brought back some stuff. Stuff you didn't know much about.'

'What stuff?'

Her head droops. 'Stuff about Damian.'

'The love of your life, Damian?'

'Yeah.' She stares up at me, grimacing. 'He wasn't the nice guy you thought he was.'

'What do you mean?'

Em gulps.

'Em? What did he do?' My pulse quickens as an unknown fear crawls over my skin.

'He... he had a temper,' she says, grabbing the bottle of wine and pouring it up to the rims. 'When he was drunk, he'd... umm... he'd lay into me, any excuse.'

'Oh my God!' My mouth drops as her words sink in. 'Em, I—' I go to her, scooping her in my arms. 'I'm so sorry. I didn't know,' I whisper as tears flow.

We sob together, united in a moment of pain, Em's raw emotions exposed. A time when only a safe embrace can offer the space for her to crumble. So that's what I do, holding together the pieces as she falls apart.

Em eventually pulls away, dabbing her eyes with the backs of her hands. 'It's not that I didn't want to tell you. It's just I … I was ashamed.'

'Of what?' I wipe away my own tears.

'Of what you'd think of me.'

'Huh?'

'I didn't want you to… pity me.'

'Why would I?'

'Some of the stuff he made me do. The places he took me to.' She screws her face up as if tasting a lemon. 'I worried that you'd be disgusted, would think less of me because I'd let it happen.'

I bear-hug her, overwhelmed by her admission. 'I wish you'd told me, Em. Maybe I could've helped.'

'I don't think anyone could've,' she says, pulling away again. 'I needed to figure it out for myself.'

'That's a tough call.'

'Yeah… maybe. But I figured it out eventually. Realised that he was a depraved fucking bully.'

The thought of Em being anything but bolshie seems too hard to digest. She has always been the strong one. 'Is that why you swore off relationships?'

She nods. 'There's no way I'm going to let anyone treat me like that again.'

'So, the whole thing about him ditching you because you cheated… that was a lie?'

'Uh-huh.'

'But—'

'He was the first guy I ever really fell for. Everyone loved him. Even you. I didn't want everyone knowing the truth.'

She folds her arms, signalling we're approaching a no-go zone.

'And some of the stuff he made me do... well, I'll tell you about it some other time.'

'So, you took the blame for him being a dick to you?'

Em nods.

'God, Em. You don't do things by half!'

She giggles, snuffling, and uncrosses her arms again.

'So, Ant and his fuckwit mates... they brought it all back.'

Em nods again.

'I'm so sorry, Em. I should've paid more attention. Been a better friend.' My arm cradles her shoulder and I drop my head as shame engulfs. I thought all she needed from me was a wing woman, a partner-in-crime, someone to debrief with when the raunchy nights had ended. She hid all of this because she thought I'd... what? Judge her? I've let her down.

'You're the best friend anyone could wish for,' she replies. 'I'm the one that should've been more supportive of you these past couple of years.'

I roll my eyes. 'We're both as bad as each other, eh?'

'Yeah,' Em's voice trails. 'The thing with Ant has kinda made me realise what we've been doing all this time and how pathetic it is.'

Harsh, but I nod in agreement.

'Fun, but dumb,' she continues. 'I think I need to do some serious growing up.'

'Tried that... it didn't really work out,' I muse.

'What? With Joe?'

'Uh-huh. The whole marriage-thing… I thought that meant I was growing up.'

'You did seem to change… for a while, at least,' Em says, refilling our glasses.

'I thought that's what I was supposed to do; be the dutiful wife, but I guess I was wrong.'

'Or he was wrong for you.'

Em reaches across for my hand.

'Luce, you know… I didn't help things, though. Tried to put a wedge between you 'cos I felt like you were being dragged kicking and screaming away from me.'

'Really?'

'Yeah… If I'd have been a better friend, I would've supported you more. You *and* Joe. Realised that you were trying to do the right thing.'

I shake my head. 'I don't think any amount of support would've changed the outcome… and you were, still are, the best friend anyone could ask for. Don't ever think otherwise.'

Her eyes glisten and she squeezes my hand.

'Here's an idea,' I offer. 'You could stay in Ibiza too, so we can both figure out how to grow up!'

Em leans back, laughing. 'And miss out on all those hot blokes back home?'

'I guess that's a no, then?'

'Don't get me wrong, I love it here too, but I love being home more. Besides… I think we have different needs right now.'

Em has a point, and I know she has my best intentions at heart, even if she doesn't always show it.

'So why encourage me with Brian?' I can't help asking.

'Guess I still hold some hope of finding the good guys...'

'Hmmm. Don't think I'm ready for hearts and flowers just yet.'

'I know. Maybe one day, eh?'

'Maybe.'

'But hey, no more secrets.'

She throws me a wistful look.

'Yeah. No more secrets.' I reply, staring out at the twinkling lights below.

Em and I are finishing up our packing, and with only a couple of hours left before our flight home, I'm not sure how I feel about what has happened here and what is yet to come. My head is on fast spin.

We spent the morning in town buying trashy tourist trinkets and ate lunch in a pub on the harbour. Em was quiet, contemplative. Probably still processing last night's revelations and sad at my decision to return, even though she says she understands why. But deep down, I know I've made the right decision. My life back home has been stale for so long, and if I'm honest, it started way before Joe lost his life.

It's late by the time I arrive home and begin the laborious task of unpacking my case and bag.

The house is dark, and feels cold, small and empty. I wish Em was here. I liked having her around. The two of us have reconnected as halves of the same beating heart, always there for each other, always falling in time with the same beat. But I can't help the niggling feeling she is harbouring some deeper truths she is not yet ready to reveal. Perhaps one day we can both lay all our cards on the table and bridge the gap that secrets widen.

My wedding ring is still in the inside pocket of my toiletry bag. I take it out and put it in a jewellery box on my dressing table, snapping the lid shut.

CHAPTER 22

Fixated, I watch the last of my washing spin in the machine, the highs of the holiday rinsing away. A text from Em brings me round.

'Miss you already!' it reads.

On the flight back, she kept whining about how she wouldn't have her confidante and clubbing buddy on hand to go out with. I'll miss her too, but I need this. I need to have more time away in a place where I can forget all the crap of the past few years and not have to suffer the pity and judgements.

Then it dawns on me I should contact Marj and let her know the score. What will she make of it? Will she disapprove? Will she realise I'm just running away from my grief, delaying the inevitable?

Truth is, I want to escape. I *need* to be the old Lucy again, the one who is carefree and enjoys life.

I make a list of all the things to sort out before heading back to Ibiza. I'm pretty sure Em will keep an eye on the house and car for me; I'll type up a resignation letter later; and I'll go on to my online bank account and make sure all my bills are sorted by direct debit. But will Darren agree to rescind my notice period from four weeks to two?

By late evening, I've written a to-do list and my resignation, is printed, signed and put in an envelope ready for work tomorrow. I resolve to call Marj at lunchtime and see if I can schedule a session to see her on Friday. Even though I have no obligation to keep up the counselling, I feel as though I want to reassure her, and myself, I haven't given up. That Ibiza is a minor detour in this journey away from pain. That I will eventually return to patch it all up soon enough.

But I stall, deciding to phone my cousin, Jen, to let her know my news.

'Lucy! So good to hear from you. How was Ibiza?' Jen's shrill almost pierces my eardrum.

'Good. Really good. How are you?'

We chit-chat about the holiday and what she's been up to.

'I've got some news,' she says once I've finished my spiel about all-things Ibiza, her voice squealing like an excited toddler. 'Marcus asked me to marry him… and I said yes!' She screams with delight.

'Oh my God! Jen, that's fantastic! When? Where?' Questions pop out at lightning speed.

'He proposed last week when we were in London for a show,' she gushes. 'I'll send you a snap of my ring.'

'I'm so happy for you, Jen. Are you getting hitched soon, or waiting a while?'

'Soon. October, maybe.'

'That *is* soon. You're not pregnant, are you?'

Jen lets out a belly laugh. 'As if! No, we want to get hitched before Christmas. Marcus's grandma is sick, and he really wants her to be at the wedding.'

'Ah… I see. You'll have to let me know the date so I can make sure I'm back.'

'Back? From where?' she asks.

'Um… Ibiza. I'm going back there for a while.'

'But didn't you just get back?'

'Uh-huh. But I kinda got myself a job there. Just for a few months.' I inhale sharply and hold my breath as if waiting for approval.

'Wow. Way to go Luce! I thought you sounded different.'

'Different?'

'Yeah. You know… happier?'

'I feel happier,' I reply, and it's genuine.

'Is Em going too?'

'No. Just me.'

'Bloody hell, Luce. You don't do things by halves, do you? But I'm happy for you. It's about time you stopped moping around and did something exciting.'

She means well; I know she does, so I don't bite back. We've always been on the same wavelength even though she's eight years younger and we only get to see each other a few times a year.

I feel a mixture of euphoria and sadness. Happy that Jen is marrying the love of her life and approves of my jaunt back to Ibiza, but sad I won't see her for a while to celebrate.

It's getting late, and I stretch out, yawning as jet lag kicks in with a vengeance. I'm exhausted, and it makes what I'm about to do all the more real.

CHAPTER 23

I've spent the morning in my Darren's office going through my resignation. 'It seems a hell of a risk for a couple more months in the sun,' Darren says, frowning. 'Perhaps we could arrange a sabbatical, or something?'

I struggle to look him in the eye. 'Darren, I'm really grateful for all the opportunities I've had here, and the patience and kindness you've shown me since... well, you know. But I've made my mind up and want to keep my options open when I come back.'

'But what will you do for money? And what about your family, your friends?'

'Money's not an issue for me anymore,' I reply flatly, wrapping arms around my stomach. 'And as for friends and family, well, like I said, it's only for a few months.'

He shakes his head.

'Darren, I need to leave in two weeks, which means—'

'You need me to rescind your notice period?'

'Yeah.' A flush creeps up my face.

He sighs, pausing before replying. 'Well, if it's what you really want... I'll need to clear it with HR first, though.'

'I'd appreciate it.' I toss him a smile.

'I wish you'd reconsider. When you're on form, you're one of my best workers,' he continues. 'There's nothing I can say to change your mind?'

I shake my head. 'It's a done deal.'

'I'll let you know what HR says ASAP.'

'Thanks,' I say, heading out of Darren's office and back to my cubicle.

I still need to phone Marj.

Nervously, I pick up the phone and call her. Her polite, softened voice answers after a few rings. We exchange pleasantries before getting down to business. I schedule the usual Friday night session with her, giving no mention of my plans. What will I tell her? How will she react? And why am I so bothered by it?

It's lunchtime, and Darren approaches my desk just as I'm stuffing a smoked salmon bagel into my mouth.

'Lucy, hi. Erm... HR have emailed me.'

I gulp down the bite and stare up at him, eyes wide like saucers.

'They've agreed to me rescinding your leave by two weeks as long as you cash in the rest of your holiday entitlement. Does that work?'

I nod rapidly, perhaps a little too eager. 'That's great.'

'You'll need to spend the next couple of weeks handing over your work to Janine. I'll let her know before the end of the day.'

His tone seems clipped.

'Okay, so starting from tomorrow?'

'Yes.'

'Thanks, Darren. I appreciate it.'

Darren walks back to his office, head lowered.

I'm so relieved. The thought of not going is too much to bear right now. Escaping the humdrum is what's keeping me going, regardless of the dour mood Darren seems to now be in.

Even though Darren has only just confirmed my being able to leave, word is getting around, courtesy of Stella, that I'm going. And before I know it, she has organised a leaving do, inviting all my workmates.

I wanted to go quietly, but after much peer pressure give in to the idea. I suppose it would be rude not to, and besides, my days of avoiding social events seem to have fallen by the wayside. But I am fond of most of them and realise they need and ending as much as I do; it hasn't always been bad. There are many loose strings I need to tie up before I go.

After work, I busy myself going through paperwork, making sure that everything is in order and up to date. I only plan to be away for three months but need to make sure nothing can go awry. I also need to let Juan and Tara know when I'll be arriving, so once I've finished with the paperwork, get on and book my flights, tingling with excitement as I fill out the details.

Everything is happening so fast I feel the need to sit for a while and take a breather. Never in my life would I have done anything like this before, even before Joe. It would've been me and Em all the way.

Alone was never a word in my vocabulary.

CHAPTER 24

The cushioned seat of my chair gives little comfort as I fidget, waiting for Marj to pop her head out of the consult room.

This week has gone so fast it's a wonder I can still catch my breath. The arrangements for my departure have kept me so busy, my mind whirring like an aero generator in high winds. What were we talking about the last time I saw her? What is there left for me to say that will let me quietly pass through without giving the game away?

These thoughts continue to cycle, and I don't hear the door creak open, startled by Marj's low dulcet tone.

'Lucy, hello. Come this way.'

I follow her into the room and take my seat in the usual chair.

'How have you been?' she asks.

'Fine, thanks. Pretty good, really.' I smile back.

'How was your holiday?'

'It was good, really good. Did me a lot of good getting away... which is something I want to talk to you about,' I say, too eager to offload.

She looks surprised, pushing her blue-framed glasses down her nose to study me. 'Okay.'

'Well...' I stutter, already chastising myself and shuffling in the chair to get comfortable. 'I enjoyed the holiday a lot. Felt a sense of peace from it.' I glance at her crinkly blue eyes, looking for warmth, acceptance, *anything*. 'And I've kind of got myself a job there for a few months.' I pause, breath held, waiting for Marj's response.

'You enjoyed your holiday enough to want to spend more time there?' she says, tilting her head, her usual 'I'm listening' smile flashing. 'I'm wondering what it was about the holiday that helped inform your decision.'

'Well, like I said, I felt a sense of peace, like I could leave my troubles behind for a while.' Anxiety builds like a soap bubble about to burst as I try to justify my decision, still worrying about what she's thinking. 'I guess I reconnected with a part of me that hasn't been around in a long while.'

'Can you elaborate?'

'Um... who I used to be before I met Joe.' I suddenly feel foolish but continue. 'I used to love going out, you know, clubbing and all that. But when I settled down, it all stopped, and on holiday, I realised how much I missed it.' I'm the naughty child with the ball and broken glass waiting for a parent to scold me.

'It sounds like you rediscovered an element of yourself you once enjoyed: socialising and being around other people. Is that right?'

'Um... yes,' I say, frowning. 'I don't want to carry on with my life the way it has been for the last few years. Not yet anyway. I want to go back to the island and enjoy myself for a bit longer.' I pause, contemplating what I'm going to say next to avoid sounding like a hermit crab running off to find a new shell.

Marj says nothing, expectation etched in the wrinkles mapping her face.

'I'm not saying I'm over all the guilt and stuff about Joe. I can come back to that, *will* come back to that. It's just... well, for now, I want a bit more time away from it all. Y'know?'

Marj frowns, inhaling sharply. 'Do you feel you need my approval, Lucy?'

'I thought you'd need to know where my head's at and hopefully understand why I want to go,' I reply, half-nodding.

Her voice softens, and she leans forward. 'I'm not here to approve or disapprove of your choices, Lucy, just to help you explore options so you can figure out which ones to choose for yourself.' She jots something down on her notepad. 'It seems to me that you have thought about returning to the island as a means of getting more time out from the challenges you face. My concern is where you feel that leaves you regarding blaming yourself for Joe's death.'

'What you mean?'

'I'm wondering if your feelings around Joe's death have changed, or if you are just putting them aside for a time to return to them later?'

'They haven't changed,' I say, sighing. 'I will be coming back, but figure if I can get some more headspace, surely it will do me good.'

'All that matters is that *you* are happy with your choice right now.'

'I am,' I say, certainty cementing itself. 'I *will* come back, though.' The feelings about Joe's death will not just disappear; two years of cave-dwelling and beating myself up about it have proven that. But I know I should take this opportunity while I can, safe in the knowledge I will come back to Marj when I feel ready to deal with the fallout. 'I'm leaving a week tomorrow and my work mates have organised a leaving do for me next Friday, so... I guess this will be our last session for a while.'

Marj's eyes widen. 'I guess it will, Lucy. I do hope you find what you are looking for during your time away,' she smiles. 'And I'm here if you feel you want to talk to me about anything.'

'Thank you. I really appreciate it.'

We sit silently for a few moments, an air of awkwardness descending.

'Marj, I'm not sure there's anything else to talk about right now.' I twist my fingers, eager to leave. 'Can we call it a day now?'

'Okay, Lucy. But I will still need payment for the session,' she says softly.

I nod, reaching in my bag to pull out her envelope, and hand it to her.

'Thanks for all your help so far... I do appreciate it.'

'It's what I'm here for,' she says smiling. 'It's what I'm always here for, should you need it.'

'Thanks, Marj.'

To my surprise, Marj walks around the table dividing us and hugs me. We say our goodbyes and I make my way out, a rare feeling of lightness coming over me as I head outside and over to my car.

Once inside, I sit pondering, allowing doubt to creep in like a slithering snake and black it all out. *Am I just running away again? What if it all goes pear-shaped and I end up back at square one again? Would I have the nerve to come back if the shit hits the fan?*

A craving for nicotine takes hold as I buckle up and start the engine. Once home, I go straight out back and light up. Somehow, it calms the ebb of uncertainty flowing through me. Is it a natural response to a big change such as this?

CHAPTER 25

Em and I are in the city centre shopping for decent clothes for me to take to Ibiza. I've spent most of my working life wearing formal dull greys, blacks and brilliant whites, finished with a floaty scarf or sparkling brooch. All very conservative.

What I'm about to do hasn't sunken in with either of us. It's all so out of character for Lucy Morris—latent party girl, failed wife, husband killer—who has been treading water for the past few years. But that's the thing. All these, 'so unlike me' things I've done recently *are* part of my character, just ones buried a long time ago. This whole situation smacks of rediscovery. What makes me tick; what do I really like; and importantly, what do I really want? Or is it, as Em and Marj have both alluded to, that I'm just running away again?

By mid-afternoon, we're shopped-out. Em has had me trying on the skimpiest of outfits. Our time in Ibiza seems to have given her the green light to fully resurrect Lucy Fraser, socialite. As usual, she wore me down, coercing me into buying several club-appropriate style dresses, several pairs of jeans and tee-shirts for the bar work, and a whole new drawer full of matching lacy undies.

We're chatting over coffee and cake when she pipes up, 'What happens if you see Brian again?'

I almost spit out a chunk of carrot cake. 'Where'd that come from?'

'Admit it. You liked him, I mean *really* liked him, and you seemed disappointed when you didn't see him that one last time, even though you wouldn't say as much.' She winks, but her arrow hits the bullseye.

'I really don't know. My head would say leg it, but—' Heat rises.

'But what? You'd go for it?'

'No! Well... I don't know!' I frown, shaking my head and cupping my cheeks.

'I think you do. You just don't want to say it out loud.'

Her eyes crease as she's consumed giggles, enjoying making me squirm.

The tingles down below at the mere mention of his name tells me all I need to know. But my plan is to work hard and play hard. To blend into the background, and definitely no ties.

For now, I'm exhausted. Em can shop like it's an Olympic sport, but my feet ache from traipsing around so many stores. We finish our drinks, say our goodbyes and go our separate ways.

There's a message from Tara on my answer phone telling me she's emailed some stuff over, so I pull out my laptop and log in to my email, anticipation building like a tsunami. She's sent me the lease agreement and some pictures of her place. Glancing over the photos, excitement piques. I picture my days lazing on the russet-red sofa or smoking on the small balcony while reading a love-swept novel. And my nights spent serving partygoers rife with anticipation or dancing the night away with captivating strangers. I complete the form and email it back to her, confirming my arrival date in the process. I feel giddy at the prospect, but there's still a week to go before I leave and plenty of things still to do.

After grabbing a bite to eat, I head outside for a much-needed smoke. It's a drab, drizzly day, but I don't care. Thoughts of a sexy redhead interrupt my planning, corrupting my resolve. I really need to get my shit together if this is going to work.

CHAPTER 26

A weepy Em is driving me to the airport, blowing her nose one-handed and periodically dabbing Alice Cooper-like eyes. I hope she can see where she's going.

You'd think I was going away for years, not a few months. She says she is beside herself with worry and sadness. It's touching, really, and goes to show how off-track our friendship had been since Joe came and went. The holiday has bridged the gaps in many ways, helping us regain what we had lost. I will miss her so much, but I know she'll always be there for me and just a phone call away. She's already planning another Ibiza holiday to coincide with when I finish.

A few nights ago, I had my work leaving do. I've been blown away by the tributes and heart-felt goodbyes. These past few years I haven't noticed how much people really do care about me. Many of my work colleagues cried, but strangely, I didn't shed a drop.

By the end of the night we were all steaming drunk, and people trailed off to seek respite in their beds.

Only Darren and Stella remained, both telling me how much I'll be missed and how I should re-apply for my job when I get back. But it's no longer an option for me.

As we parted ways, Darren hugged me and whispered in my ear.

'It's not just the job you can come back to.'

I flashed a smiled, inwardly knowing Darren, as nice a boss as he was, would never be the type of person to blip on my radar. It's more a failing on my part than his.

As I took the last bus home, I checked through the bag of goodies my work mates had clubbed together to buy me: a shedload of sun cream, a sombrero, and a 'Teach Yourself Spanish' book. Leaving them after such a long time seems so strange, but it was because of Joe I came to work there, so in some ways it felt like I was saying goodbye to remnants of him. Circle closed.

We park and head to Departures. Em has made me promise to text, phone, email, even write at least three times a week so she knows what I'm up to and that I'm okay. I don't often see such concern etched on her face, but it is on show now. It touches my heart, causing much sadness and with it a smidgen of doubt. She throws her arms around me for the third or fourth time, embracing me as if we are never going to see one another again.

After checking-in my bags, Em suggests we go for a coffee since there are still a couple of hours to kill before my flight departs. A shred of anxiety rises from my gut again as the enormity of what I'm about to do sinks in. Fears flitter like scurrying ants through my mind. This is no holiday, and Em won't be there to keep me safe and sane. What if I don't like the job or the place, or don't get on with Tara? What if the feelings I've buried from over two years of drowning resurface with a vengeance? As we drink our coffees and chat, Em seems to sense I'm getting nervous and puts her arm around my shoulder, squeezing me gently.

'You'll be fine, Luce. It's not like you've never been there before.'

Tears well and I pluck a tissue from inside my bag. 'What if I'm making a huge mistake? What if it all goes to shit and I end up feeling worse than I did before?'

'You won't,' she replies, her tone low and soothing. 'Besides, you can just get on a plane and come home. And I'll be here, just a phone call away.'

'How can you be so sure?' I need her to say something to lock up the doubts and throw away the key.

'I just know that when we were in Ibiza, you came back to life. It was good for you, but being back here... well, it isn't.'

She gives me another reassuring squeeze.

'Just remember the good old days when you went with the flow, Luce. Live a little.'

She beams at me, but I can see tears forming.

I glance down at my watch and realise it's time to go. My heart feels heavy, made worse by Em's sullen face. The two of us plod towards the security gate, holding hands, saying nothing.

We reach the gate where a scowling man asks for my boarding card. Em and I stand by the gate hugging until she reluctantly lets me go. My heart pounds as I head through, casting one last look back at Em who is wiping streams from her eyes, feigning a smile as she waves me on.

I'm three rows away from the kid zone. The flight has been turbulent, not just because of tears and tantrums from toddlers, but also because my mind has whirred like the rotating jets of the plane. Picturing Em's teary face, I'm hoping the Ibiza I knew on holiday hasn't changed in the last few weeks.

'Stop that, Harry,' shouts a mother across the aisle as little Harry runs across it and pokes a snoozing old lady.

A baby girl snivels in response, chorusing the tuts coming from her disgruntled father who's been binge-watching Top Gear on the inflight entertainment system.

My nerves fray.

'Ladies and Gentlemen,' an announcement blares out. 'We will shortly be arriving in Ibiza Airport. Please fasten your seat belts, stow your luggage in the overhead lockers or under the seat in front of you, and fold up your tables. The time at our destination is four-fifty-one pm, and the temperature is a lovely twenty-four degrees. We hope you have enjoyed your flight today, and on behalf of Thomas Cook Airlines, we wish you a pleasant trip.'

The seatbelt sign pings on as I click my belt together, craning my neck around the man sitting next to me to get a glimpse out of the window. And then the familiar coastline of Ibiza island comes into view. The azure seas, the golden sands littered with tiny specks of holidaymakers, the white-washed buildings and looming hotels. My heart gallops as a mix of euphoria and apprehension collides.

Tara's at work when I arrive at my new apartment in Ibiza Town but has left a note on the kitchen bench with her contact number and some basics. It's just before 7.00 pm and I'm exhausted, sprawling on the sofa in the scant apartment that is to be my home for the next few months.

Tara's left a bottle of red wine on the countertop as a welcome gift, so I hunt down a wine glass and head out to the balcony. It's just what I need.

Several glasses of wine and many cigarettes later, I feel myself unknot and relax a little. Dark, but still warm outside, the lights from the town twinkle around me creating a glow against the almost still black ocean. The apartment is only a few minutes from the town centre, on the port side, part of a complex of about fifty or so homogenous units spread over three floors. It's small and clean, with two bedrooms, a shared bathroom and living area, and a small kitchen and dining area. Whitewashed walls and terracotta tiles give it that distinctive Spanish feel.

It'll be fine, I keep telling myself, taking another sip of wine, but I can't help feeling incredibly alone.

CHAPTER 27

The sun has reached its peak in a cloudless cyan sky. I'm sitting on a plastic chair on the balcony of my new home, flicking through my Catalan language book, paying lip service to the words on each page. It's not like I really need to learn the language. Most people in and around the main towns of Ibiza speak English. But as a matter of courtesy I want to get the basics mastered so I can at least figure out the directions of where I may end up on a night out. Thoughts of Brian flit through my mind.

Stirrings coming from the kitchen pull me out of the delicious daydream I've become immersed in. I turn around to see a sleepy-looking Tara smiling down at me.

'Hey! You made it okay,' she says, grinning, her blonde hair knotted around her tanned face.

'Hi!' I reply, rising to hug her. 'Yep, here in one piece.' For some reason, I expected to see Em.

'Welcome back! So, how was your flight?'

'Yeah, not bad. I ended up seated next to some old Spanish guy who slept most of the way. His snoring was terrible!' I giggle at the thought of it. 'Thanks for the wine, by the way. It helped!'

'No worries. Start as you mean to go on!'

Tara flashes me a brilliant white smile.

'I'm just going to grab a coffee then I'll join you.' She heads back inside to get her coffee, so I light up a cigarette realising I haven't yet told Tara I smoke.

'Is this okay?' I ask when she returns, lifting my cigarette.

'No worries. Just not inside. Okay?'

'Sure,' I reply. 'So, tell me, what's Juan like?'

'Juan? He's an absolute sweetie, maybe too soft at times. It gets him in to trouble with the owner.'

'He doesn't own the club?'

'Nah, just manages it. The owner has two clubs here, but we don't see much of him, except when Juan's in the shit,' she says, giggling. 'You're starting tomorrow, aren't you? I think Juan's put us on the same shifts this week so I can show you the ropes.'

'It's a relief we'll be working together to start off with, kind of helps take some worry out of starting at a new place.' I flash her an appreciative grin.

'Glad to have you on board. Don't get me wrong, most of the staff are nice enough, but a lot do their own thing when they're not at work. I'm just rapped to have a roommate and a work mate. It'll be heaps of fun!'

She sounds like Em, and I can't help wondering if this is a good thing or not.

After eating and showering, Tara shows me the apartment and all its little quirks. It gives me a chance to study her in more detail since I've only seen her in a dimly lit bar and via her pictures on social media. She's a pretty girl: petite and lithe, with brown eyes and long glossy blonde hair tied into a ponytail. Everything you imagine a stereotypical Aussie to look like, with an open and friendly manner to match. I hope we'll become good friends, but in this moment, I can't help pining for my Em.

We head off to a local supermarket to get some food. She tells me more about work and what I'll be doing. I feel reassured I haven't jumped out of the frying pan and into the fire. The more we chat, the more I warm to her, and even though she's several years younger than me, we seem to click on many levels.

By late evening, we're both sat out on the balcony drinking wine, me smoking, and planning out the next day. I feel jittery, but Tara reassures me I'll enjoy it, with the bonus we get discounted drinks and free club entry as one of the perks of the job. Turns out, she's a bit of a clubber, but more for the rave and techno scene.

'Most of the guys here only stay here for the season. They follow the big-name DJs around and work in the smaller bars to fund the drinks and err... other things,' she winks. 'It's nearly impossible to get work in town, so I was rapped when I got this job.'

'Are you here just for the season?' I ask.

'Not sure yet.' She looks contemplative. 'I mean, I enjoy the big clubs like Pacha and DC10, but I'm not obsessive about the club scene. I have some more travelling to do, but for now I like it here. It's so free and easy going. Homely, you know?'

I'm relieved she's not buggering off too soon and agree with her about how easy going the place feels.

When Em first told me about her parents' villa, I had visions of thousands of sweaty bodies dancing in unison in the equivalent of a ginormous, smoke-filled mosh-pit. Santa Eulalia was such a pleasant and welcome alternative to Ibiza Town. Even though Em and I are clubbers, we're old-school, and Santa Eulalia didn't disappoint. But there's something to be said about being close to the action and amongst the revellers all seeking escape. And the apartment is near the beach rather than perched on a hillside, so my feet will be spared.

CHAPTER 28

An hour and a quarter into my first shift and bar work is slowly coming back to me, even serving a few customers without hiccups. Tara's right about Juan, he seems nice, very helpful and concerned I'm doing okay. But he's an absolute pushover to the point where several members of staff take the piss, like bunking off for longer than scheduled breaks, and helping themselves to the optics on shift.

I get a break at around 11.30 pm and head out of the back of the club to have a smoke in a small courtyard designated for staff. It's been a fun evening so far, but my feet are hurting a little. I'm just about getting used to having to lip read customer orders over the din of the constantly pulsating music but am still drawn in by the buzz of it all. Doubts have flittered away.

Tara has been great at showing me the ropes and introducing me to some of the staff, and Juan has gone through paperwork and my shift plan. This week, I'm doing Monday to Friday nights, but from next week I'll be doing Saturday to Wednesday nights, with only two nights on the same shift as Tara. I only hope I'll get used to the new people, the late nights and sore feet.

CHAPTER 29

I've been here nearly a week, and it's flown. Work's been going well. Tara has been a godsend on that score, and strangely, I feel settled.

Tara and I have been getting on really well too, spending most of the week together. She's a character, especially around the blokes, so much like a younger version of Em.

Tonight is my first shift without her, and it feels like I'm finally being let loose. I've got to know a few more of the staff, so there are still familiar faces about. It's strange wanting familiarity now when before I wanted nothing more than to hide away in my cave.

I take my break at around 11.35 pm, as has become my pattern, and head off to the courtyard for a much-needed smoke. Staff breaks are staggered, so I'm usually on my own.

I'm sitting on a step near the back door enjoying a few moments of peace and much-needed foot relief when the door creaks open. I swivel around to see who's there, but it's dark and can't make out who it is.

The figure steps past, leans down and says, 'Can I get a light?' The silky voice is familiar, and all at once the air in my lungs is sucked right out.

I stare up, speechless.

The person squints, and then recognition sweeps over their face and they bolt upright.

'Lucy?'

Shit, shit, *shit!*

'Brian?' I squeak. 'What are you doing here?' My heart pounds like a kettledrum, my mouth sucked dry of moisture. He's standing right by the door, blocking my exit, curbing my desire to run the fuck out of there.

'I could ask you the same thing,' he replies, mouth gaping.

'I... I work here,' I say, trying to remain calm as my pulse rate hits treble figures.

'Do you now?' He pauses momentarily as if searching for something to say. 'So, can I get a light?'

He places a cigarette in his mouth and leans towards me, a peep of lithe neck coming into view.

'Oh... sure.' I pull my lighter out of my pocket, flicking on the flame and hold it to his cigarette, my hand trembling He cups his hands around the flame and inhales deeply. 'What are you doing here, Brian? This area is for staff only.'

'I guess I must be staff then.' His reply is deadpan.

'What do you mean?' My face must look like a rabbit caught in headlights.

He tosses a wicked grin. 'I own this place, so I guess you could say I'm staff.'

He cocks his eyebrow as though mocking me.

All I can do is stare, mouth open, as his words sink in. *He's the owner?*

The air between us hangs heavy as Brian takes several drags of his cigarette. The realisation smacks me in the face that the guy standing in front of me, the man who could map out the contours of my body, is in fact my boss. My boss of only five days!

Shit! I'm going to get fired.

Finally, I string a few words together. 'I guess this means I'm out of a job, then.' I take a long drag of my cigarette, hoping it will calm the butterflies now performing acrobatics in my stomach.

'Oh? Why would it?'

'Because we... you know.'

'Look, it's not a policy of mine to sleep with my staff but given the circumstances I don't think it's necessary to fire you. Unless Juan thinks you're a crap worker.'

'I guess I should be thankful to you for that.' *But what about my dignity? And what if other members of staff found out? And what about my plan to keep my head down and not get embroiled in any emotional crap?* Panic rises and I stiffen.

'So, what are *you* doing working here, Lucy?' Brian asks.

He provides momentary release from my wayward thoughts.

Oh god, this is awkward. 'I... err... well, I needed some more time away. This seemed like a good solution.'

'Escaping again, eh?'

'No, not at all! Not that it's any of your business.' My irritation bubbles like the Kasane Hot Springs, forgetting I'm talking to my boss. Thank God I've nearly finished my cigarette as the desire to flee takes hold. 'I have to get back to work. Thanks for not firing me.' I stub out my cigarette and bolt for the door, pushing him aside.

My heart is pounding, echoing the beats coming from the dancefloor as I head back up to the bar. It's times like these I wish Em was here. She'd know what to do. My only other option is to talk to Tara tomorrow and get her take on it. Only, can I trust her?

By a stroke of luck, she's standing by the bar when I return, glammed up, ready for a night out.

'How's it going?' she says, yelling above the hum of the music. With frayed nerves, I scan the room checking that Brian is nowhere to be seen.

'Yeah… okay. Um… listen Tara, can I talk to you for a second?'

'Sure, come around. We'll go to the bathroom.' She looks puzzled.

I look over to Jason, one of the bar staff on shift, and mouth to him I'll be back in five.

'You okay?' Tara says as we enter the ladies' toilet.

'Kind of.' Damn it, I need help. 'Um… you remember when I was here on holiday?'

'Yeah. What about it?'

'Well, I kind of hooked up with a guy a couple of times, and it… well, it turns out it was the boss,' I cringe.

'What, Juan?' She looks like she's been slapped with a wet fish.

'Of course not!'

'Who then? Brian?'

I nod.

'You fucked Brian?' she says, eyebrows raised, her lips curled into a bemused smile.

'Um… yes.'

'Wow. Way to go Lucy!'

'I'm not sure it is. I've just seen him in the courtyard and found out who he is.' I shiver from head to toe.

'I wouldn't worry. He's barely ever here.' Her eyes bore into me. 'I'm surprised though, he's err… quite private, from what I gather. I know a few girls here who wouldn't mind a piece of Brian. Me included.'

A green-eyed monster claws at my gut.

'Does he make a point of having one-nighters with holiday makers?'

'I don't really know. He's not in this club much, but from what I've heard from people working at his other club he doesn't *seem* to put it about much.'

I feel relieved, if not slightly puzzled. *What was I then?*

'I see. Well, at least he said I wouldn't be fired, but I'm hoping it won't affect my working here.'

'You'll be fine. Just stay out of his way. Like I said, he's never here. Only when Juan's being bollocked for something.'

'You're right, I guess,' I rasp. 'I probably won't see him that often. Just... don't tell anyone about it, okay?'

'Sure, no worries.' Tara gives me a reassuring squeeze. 'You'd better get back to work. Guess I'll see you sometime tomorrow.'

We both walk back out to the bar, and I double-check Brian is definitely gone.

When Brian said he was into hospitality, I assumed he meant hotels, not clubs. But if Tara's right, I won't see him so my pride or dignity, or whatever it is that is feeling vulnerable, can stay intact.

My wobble over Brian soon passes, and I relax a little as I get on with work. Time passes relatively quickly.

CHAPTER 30

As the end of my shift fast approaches, thoughts of Brian have drifted away and I'm looking forward to getting back to the apartment and having a well-earned sleep.

The end of each shift has a surreal edge to it. The music stops, the lights come on changing the whole place from a mysterious, intimate dance floor into a vast industrial-looking warehouse, save for the stylised bar. It's followed by a buzz of activity to get cashed up, cleaned down and organised before the club closes and everyone disperses to catch their taxis home.

I'm just logging off the till when someone walks past me, brushing lightly against my behind and stopping at my side. I turn, coming face to face with Brian, and gasp. So much for not running into him that often!

'Lucy, hi. Can we have a quick chat before you leave?'

Dread rises from my belly.

'Um... what do you want to chat about?'

'Finish up, then meet me down in Juan's office.' His voice is stern, lacking the curls and softness it has in the past.

My heart thumps. 'Oh... okay.' I finish what I'm doing then head through the back of the bar and down towards Juan's office. Every inch of me is trembling, in part from the fear of losing my job, but also with anticipation. Brian said he wouldn't fire me, so why has he changed his mind? Is he worried about how awkward it could get, or perhaps he's concerned I'll tell everyone about our nights together? A million different thoughts spin as I approach Juan's office. Taking a lungful of air, I open the door expecting to see Brian and Juan poised to fire me, but it's just Brian sitting in Juan's chair, elbows on the desk, a pen twirling in his long fingers.

'What did you want to chat about?' I fold my arms across my chest and stand against the door, hoping I'm the only one hearing my heart's rapid beat.

'Take a seat.' He motions to the chair opposite.

I sit down, looking at him through furrowed eyes.

'How're you enjoying being back here?' he asks.

'It's fine,' I reply, irritated and nervous at the same time.

He bores into me for what feels like ages, blue eyes piercing through me as if seeking the answer to some unspoken question.

'I'll get straight to the point.'

Oh shit, this is it.

'I was disappointed when I didn't get to see you again before you left so you can image my surprise when I found you here, working in my club of all places! Are you stalking me, Lucy?' He smiles from ear-to-ear, his eyes dancing, challenging me.

'What?' I almost fall out of the chair.

He chuckles, rubbing his stubbled chin. 'Kidding.'

'That's not funny,' I snap.

'So, what *are* you doing here?'

'I told you before. I needed more time off.' I clasp my elbows around my chest ready to plead my case. I just wish he'd get on with it.

'I see. You don't give much away, do you?'

I look away, involuntarily tutting in response. 'What do you want, Brian?'

'To see you again.'

'I'm sitting right in front of you,' I reply sarcastically.

'You know what I mean.'

'Are you kidding me? *Why*?'

'Because I like you.'

'I didn't come here to get involved with anyone.' My reply is deadpan.

He pauses momentarily. 'What did you come here for, Lucy?' The way he says my name sends a sonic boom through every fibre.

'I already told you.'

'You said you needed more time off, but not why you came back *here*.'

'That's none of your business.'

'I'm curious. Indulge me.'

'Look Brian, I'm tired, my feet hurt, and I want to go back to my apartment and get some rest. I'm not here to get involved with anyone, or any other shit, so if you're going to fire me can you please just get on with it.'

'I'm not going to fire you.'

'You won't mind if I go, then.' I rise to leave, but he shimmies around the table, blocking my exit.

'Could we not have some fun together?' His voice is low and seductive as he brushes my arm with his fingers.

I panic. 'I told you. I don't want to get involved with anyone.' I yank my arm free from his touch.

He lowers his eyes as if deep in thought and I reach for the door handle.

'An arrangement then? Something agreeable for us both.'

'What do you mean?' I reply, curiosity biting despite my better judgement.

'We hook up regularly, but no ties.'

His words jolt me, and at first, I'm stuck for a reply. 'No ties?' is all I can muster.

'If that's what you want.' I swear he looks disappointed as I scrutinise his face, digesting his words. 'What do you think?'

'I... err... No! I mean, I don't know. I need time to think about this,' I reply, my head starting to spin. 'When would you propose starting this *arrangement*?'

'At least that's not a definite "no" then.' He grins and continues, 'Well, it's officially my day off now, and I was planning to go to Space... Why don't you come with me, see how you feel?'

His eyes dance a devilish invitation as he throws me a coy smile.

'Brian, I'm tired and it's already silly o'clock in the morning,' I whinge, yet part of me is already out the door and in the queue for the club.

'You're in Ibiza now, Lucy, where the nights are for dancing and drinking and the days are for sleeping. Come on, it'll be fun. I promise.'

He winks, grabbing my hand and tugging.

I already know this battle is lost.

'Besides, I have something that might help keep you awake.'

I am not going to sleep with him. The words go on repeat as I wait for Brian to return from the bar.

Dry ice puffs out from the base of the god-like DJ's sound deck. A kaleidoscope of sound intertwines within my ears, masking all thought. Colour and shade intersperse, animating everything around me as the sea of bodies beckons. Raised arms, eyes closed; all ebbing in unison to the 'doof, doof' beat.

My brain is bombarded. It's too hot, too dark, too bright, too...

I squint, stilling myself, seeking normality. My magnetised flesh anticipating what's to come.

Limbs and torsos bump and grind around and against me, the stench of sweat lingering in the air like smog. The addictive pulse infiltrating my every pore until I'm a willing traveller in this hypnotic world. Digested and regurgitated into something unreal, nothing makes sense, and yet it all completely does. I'm feeling it... bliss.

I drift, embracing these strange, yet familiar sensations.

A tap on the shoulder tugs me back, and with heavy eyelids, I acknowledge him.

He says something. I can't hear him, so he closes in, cupping my ear.

'I was worried you'd done a runner.'

His voice is like mellow whisky pouring into my ears. Soft whiskers brush against my enflamed cheek, a hint of alcohol wafting from his delicious mouth.

'No, I'm still here,' I say, steadying myself.

'I'm glad you came tonight.'

'So am I,' and there is some truth in that.

My body betrays me, and I melt into him. We sway together, immersed in this synesthetic world drawing us closer to an inevitable climax.

Damn.

Brian gets in the taxi beside me and instructs the driver. He turns towards me, clasping my face and pulling me in. His kiss is hard and intoxicating. A moan seeps out of me as his hands move down my neck and the sides of my breasts, oblivious to our surroundings and responding only to his magnetising touch.

By the time we arrive at his place, I am aching for him. If he'd have wanted to have me in the car, I wouldn't have stopped him. Pure lust has consumed me.

Brian pays the driver and we both get out of the taxi and head towards the metal staircase leading up to his door. A feeling of déjà vu sweeps over me in recognition of our previous nights here. He quickly unlocks the door, grabs my hand and pulls me in, the door slamming shut behind us, then pins me up against the nearest wall finding my mouth again with his.

I grab his waist, tugging his shirt free, desperate to feel his skin.

In swift movements, he removes my top, tossing it to the floor, his hands exploring me once more.

'Lucy,' Brian moans.

He kisses me hard as I undo the buttons on his shirt, slipping it over his shoulders when I'm done.

He makes quick work of my bra, engulfing my nipple, tugging and flicking it with his tongue. His breath is molten against my skin causing sparks to course through every inch of my body creating a drunken achiness.

He pulls away to remove the rest of his clothes and shoes, his breath hitching, eyes loaded with desire, skyrocketing my need for him.

I follow suit, removing jeans and shoes but leaving my knickers on as if challenging him to complete the task. And he doesn't disappoint, dropping to his knees to ever so slowly slide them down my thighs and legs, trailing hot kisses in their wake.

I feel lightheaded, spaced out, except for the pulsing rapidly building between my legs.

He kneels up against me, his breath searing my flesh.

I reach for his hair, closing my eyes as he parts my legs and kisses me around the top of my thighs before trailing his lips to the middle. He lets out an appreciative moan as his tongue pushes between my legs and rhythmically flicks against my clitoris. I gasp as his tongue finds my sweet spot, revelling in this delicious torture.

'Lie down,' he growls, pulling me onto the floor.

I obey, desperate for him to relieve me, and slink to the floor, gasping as the cold tiles press against my flushed back.

Brian parts my legs and continues his onslaught.

I don't know how much more I can take, ecstasy is building so quickly, gasps and moans seeping out uncontrollably.

'I'm gonna come!' I yell, arching and reaching for my orgasm, exploding as the heat of his tongue rips through me.

When I've come down, our eyes lock. 'Suck me, Lucy,' Brian rasps, his erection primed and ready to go.

Mustering strength, I clamber onto my knees, pushing him onto the floor and straddle him, trailing kisses from his jaw, down his chest and to his taut belly. He moans as my lips suck and bite at his skin, beads of sweat clinging to his chest. Red bristles of hair prick lightly against my mouth as I taste him.

I part his legs with my knee, positioning myself in between, and in slow motion, sink my mouth down onto his poised erection. He groans loud and fierce as I flick my tongue around its head and slowly suck up and down his hard length, building a rhythm, increasing with his moans until I sense he is ready to come.

In one final onslaught, I suck hard and deep.

'Oh God!' he yells as he explodes into my mouth.

I gulp quickly as the warm, soapy, salty fluid hits the back of my mouth.

Brian throws his head back, panting and I release him and lean my head against his thigh.

His hand brushes through my hair as he breathes a deep, thankful sigh.

We lie together, satiated, coming down from our shared ecstasy.

Eventually, Brian sits up and gazes down at me.

'I like what you do to me,' he says stroking my cheek, a drunken smile on his face.

I like what you do to me, too.

'Shall we have a drink?' he says, pulling me out of my dream-like state.

'What time is it?'

'Four-thirty-six. Are you sleepy?'

'A bit. Aren't you?'

'Wide awake now.' He grins like the cat that's got the cream.

He helps me up from the floor and heads to the kitchen.

Obediently, I follow.

'Red wine okay?'

I nod, wrapping my arms around my chest.

He goes to a cupboard and grabs glasses and a bottle of wine, opens and pours, then hands me one.

I gulp a few mouthfuls hoping to get rid of his taste in my mouth and the threads of discomfort swirling in my gut. He grabs his glass and moves closer. I steal a moment to look at his lean body; not overly sculpted, spattered with red hairs. Doubts are soon replaced with a teasing tingle.

He takes a sip of wine. 'I think I'm going to like this arrangement.' He runs his free hand down my cheek. 'I'll get some robes so we can go for a smoke.'

'I haven't agreed to it yet,' I call after him, knowing full well it is already a done deal.

'You will.'

He returns with the same white robes we wore on our first night together, as if it was days rather than weeks ago. He leads me through the bedroom to the balcony, wine and cigarettes in hand.

I really liked what we did, how he made me feel. So free and natural, but I don't know him, don't *want* to know him, and yet he is systematically ripping through my carefully constructed boundaries.

His voice breaks my thoughts.

'Just in case you have any ideas about sneaking off again I want your mobile number, and there's a card on the kitchen bench with a twenty-four-hour taxi service.' He smirks.

'Is that really necessary? You know where I work after all?' I say, making one last stand, futile as it may be.

'For discretion's sake, I think we should text arrangements.'

'I guess,' I reply, mulling it over. 'My mobile is in my jeans pocket. I'll get it in a minute.'

We finish our cigarettes and head back into the kitchen to retrieve our phones and swap numbers. It feels awkward and unnecessary for something so casual.

The wine has made me drowsy and I stifle a yawn.

'Shall we go to bed?' Brian asks, finishing his glass and holding his hand out to me. I nod, too tired to protest, and take hold as he leads me to his bedroom. We disrobe and get into bed, our naked bodies mere centimetres apart.

He plants a soft kiss on my forehead. 'Goodnight, Lucy. I guess I won't see you in the morning.'

Exhaustion finally catches up and I rest my head on his chest as my eyelids fall.

The sun peeps through the French-style doors in Brian's room.

My eyes blink open. I'm still so tired and my head feels numb. Brian is fast asleep, snoring softly. I watch his torso rise and fall for several moments until gripped by the familiar feeling of wanting to flee.

I grab the bottle of water sitting on the bedside table and gulp until it's nearly all gone. Dehydration is a bitch, I ruse. I need some headache pills and a lot more sleep, but the bathroom beckons.

After a toilet stop and freshening up my face, I check through the bathroom cabinets for pills, downing some paracetamol when I find them.

My clothes, entwined with his, lay in a heap near the entrance and I retrace my steps, picking them up and putting them on until there's only shoes left.

One final sneak into the bedroom to steal another look at the sleeping Brian. Not a pretty-boy, but handsome nonetheless, with experience etched into his face; something alluring that draws me in. And I'm sure he knows it.

Clicking the front door shut as quietly as I can, I reach for the taxi card now in my jeans pocket and dial the number on my mobile. There's a wall at the entrance to his place, so I plop myself down and wait for the taxi, hoping my footsteps crunching on the gravel haven't woken him.

My phone pings. I stretch over to the bedside table and pick it up.

'Are you always going to leave so early?' It's a text from Brian.

I'm irritable, annoyed it's woken me. This is not what I wanted to happen. I quickly type, 'yes' and press send, then switch the phone off and go back to sleep.

I'm woken up later by Tara clattering around in the kitchen. My bladder wakes up too, so I drag myself out of bed and head for the bathroom. It's nearly 3 pm. I can't believe how long I've slept.

After showering and grabbing some coffee from the kitchen, I head to the balcony for a smoke. Tara comes out to join me just as I'm lighting up.

'Good afternoon, sleepyhead,' she says, giggling. 'So where were you last night?'

'Morn—I mean, afternoon,' I reply. 'Went clubbing with some of the staff,' I lie, crossing my fingers and hoping she doesn't ask any of the others about it.

'Which club d'ya go to?'

'Space. You?'

'DC10. Great DJ on, not that I can remember that much,' she winks, knowingly. 'You'll get used to the late nights. Comes with the territory.'

We're both working tonight, and I don't get a night off until Thursday, so I'm still in the throes of work-induced jetlag. Tara and I go to the beach for a few hours and grab some dinner before getting ready for our shift.

As I'm getting ready, I switch my phone back on. No further

messages from Brian.

Maybe this can work, I muse. It might even be fun, as long as we're clear about the boundaries.

CHAPTER 31

The older I get, the greater the impact of late nights. I'm knackered, the sagginess under my eyes resembling two dark holdalls, and I've broken out in pimples.

I've heard nothing from Brian, and I'm confused by it. Is he waiting for me to make contact? Or do I wait for him?

As lunchtime fast approaches, I plonk myself in my new favoured seat on the balcony and rip open a fresh packet of Marlboro Lights. Tara has gone out to do some laundry leaving me time to enjoy these solitary moments, in total contrast to the self-imposed isolation I had back home. It feels refreshing, steadying. I don't have to explain myself to anyone or pretend to be strong, so others don't worry. My unsettled, guilt-infested existence seems like a distant blip on the timeline of my life.

My mobile pings, the precious moment of bliss interrupted. A message from Brian flashes on its screen.

'Tonight?'

A tingle runs through me. 'When and where?' comes my swift reply.

'Space 9.30.'

'OK.'

And just like that, our next hook up is arranged. A contemplative sigh escapes me as I light the cigarette I've been holding during the exchange. Tonight's plan takes shape in my mind. Tara's not on shift so a night out has been arranged. A few drinks after dinner, then I'll tell her I'm heading home while she goes off clubbing. Simple. The less she knows, the better.

My make-up skills have vastly improved again, due in part to Em and the holiday. The minimal conservative look I'd been sporting now elevated with smoky eyes, recently cut hair, and killer ruby-red lips. All this creating a sultry reflection, tired lines caked over. My hair curls softly around my shoulders, its golden hue from days in the sun adding much-needed warmth. I brush my hands down the close-fitting dress hugging my frame like a sweet caress. Tick.

Tara and I make our way to a beachfront bar, meeting up with a couple of the other girls from the club. Already crowded, the girls have commandeered a wooden umbrellaed bench and several pitchers of sangria to get the night started, pouring glasses for us as we take vacant spots. They're already drunk and pressuring us to 'neck' the drinks to catch up. It reminds me of my twenty-something days when Em and I would buy bottles of Lambrini and drink the lot before heading out to a club. Much cheaper than buying club drinks, but a sure-fire way of vomiting in the wee hours.

The sun is bobbing over the ocean to the west, streaking the sky with deep purples and pinks. The sea's gentle breeze plants salty kisses against our cheeks and exposed flesh, and I shiver, not from the cold, but from the anticipation of what comes next.

Two glasses down, and that delicious distancing from all the ills of the world starts to take effect. The girls, more youthful in their outlook and hopeful of finding a knight in shining armour for tonight, are loud; shouting and shrieking in an animated dance designed to attract predatory guys. No natural mating rituals, just over-zealous attempts to 'pick me'. As I watch these acts of enticement, an unwelcome thought crosses my mind. *Were Em and I like this? Were our nights out all about attracting guys?* The answer forms too quickly, and I shake my head hoping to slough it away.

A discreet check on my phone reveals it's 9.11 pm. My real night is about to start, and tingles have gripped, coursing through me like I've just laid on a bed of nails. I scull my drink, glancing around to make sure no one has sussed my intentions. Tara is miles away, chatting to a bronzed boy-man on a nearby bench. I look over at the other girls still performing their mating calls and rise, squeezing through the narrow seat to reach Tara, and tap her shoulder.

'Hey T, I'm heading back.'

She turns, frowning, her cheeks glowing from the toxic mix of alcohol and salt air. 'It's still early,' she says, puzzled.

'I know, but I'm really knackered and could do with an early night.'

She pauses, tipping her head towards the bronzed guy, a subconscious gesture to let me know she doesn't want to leave just yet.

'You stay,' I assure her. 'Enjoy your night.' I flash her an approving smile and she grins back.

'Cheers, mate.' She plants a kiss on my cheek, and we part ways.

Anticipation builds as I totter along the paved back streets to Space. By now, the butterflies in my gut have become acrobats on ecstasy, performing cartwheels and headsprings as perspiration pools in every nook and cranny. As I approach, a thought flashes through my mind. *Is this his club, or neutral territory?*

I join the line, and eventually, a tall heavy-set tattooed bouncer ushers me through. I am deafened by a revved-up version of *Titanium* as I enter the cavernous main dancefloor. Revellers are everywhere, with no tangible gaps between each body already electrified by the pounding beat.

How the hell am I going to find him?

Fright and flight soars as I push and slide through the masses to reach the bar, scanning and squinting, bobbing my head around and through the crowds trying to spot him. All the while the voice in my head telling me to forget it and go home. I reach for my phone but realise he might not hear his. Panic wells as I shuffle to the front of the bar, the stench of sweat and alcohol ravaging my nostrils.

A hand grabs hold of my shoulder. I whizz around and find Brian gazing down at me, his eyes flickering under the strobe lighting. Relief and terror intertwine as I stare back, transfixed.

'Hi,' he says, leaning towards my ear, brushing my cheek with his hot breath, the waft of spiced aftershave dancing around me.

'Hi.' I quiver, trapped in his magnetic pull.

'You okay?' His lips touch my searing cheek.

'Fine,' I shout, praying my trembling has gone unnoticed. 'Is this one of yours?'

'No. I thought this would be more discreet.' He grabs hold of my hand. 'Dance with me,' and leads me to a clearing right in front of the DJ's box.

He pulls me close, his hips swaying against mine as we meld into each other, desperate for contact. I'm lost in a bubble of music, movement, and most of all, Brian.

We dance, kiss and drink into eternity until the searing lust is just too much, like a volcano about to blow.

As if acknowledging the urgency, his mouth trails chaste kisses to my ear. 'Shall we go?' The words somersault through my ear canal and into my brain.

I nod, more than happy to oblige, and he takes my hand, leading me through the crowds towards the exit.

The cooler night air refreshes my senses heightened from our mating ritual. We seek out a taxi, no words needed to discuss what comes next. And when we reach Brian's place, we tumble into bed and fuck the night away as if nature herself has decreed it an essential act.

And just like that, the foundations for our arrangement are laid bare. I work my shifts, rest my weary bones as and when I can, take care of day-to-day living, and spend most Fridays enjoying the best sex I've ever had. Remnants of my life in the slow lane cast firmly aside.

CHAPTER 32

The late afternoon sunbathes my weary body as I sit by the balcony table, legs stretched onto another chair, engrossed in a book, ignoring the ping from my mobile phone.

Ten or so minutes later, my phone rings out. It doesn't register at first. I'm not used to it ringing on days like these, but the caller's persistence pays off and I reluctantly get up and go to answer it. Brian's name flashes across the screen.

'Brian?'

'I sent you a text. You haven't replied yet.' There's a curt edge to his voice, his usual mellow tone clipped.

'I thought it'd be the usual,' I reply in all innocence.

'It's not.' Deafening silence ensues.

'Are you okay?'

'I've had a really bad day. Can you to come over?'

Uneasiness lingers as I contemplate a response. 'Why, what's happened?'

'I'll tell you later. Are you coming over?'

'But it's not Friday.'

'Fuck Friday! I've had a shitty day. I just need to see you.' He says, almost shouting.

I really don't like where this is heading. 'But... our arrangement?'

'Fucking hell, Lucy. I'm stressed beyond belief and I just want to see you. It's just one fucking night!'

'What? So I'm your stress reliever now?' I can't help myself; my hackles are up.

Fog descends and an uncomfortable silence prevails. He sighs, and then in a much calmer voice says, 'I'm sorry. I really want you to come over. Please come.'

My head is spinning. If I allow this to happen, it promotes the message I'm at his beck and call. I don't want that. But my judgement nosedives and I cave in. 'Give me thirty minutes.'

'Good. I'll see you soon,' and he hangs up.

Irritation bubbles under my skin as I head off to my room to get changed. I'm annoyed at him for asking, and even more angry at myself for agreeing.

Against far better judgement and attempting to create the illusion of sultriness, I change into something sexier, although it seems pointless; my clothes won't be staying on for long. But this... whatever it is, unsettles me. I feel... *vulnerable*, like the situation is outside of my control. Unsafe. And yet, I'm still going... *why*?

I call a taxi and pace outside the apartment block as I wait for it to arrive. I can't reconcile what's going on, questioning whether I should just ring and cancel the whole damn thing. Let him sort himself out.

The taxi arrives much later than expected, so it's getting late when my taxi pulls up at Brian's place. I pay the driver and, with trepidation mixed with unwarranted excitement, head up the staircase.

Before I get the chance to knock, the door swings open and I'm greeted by a dishevelled Brian.

'I was beginning to think you weren't coming.'

He bends forward to kiss my cheek, any semblance of a smile absent, his expression set like concrete.

'The taxi was late,' I reply, still standing at the entrance, tempted to edge away and leave.

He motions for me to enter, shutting the door with a slam behind me. The usual adrenaline rush I get before seeing him wanes, replaced by a sense of foreboding. I follow him to the kitchen bench feeling like a chastised child. He pours wine into glasses already on the counter, taking several gulps of his before slamming the glass back down and grabbing hold of my face. I can smell the alcohol on his breath. He's been drinking... a lot, but before I can say anything, his mouth is on mine, kissing me hard.

I push him back. 'Wait—'

His eyes probe mine. 'Lucy?'

'I don't want to do this. Not like this.'

He closes his eyes, his head shaking. 'Sorry—' and then his face softens. 'Drink with me?'

'Fine,' comes my clipped reply.

He tops our drinks and beckons me to follow him, making his way to the balcony.

'Are you going to tell me what's going on? Why I'm here?'

'Let's just say the shit's hit the fan at one of my clubs.'

'Oh... I'm sorry. Is there anything I can do?'

He reaches over and grabs my hand. 'Help me escape for a while?'

I take a glug of wine and nod knowing it's futile trying to resist. Every inch of me ignites as I know I am a willing participant in his journey away from reality.

I roll off the bed, find my clothes and quickly dress. *Now what?* Do I just leave now he's got what he needed?

Brian returns from the bathroom, striding over and grabbing my face in his hands, planting a lingering kiss on my lips.

'Thank you,' he breathes.

'What was that?' I ask, annoyance seeping through my pores.

'The best kind of stress relief there is,' he replies, a wry smile crossing his face as he releases me and grabs a gown from his wardrobe.

'Well I'm glad you got what you needed.' Anger seethes through my veins, and I stomp towards the front door, smoothing down my skirt on the way. He rushes after me.

'No... don't go!'

I ignore him, but he follows me to the door, grabbing hold of my shoulders and spinning me around. 'Lucy, wait!' But before I even reply, my hand rises, smacking hard against his cheek.

Silence.

He lets me go, cups his cheek and stares, eyes wild, nostrils flaring.

'What the fuck was that?' he balks, eyebrows furrowed.

'Stress relief!' I bite back.

He reaches out, grabbing my hand again, pulling me in.

'I'm sorry. I'm really sorry, Luce,' he says, whispering, and strokes my hair.

'Don't call me that!' I spit back, shaking myself free, tears tumbling freely. 'Who the hell do you think you are?' I bolt to the door. 'I knew this was a bad idea,' but he grabs me from behind, folding strong arms around my waist.

'Let me go!' I wriggle to free myself. His breath scorches my neck as his lips brush against my skin.

'Lucy, I am sorry,' he says as he nuzzles into me. 'Please don't go.'

I'm rooted to the spot, treacherous feelings coursing through my body. Involuntarily, I lean back into him as his mouth trails up over my jaw towards my mouth.

'Please stay,' he says.

He twirls me around and claims my mouth. I want to protest, to run away, but I'm overwhelmed, trapped between repel and attract.

Moments later, he pulls away and gazes down at me. My judgement has faltered. Instead of fleeing, I am rigid, staring blankly at him.

'Have another drink with me. A smoke,' he says, his tone silken again, more inviting.

I nod, the lava flows of anger now cooled, grabbing my drink and following him sheep-like to the balcony again, questioning why I have let myself do this. All I know for sure is this territory is unknown and I need to keep my wits about me.

After a few drags on his cigarette, Brian lets out a sigh and finally speaks. 'We had a drug bust at Roca last night.' He takes another long drag. 'It's been shut down pending further investigation.'

'That sounds bad.' Now I understand why he was in such a shitty mood.

'It is. I need the income from both clubs to keep them going and pay my bills and staff. Shutting one down over the summer is the worst thing that can happen; a nightmare. It's when I do most of my trade.'

'I'm sorry,' I reply, proffering a sympathetic smile.

'I just hope the investigation doesn't take too long.'

'Why are the police wanting to investigate?' I ask, my concern genuine.

'Because they suspect that a lot of the clubs in Ibiza have special arrangements with dealers, letting them peddle on the premises for a cut of the profit. They shut two clubs down last year for doing it. It's the rave clubs that are usually targeted.'

'So why do you think it's happening now?'

'No idea. Tourists are the main problem when it comes to drugs coming into the clubs. They come to Ibiza looking to party hard and get sloppy.' He rubs his face. 'Some post-teen twat has probably brought something in with him and someone's noticed and called the police. But unfortunately, it's not just the tourist who gets into trouble. I could lose my licence.'

He glugs down the rest of his wine and I notice the frown lines on his face deepen, highlighting the seriousness of the situation. It all makes sense now, but my uneasiness hasn't quelled.

We carry on talking for some time, Brian's mood gradually tempering. This is far more conversation than usual, albeit censored on my part, revealing only that I was married and snippets of my life back home. But Brian has told me a lot about himself, his lips loosened by alcohol, and I've discovered he came to the island about eight years ago after a messy divorce. He has no kids and came here to escape for a while, but the freedom and hedonism Ibiza has to offer seduced him. We have more in common than I give him credit for.

'It's getting late,' Brian says. 'Come to bed?'

By now we've downed several more glasses of wine and smoked numerous cigarettes. He gets up and holds his hand out to me.

As I follow him to the bedroom, my mind whirs into action. Tonight has gone against my better judgement.

'Back in a tick,' Brian says.

I'm left standing by his bed wondering whether we're going to sleep or have sex.

Tentatively, I undress and perch on the edge of the bed as if this is a new experience. Brian returns and disrobes, flopping onto the bed and patting the side for me to join.

I clamber in beside him and lay my head against his chest, his arm cradling my shoulder. 'Do you want to have sex?'

He strokes the side of my face.

'Only if you do,' he replies. 'Just make sure I'm fit and fresh for my hot date tomorrow night.'

'What hot date?' But it is too late. He's falling asleep.

I lay on my side and look at him for a while, watching his chest heave up and down and surveying his face as if creating a mental map. His closed blue eyes are framed with dark red lashes, his straight nose dappled with freckles that have merged over time creating a tan-like hue, his mouth and chin spattered with fire-like stubble. He is breathtaking.

As I lie against him waiting for sleep to take me, something feels off. This evening has been a game-changer.

CHAPTER 33

I wake and stretch out, gazing up at the ceiling, adjusting my eyes to the lack of light.

Turning over, I realise this is not my bed, and worse still, Brian's not in it. *Shit!* I sit up, panting as panic grips, my eyes darting to his bedside table to see the clock: 8.35 am. Confusion crashes over me like a king wave. The room is dark, and I look over towards the window noticing black blinds pulled low.

I bolt out of bed and scramble around looking for my clothes. This is bad. Not how it's meant to be. And where is Brian?

After dressing in lightning speed, I dart to the bathroom, putting my ear to the door to hear if he's in the shower. My desire to flee is now higher than Everest and I rush through to the living area but am stopped in my tracks. Brian stands behind the kitchen counter, cup in hand.

'Good morning,' he says, grinning

I stare at him, trying to assess if he's real.

'You okay?'

'I shouldn't be here,' is all I can offer. 'I have to go,' and bolt towards the door.

'Stay. Have breakfast with me.'

I glare at him, thrown by his crazy idea. 'Are you kidding? I need to go!' My cheeks flush with a mix of anger and embarrassment.

'Why would I be kidding?' And without warning or time to protest, Brian is upon me, grabbing hold of my shoulders.

'Get off!'

'Lucy?' he pulls back, frowning. 'What's this about?'

'You know what this is about! You closed the blinds!'

He looks mystified, as though he's just been told the sky is pink.

'You know I don't do *this*!' My anger whips, and I shrug him away, but his grip is firm.

'What the hell are you talking about?' His face contorts.

'I don't do this—sleepovers, morning coffee, small talk!' My arms flail, pointing erratically at the kitchen, the bedroom, the windows.

'The blinds are new,' he mumbles. 'They all are,' he gestures to the windows. 'Just stay and have some coffee.' His face softens.

'NO!' I yank my shoulders free of his hands and bolt to the door.

'You're leaving?'

'I always leave!' I throw back, gulping back the urge to whimper like an injured dog.

'Can't you make an exception?'

'No!' My hand clasps the door handle.

'Wait. Please Lucy, don't go.'

I stop momentarily and turn to face him. 'Why? Why do you want me to stay, Brian?'

He releases his grip and runs his hand through his hair, sighing. 'Isn't it obvious?'

I shrug. 'Isn't what obvious?'

'That I want to spend more time with you to see where it leads.'

'No, no, no, no, no,' I shake my head repeatedly, possessed by the urge to scream.

'Why not?'

I grit my teeth. 'Our arrangement.'

'What about it?'

'It was meant to be clear-cut, no emotional ties. You agreed!'

'I know that's what we said at the start, but can't you feel what's happening between us… or is it just in my head?'

My ice-queen persona retakes her throne. 'It's in your head,' and I push him away, turn and flee.

Exasperated, he calls after me.

'Lucy! Come back. You can't keep running away like this.'

But with clenched teeth, I race two-at-a-time down the staircase, desperate to keep my resolve firm. I make my way down the hill, almost jogging, saline tears tumbling.

As adrenaline courses through my veins, pumping life to each tributary of my weary body, the words repeat over and over in my mind. *He's changed the fucking game!*

I arrive back at the apartment just after 10.00 am and spy Tara in the kitchen as I walk in.

'Oh good, you're here,' she says, smiling, but frowns when she sees my dishevelled state. 'You okay?'

The walk and taxi ride have calmed me enough to conjure a coherent response. 'I… went into town for a walk,' I lie.

'Oh… okay,' she says, bemused. 'Coffee?'

'Yeah, that'd be great. Thanks.'

'No worries.'

She pours me a cup from the plunger.

'Before I forget, there's a letter for you.'

She reaches over the counter, picks up the envelope and passes it to me. I take it and look down at it. From England. Jen's handwriting, I think.

I haven't heard from my cousin for a while. She doesn't know anything about Brian. I grab my coffee and head to the balcony for a smoke, ripping open the decorative envelope, a wedding invitation! Jen's invited me to her wedding to Marcus Darrington on Saturday, 1st October 2011. My mood lightens and a broad smile spreads across my face. It's just over three weeks away, coinciding with the end of summer season here. A wry thought forms. I could head off a couple of weeks or so beforehand, avoiding the messiness with Brian. After the wedding, I'll go home, leaving all this crap behind me. Easy.

I re-read the invite and notice it's addressed to 'Mrs Lucy Morris + Guest'. A long-forgotten wound reopens. The words are all wrong. It should read 'Mr Joseph and Mrs Lucy Morris'. I stare down at the card, the slap of comprehension stinging. *There is no Joe.* Nausea grips, and I just make it to the bathroom as years of stashed away pent-up guilt vomit violently out of me.

A short while later, Tara raps on the bathroom door. 'You okay, Lucy?'

'Yeah, fine,' I reply, and hurl again.

After cleaning myself up, I return to the land of the living. Tara, still in the kitchen, turns to me, concern etched on her pretty face.

'Something I ate,' I lie. 'I'm going to lie down for a bit.' She nods, and I retreat to my room, collapsing on the bed as tears, raw and untamed, spill out of me.

CHAPTER 34

Juan rubs his stubbly chin, contemplating what I've just told him.

'So, you want to leave on the twenty-first? In eleven days?' he says, frowning.

'If possible, yes,' I reply. 'It'll give me a chance to spend a few days at home and sort some stuff out before I go to my cousin's wedding.' I throw him a hopeful smile.

'Will you come back?' Juan asks. 'Most of the staff are leaving soon, but we stay open for the rest of the year. I still need people.'

'I'm not sure,' I say, and I genuinely don't know. I only came here for a short while to escape the rut I'd fallen into, but recent events have conspired to send me fleeing back home. Yo-yoing back and forth won't solve anything. Deep down, I know it's time to face the music.

'Please, let me know if you change your mind. With one of the other clubs being closed at this time I can get some staff to cover, but I will soon need more. You are a good worker. It would be a shame to lose you.' Juan is so sweet. His words are gut-wrenching.

'I'll keep it in mind,' I reply, not entirely dismissing the possibility.

We finish our impromptu meeting and I return to the bar to continue my shift. But I feel drained, as if recent events and the thought of returning home have added lead weights to my limbs and sucked out all my remaining strength.

My break doesn't come soon enough, and I race to my usual spot outside and quickly light up. The quicker I inhale, the sooner I can bury any errant feelings and get back to work only, my mind is racing with a million thoughts; the wedding, leaving, returning home. My phone pings, pulling me out of my head.

'Can we talk?' I gasp, re-reading Brian's message. But what is there to talk about? He must know our arrangement is over. Part of me wants to ignore him, tell him to get lost, but the other *treacherous* part won't shut up.

After an unspoken battle between them, reason wins, and I hurriedly type, 'No,' press send, and switch off my phone as soon as it's gone.

I finish cashing up and am about to head off when a voice startles me from behind.

'Lucy.'

I whizz around and gasp. A stony-faced Brian stands on the other side of the bar.

'What do you want?' comes my icy reply.

'I missed you on Friday. You didn't reply to my message.'

My eyes dart around the bar, checking to see if anyone's in earshot. Thankfully, everyone has gone apart from Juan, who must still be downstairs in his office.

'There's nothing to talk about.'

'I think there is. Come to the courtyard and tell me what we haven't got to talk about.'

'I really don't think that's a good idea.'

'Come on, Lucy. Stop fucking around. Can't we just talk like grown adults?'

'No. Like I said, we've nothing to talk about.' I reply, hissing like a snake about to strike.

'And what about our arrangement?'

'Our arrangement is over.'

'Just like that?' He frowns. 'I don't want it to be.'

'You should've thought about that before you crossed the line.'

'What line? I have no idea what I'm supposed to have done!' He clasps his head in exasperation.

'The stress relief sex. The blinds. The "let's see where this leads" talk!' I say, my tone rising higher than the Empire State Building.

'You slapping me.' His tone is blunt.

I ignore his sarcasm. 'I don't do mornings, and I don't do relationships. I thought that was clear, so why try to force it?'

'I wasn't trying to force it, merely suggesting.'

'I need my boundaries. I thought you knew that.'

'I do, but what is so wrong with wanting to spend time with you, getting to know you more?' He throws his hands up.

Anger bubbles like molten lava beneath my flesh. 'You knew what the score was when we started this up. You knew that I didn't want any of this!' I wave my arms, gesturing to an invisible mess around me.

'So, it was just about sex for you,' he says, brow furrowed as if understanding for the first time. 'Well... if that's how you want to play,' he replies, shaking his head, face turning crimson.

'It is. Now if you don't mind, I need to finish my work.'

He pauses for a moment, his features softening. 'At least let me make sure you get back okay.'

'I'll be fine. I always am.' Tears well, threatening to spill. I will not let him see me like this. Turning, I stride away and out through to the back of the bar. He doesn't follow.

Outside, a taxi is waiting. I quickly get in and direct the driver, slouching into the seat as I cover my face and set the sobs free.

CHAPTER 35

My appetite has faded. Sitting at my favourite spot on the small, concrete balcony of the apartment, I'm sustaining myself on red wine and cigarettes. With eyes like puffed up pillows and a throbbing head, I've shed so many tears there's nothing left except a numb, empty shell.

Tara and I had a deep and meaningful this morning. Even though we haven't known each other that long and I haven't yet figured out if she's on my 'trusted' list of friends, I confided some of what passed with Brian. I'd tried calling Em, but it was too early for her to answer her phone, probably out partying the night before. I needed to vent, and only Tara was on hand. I told her about my 'arrangement' with Brian, and how last night was a game-changer. Wide-eyed doesn't begin to describe the look on her face, followed by a grin somewhere between, 'you go girl,' and, 'you did what?' She has promised to keep the gory details to herself. I just hope I can trust her. She's like Em in many ways, but she's not her and doesn't know my history. But, then again, there are things even Em doesn't know. Things I haven't been able to tell even her, my best friend of so many years.

Tara also knows of my imminent departure. We've agreed I will pay her to keep my room until the end of October 'just in case'. Surely by then I'll have decided what I'm going to do next, especially because I'm not one hundred percent sure returning home and staying is the right thing. This island has woken me up, unleashed a dormant part of my psyche that has been asleep for far too long, and I'm not sure I'm ready to give it all up.

Tara pops her head around the balcony door. 'I'm heading out, you want anything?'

'No, I'm good, thanks,' I reply. She disappears for the rest of the day. I'm on shift later so won't see her until tomorrow. This is good. I need some time for myself, to get my head around everything that's happened.

Heading back inside to get a drink, I notice my mobile on the counter, still switched off. I switch it back on and a few seconds later it pings. My heart thumps.

'I don't want it to end like this. Talk to me. Brian.'

He sent the message just after I left last night, and as I finish reading it, my phone pings again with another one, sent an hour ago.

'This is how it's going to be? Why do you have to be so fucking cold?'

Anger fizzes. Why is he doing this? He knew the score.

I switch off the phone and hurl it onto the countertop, resolute this game of his is well and truly over. My mood is foul, and there's only one person who can cheer me up when I'm like this. I call Em and tell her about Jen's wedding, hoping, she'll be my '+ 1' and forever change the 'Mr and Mrs Morris' invite line imprinted in my brain.

'Luce!' Em yells as she answers my call, countering my assumptions of a late night and hangover. 'How's it going?'

'Yeah… it's good,' I lie. 'How're you?'

'You sound off. What's wrong?' Trust Em to pick up on it straight away.

'Nothing. Well... there is something—'

'Tell me,' she demands.

I pause for a moment wondering if I should tell her all the details of what has happened with Brian but decide not to. 'Umm... Jen's getting married, so I guess I'm coming home.'

Em whoops. 'When?'

'October 1st. Will you be my plus one?'

'Of course! I'd love to.' She pauses. 'Oh... must seem weird without Joe.'

'Uh-huh,' I say as nausea grips.

'You okay?'

'I will be. Guess I need to give myself a shake and put it all behind me.'

'I'm here for you,' Em replies. 'I'll always be here for you.'

'I know.' I wipe a stray tear from my cheek and take a deep breath. 'Anyway. Jen's wedding...'

'Party time!' Em says with a little too much glee in her voice.

I feign a titter. 'Perhaps. I think it'll be formal, you know how loaded Jen's folks are. By all accounts it's a posh hotel in the countryside.'

'Is she sure she wants us to come, then?' Em laughs.

I giggle, recounting Jen's raised eyebrows every time she'd heard about our exploits. 'I think she knows us well enough.'

My spirits lift. Em's voice is soothing and constant, and she knows just what to say to bring me out of my self-dug pit.

As we finish talking, excitement simmers at the thought of seeing her again soon, and watching Jen get married. One week and four days left here, and it can't pass soon enough.

CHAPTER 36

Instant coffee. *Urgh!* Hate the stuff, but it's all I have in the house. Mail is stacked like a collapsed Jenga game on my kitchen table, and I sift through knowing there's unlikely to be anything important.

Em has been an absolute star. She picked me up from the airport last night, and when I got home, I noticed she'd cleaned the house and got some food in for me, except for decent coffee. I have promised her we will go shopping for wedding outfits this afternoon as she's as keen as ever to get glammed up for the occasion.

I still haven't told her about what happened with Brian. All thoughts of him pushed far from my mind, hopefully left buried in Ibiza. I want to tell her everything, but haven't yet made sense of it, or how I feel. Maybe I'll reveal all in a few weeks.

My home phone rings. It's Jen, giddy with excitement and double-checking arrangements. I'm staying at the hotel she's getting married in, travelling over to Gloucester with Em on Friday and coming back Sunday. Her mood is infectious as she tells me what's planned and all about her dress. My heart races at the prospect of seeing her soon.

'Oh Luce, it's going to be wonderful! Just wait until you see the place. It's a Country House and Golf Club with a spa and all sorts,' she says.

'Sounds perfect. I can't wait.'

'Me too. We'll have to go out before the wedding so we can catch up properly. I want to hear all about your escapades in Ibiza!'

I laugh nervously. 'It's not that exciting.'

We chat for some time before her voice lowers as if she's about to give me important news. 'Hey Luce, before I go there's something exciting I want to tell you.'

'What is it? Everything's okay, isn't it?'

'Yes. It's all fine. Well, remember Rob from the stud?'

'Rob?' I reply, ignorant. And then it hits me like a truck crashing at high speed into a brick wall. I gasp out loud. *Oh my God! Rob.*

'Yeah. Him and Marcus have become good mates and he's letting us use a couple of the stallions for photos at the wedding. How awesome is that!'

I can't focus.

'Luce?'

'Yep. Still here,' I reply, my pulse racing faster than a thoroughbred at Ascot. 'So... is he going to the wedding?' I take a deep breath and find some composure.

'He can't make the ceremony but will be there for the evening do. Great isn't it!'

'Sure... sounds good,' I lie, doubled over, trying my utmost not to let Jen hear my staggered breaths.

'Luce. Are you okay?'

'Yes. Of course.' I say, trying to sound jovial. 'It sounds lovely.' I'm not okay, not by a long shot, but who am I to dictate who she can invite to her wedding celebrations? We say our goodbyes and end the call.

Afterwards, I sink to my knees by the side of the sofa; the shock hitting me like a shovel to the face. I haven't thought about Rob at all. Pushed him to the back of my mind after Joe died. But I have no choice, now. I have to deal with him.

Do I tell Em? She doesn't even know Rob exists. Yet another huge secret I have kept from her. But I need to sort this out, talk to someone, and there's only one person I can think of... Marj. I only hope she can give me some pearls of wisdom to help get me through the wedding and the likelihood of seeing Rob again. But right now, I need to be alone with my wayward, spiralling thoughts. My shopping trip with Em will have to wait.

CHAPTER 37

I twiddle my fingers, nerves frayed as I sit outside Marj's room.

She greets me with what is her customary gentle smile as we settle into our usual positions.

'How have you been?' she asks, resting her notepad in her lap.

'Good,' I reply, reluctant to divulge my current issue.

'Did you get what you felt you needed from your time away?'

'Sort of—' I fake a smile, something I've become expert at doing. 'But that's not really why I'm here.'

'Oh?' She looks puzzled. 'Would you like to share with me what's going on for you?'

Taking a deep breath and struggling to string together a coherent sentence that doesn't make me sound like a psychotic bitch, I reply, 'Um... there's something I didn't tell you before. Something important.' My pulse races, throat constricting. I draw in another deep breath, hoping it will soothe. 'A couple of months before Joe died, I... well, I met someone...' I stare at Marj searching for disapproving signs, desperately trying to figure out if I should reveal all.

She says nothing: a half-smile etched into her face; eyes lightly crinkled giving no clue to what she's thinking.

'Joe and I had been going through a rough patch. We were

arguing a lot and he was snowed under with work, so we weren't spending much time together.' I clasp clammy hands together and take a much-needed gulp of air. 'He went on a business trip abroad for six weeks, and as we hadn't had a decent holiday for a while, I decided to take a few weeks off and see my cousin Jen.'

Marj stays silent, her expression unwavering.

I suck in another deep breath filling me with the courage to continue. 'Jen lives a couple of hours away in a small town outside of Gloucester. She took some time off, and most evenings we went to her local pub. That's where we met Rob.'

Still nothing from Marj. *Why doesn't she say something? Anything!*

'He owned a stud farm in the area and offered to buy us drinks. We got chatting and just seemed to click...' I drop my head, recounting the memories.

'You met Rob while staying at Jen's and got on well with him,' Marj says, her voice steady.

I nod, fixated on my hands twisting in my lap. 'Jen and I used to ride when we were kids, so Rob invited us to his farm to go on hacks with him. I thought he was keen on Jen, but he soon made it obvious it was me he was interested in.'

'And how did you feel about that?'

'Honestly? I liked the idea of someone liking me. It made me feel alive.'

'The idea of another man finding you attractive made you feel good about yourself?'

'Uh-huh.' I can't look at Marj as shame engulfs me. 'But I let it go too far.'

'You had a relationship with Rob?'

'Yes.' I feel sick. 'When Jen went back to work, I kept going to see him, or would arrange to meet up with him during the daytime, and, well... you know how this goes. Jen didn't know what we were doing, and I knew it was wrong, but felt so alive again. I hadn't felt like that for a long time.'

'You felt enlivened,' Marj responds. 'Did you ever feel like that with Joe?'

'Yes, of course I did.' Her words wound me. 'He wined and dined me. He was romantic, confidant, more worldly than me, and knew what he wanted in life. I found that really attractive at first. It was so different from what I was used to.'

'Different?'

'Yeah. I guess he was what my parents would've called "marriage material" and I really thought I was ready for all that, you know, settling down, committing; the whole shebang.'

'You mentioned that Rob made you feel alive. What do you think it was that attracted you to Rob?'

'He was attentive and fun. And I guess the idea of it all— clandestine, I suppose—was exciting. It gave me something to look forward to, escape from the boredom I was feeling.' Memories flood back, offering a chaste glimpse of more pleasurable times. 'We seemed to be on the same wavelength and laughed all the time, and the sex was, well... passionate.'

'Joe gave you commitment and maturity, and Rob gave you fun and passion. Is that right, Lucy?'

'I never thought of it that way, but yeah... I guess so.'

Marj writes something on her notepad then looks across at me, head tilted to the side. But something about her expression rings alarm bells and I want to know what she's written.

'Can I see the notepad?'

Her eyes widen a touch. 'Of course,' she says, handing it over.

Only two words are written on the page: 'Not ready.'

'What does that mean?' I hold the pad up to her.

'Lucy—' She pauses, as though unsure of where to go. 'I'd like you to continue telling me about your relationship with Rob, if you're able to. I *will* come back to the notes, but I feel it's important to carry on with your story for the moment.'

Huh?

'Oh... um, okay.' I shuffle in the chair, thrown off by her request. 'Well... err... when I left Jen's I wasn't ready to go back to my life as it was. Rob made it clear he didn't want us to end. I guess I didn't either, so we kept in touch, mostly by text messages and phone calls. We'd spend hours talking and planning meet ups. It distracted me from all the mundane stuff going on in my life.'

'Lucy, would you refer to your relationship with Rob as an affair?'

'What? No!' I glare at Marj, nostrils flaring.

'Do you feel Rob understood what the relationship was?'

'He didn't know I was married if that's what you mean. Well, not at first. But I told him... eventually.' This confession is not doing me any favours, but I'm in so deep I have no choice but to continue. 'He was devastated and wanted to break it off because he felt awful about it, but we were heading down a path we couldn't come back from.'

'You felt the relationship had gone beyond something casual perhaps?'

'I think so.' I twist my wedding ring finger, even though the ring hasn't been there for some time. 'Rob caved. Said he loved me and wanted to give it a go.'

'And how did you feel about that?'

'At the time, relieved. He gave me an escape route.'

'You wanted an escape from your marriage?'

I nod slowly as long-held demons wriggle free.

Marj's head tilts again as if contemplating what to ask next. Finally, she breaks the silence hanging heavy in the room. 'I'm wondering what made you decide to go into a relationship with Joe if what he was offering was so *different*?'

Her question destabilises me. 'We're supposed to settle down and have the whole marriage and kids' thing, aren't we?'

'But did you feel ready for that?'

Kerching!

'I thought so...'

'You seem unsure,' Marj replies, jotting something else down.

'Is anyone one hundred percent sure when they're about to get married?'

'Perhaps. If they're ready for it.'

Marj's comment irritates me. Should I have known I wasn't ready? 'I guess I wasn't, then,' comes my clipped reply, and feel reluctant to say anything more as Marj's questions poke and prod feelings I don't want to explore because they are shrouded in shame.

I wrack my mind, censoring all errant thoughts, before finally speaking up. 'When Joe returned from his business trip, I felt so guilty about what had happened that I broke it off with Rob. I wanted to give my marriage another go and be the wife Joe wanted me to be. But nothing really changed between us, and I couldn't stop craving the attention Rob gave me. So, when Rob said he loved me... well, Joe and I nosedived.'

'You realised when Rob admitted his feelings that you and Joe were no longer working?'

I bow my head again, nausea swirling. 'That's when I decided I was going to leave him to be with Rob. That's what we were arguing about.' I cover my face so she can't see the dam walls burst.

'Lucy,' Marj says, her tone softened, 'I'm wondering if this is the reason you've been unable to grieve since losing Joe. Why you say you feel so guilty?'

'It... it's my fault.' Sobs erupt and tears tumble.

On cue, Marj pushes the tissue box my way. I pluck several from the box as she waits quietly for me to compose myself. The silence is deafening.

'I'm going to Jen's wedding at the weekend,' I say, rasping, 'and Rob's going to be there. I haven't spoken to him since—'

'You haven't spoken since Joe died?'

'No. Just heard snippets about how he's been doing from Jen.'

'And how do you feel about Rob now?'

'I really don't know. I guess that's why I'm here.'

'It sounds like your feelings towards Rob have been locked away with the guilt you feel over Joe's death. Might seeing him help unravel some of those feelings?'

'But I'm... scared,' I say, straightening. 'I don't know if I can handle facing him, facing all of it.'

'Only you can decide if seeing Rob will help you move forward, Lucy.'

Can I face him? Can I reopen that gigantic wound and let all the pain ooze out? I tremble as if it's resonating throughout my body, testing the dam to see if it's ready to crumble. I've spent so long in this abyss I don't know if I can face the reality of what I've done.

But only I decide if I can face him.

'But it's Jen's big day. I don't want to risk spoiling it for her,' I say.

'Is there something else that may help you to manage those feelings, at least until after the big day?' Marj asks.

'Should I speak to him before the wedding?' I search Marj's face for approving signs.

'I can't answer that for you. You have to do what *you* think is best.'

Exasperation hits hard as I rack my brains trying to figure out what to do, but nothing avails itself to me. There is no room for reason; my mind is filled with a garbled mess of unwanted memories.

'I need your help, Marj. I know I have to face him at some point, but I just wish it wasn't on such an important day. I'll probably end up getting steaming drunk and just stay out of his way.' A nervous titter escapes, even though there is nothing funny about any of this.

'Perhaps it's just important for you to acknowledge your feelings for now and commit to working through them at some point, whether it be before the wedding or after. Having it on your agenda may go some way to helping you get through the day, knowing you'll address them when it feels safer for you to do so.'

She's right, only, I don't know if I'll have the inclination or courage to drudge it all up again.

'But what about Rob? What do I do if I see him?'

'Could you acknowledge to him that you need to talk about what's happened, but that for the sake of Jen's wedding, you are going to park it? Bear in mind he may not agree to any of it.'

I ponder her words, dabbing my eyes with a tissue. 'Maybe not, but it's good advice.'

'I'm not supposed to give advice,' she says, smirking. 'Call it an interim measure until we can talk again.'

'After the wedding?'

'Of course.' She glances up at the clock. 'Same time?'

I nod.

Our session ends, and rather than feeling like I've come undone, relief washes over me knowing Marj will be my safety net after the wedding. That she's still willing to work with me even though she knows nearly all the sordid details of how I killed Joe.

Just as I'm about to pull open the door to leave, Marj speaks.

'Lucy, sometimes just acknowledging our feelings in that moment can trigger us to choose to change them.'

I smile and nod, saying a quick goodbye. But what does she mean by it?

The drive home is clearer than those of the past, and yet my mind is racing; facing Rob, Marj knowing more of my dark secret, and choosing to change how I feel? By the time I reach my house, I know I will have to face him, but will make damn sure it doesn't happen at the wedding. Any fallout can be dealt with in the confines of Marj's office... I hope.

CHAPTER 38

Em and I arrive mid-afternoon at a beautiful five-star, sandstone hotel set on the edge of a leafy woodland and golf course. Jen's parents have chosen well. This place is sure to impress.

Thank God Em drove here because I have been on edge since getting up this morning. She keeps asking if I'm okay, but I lie and tell her it's just excitement. She knows something's amiss judging by the pained looks she keeps tossing my way. I only wish I wasn't so adept at concealing the truth from her.

After checking in, we head up to our first-floor room to freshen up. Elegant burgundy drapes frame the huge leaded windows peeking out over the golf course, and the mahogany-styled furniture and dado rail give the room a feeling of grandeur. I drop my overnight bag on the suitcase rack and take it all in. The room is huge, and Em and I have twin beds that almost feel like they're rattling around. Thankfully, a set of French doors open out onto a small balcony where I can have a smoke, so that's exactly what I do.

'What time do we need to be at Jen's parents' house?' Em calls from inside the room.

'About six-ish. She said they'll be having dinner around seven and I reckon it'll take about twenty-five minutes to get there from here.'

'Who's driving?' Em looks at me with an eyebrow cocked.

'I guess that'll be me then,' I reply, feeling guilty that Em has had to drive the whole four-and-a-half-hour trip. She claps her hands in glee. She's met Jen's parents a few times, but sometimes needs a bit of Dutch courage to get through what can be more intimate gatherings.

'Luce!' Jen squeals bolting from the door towards me. She looks fabulous. Her hair is lighter and longer, and she is glowing.

Did I look this good before marrying Joe?

We bear hug for a few moments, making up for the way too long time since we last saw each other.

Jen greets and hugs Em and leads us inside the homely detached two-story house Jen has lived in since she was eight. Jen's parents, Aunt Liz and Uncle Ron, greet us warmly, and I'm struck by how little they've aged since the last time I saw them. Aunt Liz still wears her hair in the same shoulder-length bob, her silvery-brown hair smooth and glimmering, framing her petite face like a crown. Uncle Ron still bears the handsomeness of his youth; age has been kind to him. Barely a follicle of hair gone, and his dark-blonde hair lightened by greys wisping through it. He bends to wrap me up in his tall, masculine frame. If the truth be told, I've always had a bit of a crush on him and feel my cheeks flushing as he hugs me tightly.

The atmosphere is jolly, and I feel at home. Jen's parents are clearly excited about the wedding, but who wouldn't be when their only daughter is about to get married?

The whole evening drifts pleasantly along, providing distraction from my errant thoughts about Rob. Aunt Liz has cooked a fabulous salmon fillet for dinner, reminding me of the pleasures of home-cooked food, tinging my thoughts with sadness that I no longer get to experience it with my own parents. Uncle Ron takes great delight in recounting some of Jen's more embarrassing childhood stories, some of which, to my horror, include me. Like when we tried our hand at riding the gypsy ponies on the abandoned airfield near Jen's house, only I wasn't a rider then and ended up face-planting into horse shit. And the time Jen borrowed Uncle Ron's car to go clubbing, only to end up with a dent and a parking fine.

Em cocks an eyebrow several times, telling them I haven't changed much! *Cheek!*

After dinner, I help Aunt Liz stack the dishwasher and tidy up in the kitchen. It brings back familiar feelings of warmth and safety, something I'd had countless times in the past, but which now seem from another lifetime.

I'm rinsing out a pan and humming *You Sexy Thing* when Aunt Liz asks, 'So how are you doing, Lucy?'

She has that 'pity' look I hate so much etched on her face, although I'm sure she doesn't mean to. 'I'm fine, Aunt Liz. Really.' Her eyes soften, wrinkles deepening.

'Losing Joe was tragic, and so, so young. He was such a lovely man,' she laments.

I walk over and give her a reassuring hug, fighting back tears. *Yes, he was a lovely man, but I betrayed him and now he's dead.* The thought is sobering, and after another squeeze, I pull away, plastering my face with the well-practised faux smile.

'Anything else I can do?' I ask, deflecting any further discussion.

'No, that's it. Let's go and re-join the others.'

She squeezes my arm as we head towards the living room.

Back at the hotel, I raid the minibar and head out onto the balcony for a smoke. The jitters return with a vengeance. I hope this overpriced red wine will take the edge off otherwise I'm in for a long, restless night.

Em again asks me if I'm okay. I wish I could tell her, but what would she think of me if I did? So, I do what I always do.

CHAPTER 39

My eyes flit open as light cascades through the curtains and familiar knocking sounds rattle around in my head. Suddenly, the air is sucked from my lungs and I bolt up, gasping.

In a panic, I look over to where Em is sleeping, trying desperately to breathe. Is she awake? Thankfully, she doesn't stir, and I slump back down in the bed, my PJ's clinging to my sweaty body, fidgeting as I try to get comfortable and fail miserably. It all gets too much, so I ease my tired body out of bed and head for the bathroom to have a pee and splash water on my face.

I stare at myself in the mirror for ages, searching for something, *anything*, to snap me out of my waking nightmare. I should feel excited, happy, joyous that my beautiful cousin is about to start her journey toward marital bliss. Only, my mind scorns, telling me it's all a lie, that there's no such thing as happy ever after. Too much is at stake; too much *has* to change until eventually the love, or in my case, the love and the husband, dies.

The cold water smacks hard against my heated cheeks. I splash my face repeatedly, desperately trying to wash away the sorrows and ground myself. Eventually, the woman in the mirror throws back a feeble smile. It's the best she can do.

I put the kettle on and head out onto the balcony for a smoke, still wearing my sweat-sodden pyjamas. It's chilly and drizzling outside, but I don't care.

Em wakes up shortly after, shuffling around in her bed and letting out the odd sigh. A few minutes later, she pops her head around the balcony door.

'Morning,' she says, yawning. 'You sleep okay?'

'Yes, fine,' I reply. *If only you knew, Em.* 'You?'

'I'm in a world of pain,' she says, groaning. 'Wish I hadn't emptied the minibar in the wrong order.' She giggles unconvincingly, rubbing her eyes then tousles her glorious mane.

It takes three cigarettes and two coffees for me to finally get my butt into gear. Em and I get showered and dressed and head downstairs to the dining area for breakfast. And it's a lavish affair: a vast array of hot and cold meats, cheeses, yoghurts, fruit, pastries, and a multitude of juices, teas and coffee laid out before us, calling out to be selected and eaten. Em is green around the gills, still suffering from her over-indulgence last night. I am lost in my own thoughts.

We eat breakfast in near silence, something that is foreign territory for us.

'I wish you'd tell me what's wrong,' Em finally says, pushing her scrambled eggs around the plate.

'I'm fine, Em. Honestly.' I reply, sighing.

'You've been on edge since we left your place. Just tell me what's up. Maybe I can help.'

I need to think on my feet and get her off my back. 'It's the first time I've been back to Gloucester since Joe died. It feels weird, that's all.'

'I see,' she says.

She tilts her head to the side as if this will somehow give her a better insight into the workings of my mind.

'Are you sure that's all it is?'

'Honest, Em. I'll be okay. Besides, this is Jen's day, so I'm going to give myself a kick up the arse and stop sulking.'

'I'll do it,' she says, laughing, but then turns an odd shade of grey-green and darts out of the dining room.

She returns after ten or so minutes with a sheepish look on her face.

'I'm fine,' she says, putting her hand up. 'Better out than in.'

I can't help belly laughing. She looks so sorry for herself, having just chucked up what little of breakfast she ate.

'Let's get ready.' She nods towards the exit.

'Don't you want to eat a bit more?'

'Trust me, I don't need any more food at this moment in time.'

Smirking, I follow her out of the dining room and up to our room.

The wedding starts at 11.00 am. With only forty minutes to spare, I pace back and forth outside the bathroom waiting for Em to get out.

Housekeeping refilled the minibar during breakfast and even though it's too early for wine o'clock, I can't help myself and grab a bottle of red and take it to a seat on the balcony. I'm onto my second cigarette when Em finally appears looking fresh and smart in a sleek skirt and blouse.

'Well?' she says, twirling.

'What have you done with Em?' I ask, smirking, as she poses in front of me.

She eyes over the bottle on the table and rolls her eyes. 'Thought I'd try something different.'

'Really?'

'Yes, really. Besides, your Uncle Ron said the dress code would be smart, so I thought I'd better toe the line.'

She looks so different. Is this the same fun-loving Em? She of short dresses, stilettoes and caked-on make-up she really doesn't need? Her outfit might be out of character, but she still looks gorgeous. I cast an eye at my reflection in the French door to see if I'm fairing as well, but a scowling face, like that of a dog about to bite, is all that stares back.

After I've showered, dressed and slapped on as much make-up as I can in the scant time I had left, Em and I make our way through the swanky hotel corridors to the 'Connor' suite where the wedding service is taking place. We find two empty seats on the bride's side. The room décor is gorgeous; a fusion of fresh flowers and balloons in pale greens and yellows. Marcus stands nervously at the front wearing a dark grey pinstripe suit with top hat and tails and a green cravat, a yellow carnation in his lapel.

Above the low hum of the crowd, the plinking notes of a string quartet softly stir us all to the start of the ceremony. A hush descends. All heads turn towards the back of the room as a young girl dressed in a pretty pale green and yellow silk dress walks down the aisle tossing rose petals across the floor.

Jen and her dad enter the back of the room and slow-step their way to the front of the suite. We all stand and gaze at the beautiful bride and her adoring father. Jen's ivory dress is stunning. A simple design: tight, sleeveless bodice with a sprawling skirt finished with green and yellow faux petals on the bodice. Two bridesmaids, with dresses like the flower girls', and a page boy dressed in an identical suit to Marcus's follow behind. I well up watching my lovely cousin begin the next part of her life's journey.

The service is just beautiful, almost dreamlike, and Jen and Marcus glow brightly in each other's presence under the protective and supportive wings of an awestruck crowd. I wipe away the tears now tumbling uncensored down my cheeks as the two of them exchange vows. Em squeezes my hand and casts a reassuring smile in my direction.

'Would you all please raise your glasses to the Bride & Groom,' says Anton, Marcus's best man. We all oblige, and I can't help beaming with pride.

'He's hot,' Em says, eyeing Anton from the safety of our table. 'I wonder if he's single.'

'Em! Really? He looks about five years younger than us.'

'What's age got to do with it? I don't look thirty-four! I'll find out later, anyway.'

She tosses me a wink. Guess she's on the pull tonight. I sigh, taking a large gulp of champagne, enjoying these trouble-free moments.

Our entrees of smoked trout parfait and mini toasts arrive as we chatter amongst ourselves. Jen has put me and Em on the same table as two other cousins, aunts and an uncle from further afield. It's great to catch up with them, but also sad my late parents couldn't be here to enjoy the day. But several glasses of champagne have helped quell any errant thoughts or feelings so far. My spirits are higher than they've been for the past week, and truthfully, since returning from Ibiza.

By late afternoon, the reception is winding up. I'm already tipsy, which is not a bad thing given what's still to come. Em and I head up to our room to freshen up and get changed.

'It was a lovely service,' Em says ruefully.

I know what she's going to say next, though.

'Just hope it didn't bring back painful memories.'

She tosses me a half-smile.

'I'm fine, Em. And yes, it was a lovely service. Jen and Marcus look so perfect together.' And I mean it. They do look perfect; happy, in love, and full of hope for the future. How it should be. How I'm sure Marj thinks it should be.

'If only things could've been different for you,' Em says, striding over and hugging me tightly.

My best friend always knows when I need a hug, and they usually do the trick, lifting my spirits and comforting me, but not this time. Later today, I'm likely to come face to face with the shameful secret I don't want her to know. I'll need more than Em's hug to get through that. Queasiness rolls around in waves in my gut.

Unfolding myself from Em's embrace, I feign a smile and head out to the balcony. Air and smoke; a heady combination that relieves and enhances those sickly feelings all at the same time. I need another drink.

The disco kicks off at 7.30 pm. My nerves are shot, and I've convinced myself, with the aid of wine, that I don't want to go. Wedding discos are cheesy with terrible music, and only a handful of people on the dancefloor busting outdated moves too drunk to care what they look like.

Em is in full make-up and has changed into a skimpy outfit. I am yet to change, choosing instead to have more wine and several more cigarettes.

'Come on Luce, we'll be late if you don't get a move on. I've got some chatting up to do,' Em says, nagging, while she twirls for the umpteenth time in front of the mirror.

But the more drink I have, the more my resolve solidifies. I don't want to go. I don't want to face Rob or the past. I just want to spend the rest of the evening on this balcony smoking too many cigarettes and drinking copious amounts of red wine.

'I'll meet you down there,' I lie. I can always pretend I fell asleep if she notices I'm not there.

'Fine, just don't be too long.' After yet another check of her appearance, she waltzes out of the door.

I grab another bottle of wine and head for the balcony. It's raining, but thankfully the balcony has cover, so I can still sit outside and avoid getting wet, even though the wind is bracing.

An hour or so later and I'm still there, wrapped up in my coat and puffing on a cigarette. The room door creaks open.

'Luce, are you ready yet?' Em shouts. She pops her head around the balcony door. 'You're not even changed!'

'Oh... just wanted to have another drink before heading out.' Oh shit, there's no getting out of this now. Thankfully, I have drunk enough to stop giving a shit and think I can muster enough strength to get my butt off the balcony chair and get changed.

'Get a move on!' she commands like a sergeant major and stomps out of the room.

'I'll see you down there in a few minutes,' I call after her, gulping the last dregs of wine and finishing my cigarette. I get up and head to the bathroom knowing it really is time I faced the music.

The suite has been reworked so the tables, still adorned with their balloons and flowers, are arranged around an uncovered wooden dancefloor. As I enter the darkened room, music booms but no one is dancing yet. My stomach churns as I look around for Em, eventually spotting her at the bar talking to Anton.

'Finally!' she says snorting as I reach her and tap her shoulder.

'I was starting to think you were bailing on me.'

She beams as she introduces me to Anton.

'Nice to meet you.'

He stretches out his hand to shake mine, and I now see why he's got Em so hotted-up. He is *very* good looking in a Liam Hemsworth kind of way.

'Hi,' he says, grinning, then gazes back at Em, clearly besotted.

I shake my head, knowing what's to come. *Poor sod.*

We chat for a while, affording my nerves the chance to calm a little. The DJ ups the volume and finally some younger folks make their way to the dancefloor. A pang hits as memories of my time in the clubs in Ibiza pop unsolicited into my mind, along with the image of a very sexy red-haired Irish man.

Jen and Marcus take to the dancefloor, now surrounded by kids and adults alike. They look so happy.

Em jabs me in the side, pulling me out of my reverie.

'Don't look round, but there's a tall, dark and very handsome guy over there who's been staring at you for ages.'

Following the carrot, I turn around to look.

A gasp escapes me, and I'm rendered dumbstruck, eyes locking with Rob's. And judging by the frown on his face, he's not at all happy to see me. *Shit, what do I do now?* But before I can do anything, he strides over. Instinct tells me to run the hell out of there, but my feet are glued to the spot and nerves zoom into overdrive. *Breathe, Lucy, breathe!*

'Hello Lucy,' Rob says, surveying me, his face set in stone.

'Rob. Err... hi,' I reply, not knowing where to look, feeling the trembles running up-and-down my body.

'You're looking well.'

He lowers his eyes, scanning me, still no semblance of warmth on his face.

'Err... thanks. You too,' I reply, trying not to make it obvious as I take him in. An unsolicited flutter makes itself known.

'How have you been?'

'Yeah, um... okay. You?'

'Fine, considering—'

My discomfort goes off like a V2 rocket, but as I'm staring down at my feet desperately trying to think of what to say, a young blonde woman approaches and parks herself between us.

'There you are!' she breathes with fake glee. 'Have you got me that drink yet?'

She turns and eyes me up and down, draping herself across Rob's free arm.

I look over at Em, who is wide-eyed, mouth agape.

'I have to go,' I mumble, and hot foot it towards the exit.

'Luce? Wait!' Em calls after me. When she catches up, she asks, 'What was that about? Do you know him?'

'Err... kind of. He's an ex,' I reply.

'An ex? How come I didn't know about him?'

'Not now, Em. I'll tell you later.' This is all too much. I'm struggling to keep myself together and push past her, primed to bolt.

'Where are you going?'

'Back to the room.'

'Why? You're not going to let some stupid ex spoil your evening, are you?'

'No... but there's more to it, and I can't explain it all right now.'

'What do you mean? What aren't you telling me?'

'Later, Em. I'll tell you later. I just need to get out of here.'

She grabs my arm and pulls me back towards the bar.

'Em!' I protest, but she's having none of it. 'Just make sure we're not anywhere near him!'

She frog-marches me back to the bar, casts an eye around, and yanks me towards the far corner.

Em and Anton are slow dancing on the dancefloor, leaving me to prop up the bar in a drunken haze. Fortunately, Rob seems to have disappeared since our earlier encounter, but it hasn't stopped me being on high alert for most of the night.

Being a smoker again comes with many drawbacks as a nicotine slump signals the need to replenish. So with careful steps, I make my way through patio doors to an alfresco, the designated 'smoking' area. Puffs of acrid smoke greet me as I find a vacant cast-iron chair.

Raised, drunken voices resonate from across the garden. It's reached that time of night when the effects of too much alcohol on occasional drinkers have kicked in. But I don't care. The chilly night air refreshes as I puff away, surveying the other smokers around me as if we're part of some special clique when the reality is, we're ostracised by the masses for our anti-social tendencies.

I drift into a tranquil bubble, distanced from reality thanks to too much wine, but the bubble bursts as a chair next to me scrapes over stone slabs.

'Lucy, can we talk?' Rob asks, his voice softer than before. Inviting... almost.

'Nah,' I reply, brazen from Dutch courage, but struggling to focus fully on his face. 'What's there to talk about?'

'I think we have a lot to talk about, don't you?'

I gaze into eyes that still hold the power to pull me in.

'It's Jen's wedding. Not the best time for this.' I take another drag of my cigarette, trying to recall what Marj suggested for me to say or do, but come up with blanks.

'When *is* going to be a good time to talk about it? I haven't seen you for over two years,' he replies, struggling to temper his annoyance.

I'm barely stringing coherent words together, let alone able to have a deep and meaningful conversation with the source of my guilt. 'I—' No other words come out.

Rob bows his head, leans towards me and whispers, 'Talk to me, please. I've missed you.'

'Don't say that!' I bolt upright.

'But it's true.'

I look across at him and see nothing but despair in his eyes. 'I'm sorry,' I reply, awash with guilt.

'Are you?'

'Of course I am. I didn't mean for any of this to happen.'

'You hurt me, Lucy... badly. I was a wreck. I didn't know what had happened to Joe until Marcus told me. Why didn't you contact me?'

'I couldn't. It all hurt too much.' I tear up, the alcohol now debilitating instead of freeing.

He touches my arm, brushing his hand along my bare flesh. I don't want to feel the thrill he created when he used to touch me, so shake him away.

'Don't brush me off, Lucy,' he says, clasping my arm. 'Help me understand why we came to an end. I need to know. Please. I just need to know.'

Pangs of guilt and regret all roll into one, but what do I say? How can I tell him the truth of what happened? 'I'm sorry. I just can't,' I whisper, wiping away stray tears. 'Besides, you'd better go. Your girlfriend will be wondering where you are.'

'Girlfriend?'

'The blonde hanging off your arm earlier.'

'She's not my girlfriend,' he replies, lips pursed. 'I haven't had a girlfriend since—' He runs his hand through his hair. 'Why didn't you talk to me? Answer my calls?'

My hackles raise, and I glare at him, mouth gaping. 'My husband had just died. What the fuck did you expect me to do?'

Rob's eyes widen as I crumble before him, anger and nerves consuming me.

'Lucy,' he says, lowering and softening his voice again. I try to stand up, but he grabs my hand. 'Don't go... please.'

I want to bolt, but his hand is firm. I fight back the tears welling and turn my back so he can't see.

He stands up, releasing my hand, gathering me into his arms. Motionless, I turn to stone as he embraces me, streaks of grief staining my cheeks.

'Let me go,' I whimper.

'I can't. Lucy, I can't.'

His words sting, my defences battered as strong arms tighten around me. His warmth envelopes me, and I tilt my head up to breathe him in. 'Rob, no—' But it's too late. His lips meet mine and instinctively, I encircle my arms around him, drawing him closer and losing myself in his kiss.

He pulls away for a moment, staring down at me.

'We really need to talk, Lucy. Come with me,' he says.

He clasps my hand and pulls me in the direction of the function room. With all sense of reason now lost, I dutifully follow, and as we pass the dance floor, I glimpse Em glaring at me. I shake my head to tell her not to follow as we head out of the door towards the main reception.

We walk to Rob's hotel room in silence. My heart races, a dizzying feeling threatening to consume me. He releases my hand as we enter the room, flicking on the lights then heading over to the minibar.

I sneak a chaste look at him, and he looks as good as I remember. His tall frame still lean and sculpted; chestnut brown hair flopping around his face; blue come-to-bed eyes. Lust stirs within me.

'Drink?' he asks, bringing me back.

'Wine please,' I nod, shifting from foot-to-foot.

He gathers some glasses and pours, gesturing for me to sit next to him on the bed.

'Can we talk now?'

I don't respond, *can't* respond. All thoughts of talking have gone out of the window as desire grips, and I do the only thing I know how in situations like this. Lean up to kiss him knowing full well he won't be able to resist.

'Lucy... no—'

But I don't let him finish, curling my hand around the side of his head and pulling him down onto my lips. My tongue explores his mouth as my other hand moves up to the top of his shirt and starts undoing the buttons.

His breathing sharpens, and he folds his arms around me, surrendering. I clamber onto his lap as I tackle each shirt button. He groans as my fingers brush against his skin.

'Lucy, we can't—'

He moans into my ear as I reach his fly and stroke him, his erection hard beneath my hand.

Fire rages beneath my skin as his familiar fingers follow well-trodden lines.

'Stop!' he yells out, pushing me away.

I bolt upright, hovering motionless over him, shell-shocked. 'Don't you want me?' I whimper and slide off.

He gets up, his hands running through his hair as he strides the length of the room.

'Rob?' I feel raw, rejected.

'Of course I want you. I always have. But not like this.' He shakes his head, eyebrows furrowed.

I feel numb. No words to explain away my actions.

'We need to talk. I need to know... where have you been?'

'I... I... don't know what to say.'

Rob paces as if it will somehow help him conjure what he needs to say. 'Say anything! Give me something to help me understand.'

I need to tell him the truth, only I'm afraid. Afraid he will realise what an evil, uncaring bitch I really am. I don't want him to hate me.

'Lucy!'

His eyes bore into me as he demands answers I don't want to give.

'Okay,' I reply, whispering, pulling my knees up to my chin and heaving for breath. And sensing defeat, a moment of clarity provides the impetus to reveal all. 'Joe died after he found out about us.'

'What?'

Rob freezes in front of me, hands clasping his head as shock and disbelief harden his handsome features.

'He overheard us talking on the phone. Overheard our plans.'

'My God!' His eyes cart from side-to-side as the awful truth sinks in.

'I was going to tell him, but he found out before I was ready.' My voice falters as sobs catch in my throat.

'And what happened?'

'What do you think happened? He went ballistic.' I bury my face in my knees as shame engulfs.

'And?'

'We had a huge fight...'

A moment of stillness, neither of us knowing what to say or do next, before clouds descend and the events of that night play out in my mind. 'He... he—'

Rob rushes over and wraps his arms around me.

'I'm so sorry, Lucy. I'm so sorry,' he says

He makes shushing noises into my hair as I curl into him and release the pain as pitiful sobs.

We are treading water in a sea of despair, holding on to each other to keep afloat as the enormity of that awful night sinks in. Rob strokes my hair and wipes away tears staining my cheeks, and as I look up at him, I realise his own guilt has burst from its dam and is cascading down his face.

I reach up with trembling fingers to wipe it away, and as I do, he leans into them, planting sorrowful kisses.

Naked and consumed, I rise in his lap and sink down, gasping as he fills me, building a delicious rhythm. His arms encircle me, his lips brushing my cheek. Every moan, every gasp an exquisite reminder of the ache building between us. I quicken my onslaught, grinding up against him, rubbing myself against him as he thrusts upwards.

We move together in perfect rhythm and when I sense he's close to coming, speed up for the finale.

'Oh God, Lucy!' he cries out.

It tips me over the edge and my orgasm explodes. I yell out and collapse into him.

For a few moments we are still, save for the heaving of our chests. I lean against his shoulder and his lips brush the side of my ear. 'I love you,' he whispers.

Reality slaps. 'You loved me two-and-a-half years ago,' is all I can say.

He moves from beneath me, a discomfort made visible.

On cue, I clamber off him and head to the bathroom, clenching my thighs to avoid any mess.

He follows me, and we stand facing each other for what seems like ages before Rob finally breaks the silence.

'That reunion went better than I'd hoped.'

He grins, but I can still see a sadness in his eyes and offer a feeble smile in return.

My head is spinning as I freshen up and head back towards the bed. *What the fuck have I just done?* Still tipsy and feeling the effects of dehydration, I go to the minibar and grab a bottle of water.

'You okay?' Rob says, emerging from the bathroom.

'I'd better go,' I reply.

'What? Why?'

'We shouldn't have done that. *I* shouldn't have done that.'

'What? Made love?' His eyes widen.

'That wasn't *making love*, Rob. That was sex. We were both

vulnerable, and now we've muddied the waters.'

'That's all it was to you? Just sex?'

'I'm tired. It's been a long day and I just want to sleep,' I reply, avoiding his glare, irritation building.

'I don't understand.'

'What's to understand?'

'There's still a connection between us, otherwise—'

He searches my face for some conformation, but I remain steadfast.

'Stay, Lucy. Stay with me tonight,' he says, eyes pleading.

I gather up my clothes but am so tired there's no strength in me to argue. I take a long glug of water and clamber back into bed, inwardly chastising myself, knowing full well the waters between us are now like treacle. Rob follows suit, snuggling up against me, holding onto my hand like a child holding a blanket.

It doesn't take long for the events of the day to drift away as sleep beckons.

CHAPTER 40

'Luce, wake up!'

I'm being violently shaken from my sleep.

'WAKE UP!'

When I open my eyes, Em's standing over my bed, rocking me, trying to wake me from a deep slumber.

'What time is it?' I reply, stretching out cat-like.

'Ten-thirty-six. We need to check out by eleven.' Her face is flushed.

Christ, I must've gone back to sleep when I got back to the room, after leaving... OH SHIT! WHAT HAVE I DONE?

'Give me fifteen minutes,' I reply, launching out of bed.

The next moments flash by in a blur as I dash to the bathroom and jump in the shower. My head is throbbing, even though I took a couple of painkillers when I got back to the room at sunrise.

Em hands me a coffee as I come out of the bathroom and the balcony beckons for a much-needed smoke. A gazillion thoughts race through my mind, my heart pumping faster than a thoroughbred in full gallop.

Swiftly drinking my coffee and smoking a cigarette, I come back into the room and dump all my stuff into the suitcase Em has laid out on the bed for me. In our rush to get ready, she hasn't asked about my whereabouts last night. But as I snap the case shut she breaks her silence.

'You ended up with Rob last night, then?'

And it's more of a statement than a question because it's bloody obvious that's where I was.

I nod, averting her gaze.

'Oh my God, Luce! You are so back on form!' she laughs. 'But I thought he was strictly a no-no?'

I'm mortified and don't yet know what to say, so deflect her questioning by asking about Anton. It does the trick. Em gushes as she tells me all about their night, a night spent talking and kissing, but no sex! Not only that, they've agreed to meet up in a few weeks. She *likes* him. Shocked is not the word for it.

But my deflection doesn't work for long and she soon probes for more info on Rob. I fob her off, telling her it was a casual thing, but inwardly I'm chastising myself for creating a bigger pile of shit than before. Truth is, after our very brief deep and meaningful, lust took over. And yet again, when it does, all sense of rhyme or reason goes out of the window, falling ungracefully onto sodden grass. Only stealth can save me from an awkward encounter from here on in.

We just make it to reception before 11.00 am and stand in the queue waiting to check out. I glance around, my heartbeat quickening every time a man comes into view.

After paying our larger than expected bar bill, mostly my doing, and handing over the key cards, the receptionist passes me an envelope. Thinking it's just a copy of the invoice, I shove it in my bag, and we make our way out to the car park.

Realising I'm hungover, Em offers to drive us home. Even though we both had late nights and are sleep deprived, Em is in a far better state. An entire day spent drinking and sleeping with the guy you had an affair with didn't factor into my equation.

Forty minutes into the drive, I open my bag and pull out my phone to text Jen. She'll be on her way to the airport for her honeymoon in Barbados by now. As I fumble around for my mobile, I pull out the envelope the receptionist at the hotel handed me and notice my name is handwritten on the front. Curious, I open it.

'Lucy,

Please don't leave again. Didn't last night mean anything to you?

Call me. My number hasn't changed.

Rob.'

This is bad, really bad.

'You okay, Luce? What is it?' Em asks, glancing over.

'A note from Rob,' I reply, feeling the blood drain from my face.

'Oh? What does he want?'

'He wants me to call him.'

'And are you going to?'

'No!' I reply.

'I see.' She tuts. 'So, are you going to tell me more about this Rob guy, seen as yesterday was the first I knew of him?'

'There's not much to tell. He's just an ex who needs to stay *ex*.'

After an uncomfortable pause she changes the subject, hopefully realising I don't want to talk about it further, and chit-chats about the wedding and how wonderful it all was, especially meeting Anton. She is smitten, but I'm barely listening.

We reach my place by late afternoon. All I want is to get inside and shut the door, and retreat into my cave for a few days. Just me and my wayward thoughts. Rob was spot on in his note, though. I am leaving him again. It's the only way I know how to lock away what I don't want to feel.

CHAPTER 41

Marj tosses me a kindly smile as I shuffle in my seat and pick at a broken fingernail. I can hear the ticking of the room clock as she waits for me to say something. But I've nothing to give.

She seems to sense my discomfort and breaks the silence hanging like a lead weight between us. 'How are you feeling at the moment?'

'Not great,' I reply, moving on to a minute piece of fluff on my jeans.

'Do you want to talk to me about it, Lucy?'

My hackles go up as if she's just thrown down the gauntlet, and I fight the disparaging voices in my head telling me to confess all, my body stiffening, priming itself to flee. And after taking a deep breath to calm myself, it bursts right out, 'I... I slept with Rob. At the wedding.' I perch on the edge of my seat, breath held, waiting for Marj to respond. She doesn't at first as if taunting me, letting me stew.

When she finally replies with, 'How do you feel about it?' I am poised to get up and bolt for the door.

'Really bad.' Guilty as charged.

'What is it about sleeping with Rob that makes you feel bad?' she asks.

'I don't know. I... I didn't mean for it to happen.' *And yet I knew it would.* My breath hitches at the realisation. Much as I'd tried to keep control and avoid *any* kind of confrontation with Rob, part of me was covertly seeking the thrill he once gave. The part of me that can't be trusted.

Marj's blank expression irks me. She's waiting for the gory details, I'm sure of it. 'It was really awkward when I saw him, and I tried to avoid him for most of the evening, but we crossed paths again when I went outside to have a smoke.' A lump swells in my throat. 'I was drunk, and things were said.'

'Things were said?'

'He said he missed me, although how he could after so long is beyond me. I tried to get away, but he grabbed a hold of me and I just... gave in.'

'You gave in to your feelings?'

'No!' I reply trying to cement in dislodged bricks. 'He wanted to talk, so I agreed to go to his room.'

'To talk?'

'Yes.' I look up at her, yet again seeking signs of approval. She gives me nothing. 'We talked, albeit briefly, but—'

'But it became something else?'

I nod, head bowed.

'I'm wondering if in that moment sleeping with Rob became preferable to talking to him, to talking about how you both felt?'

'What do you mean?'

'Perhaps you felt talking about your past relationship would cause more uncomfortable feelings to arise, conflict even, so sleeping with him avoided that.'

Did I put a stop to talking about those painful times by having sex with him? Or was it just lust taking over? 'I'm not sure,' I reply. 'Maybe.'

'Lucy, last week you told me about the passion you shared with Rob and how he made you feel alive and wanted. I'm wondering what role the need for passion, for sex, has played in how you relate to men in your life?'

I stare at her wide-eyed.

'Can I be direct?'

'I guess.'

'What does sex give you?'

I think about it for a few moments, confused and slightly embarrassed. *What does it give me?* 'Well... I enjoy it, who doesn't, and I guess I feel... in control.'

'What is it that you feel in control of?'

'Me.' Something clicks inside my brain like a jigsaw piece falling into exactly the right place. 'I don't have to *feel* anything, emotionally.'

'Sex enables you to control your feelings and avoid what you don't want to acknowledge?'

I feel weird, nauseous. Deep down I know she's right, but I don't want to accept it. But then the connections in my psyche suddenly solidify and words tumble out. 'In that moment, I'm in a place where I don't have to think about day-to-day stuff... or what the other person feels.'

'Sex enables you to escape?'

'I guess so.' Bullseye!

'Was it the same with Joe?'

Marj is not letting up.

'At first.'

'At first?'

'You need to understand that before I met Joe I was, well... I liked clubbing and meeting men. Sex was a big part of that; one-nighters, and all that.'

'One-nighters?'

'You know, one-night stands.' Heat flushes over my face as embarrassment takes hold. 'I never intended to get into a full-blown relationship with Joe, but he was persistent, which I kind of liked. But once we started getting serious, it all became more... emotional.'

'Sex became something different when you and Joe grew closer?'

'Not just the sex!' I reply, vexed. 'Everything changed, more for him than me. I just followed his lead, but—'

Marj jots something down on the pad and waits.

I glare at her, struggling to piece together the right words so I don't sound like an emotionally detached whore. 'But it took some of the passion away for me.'

'Joe introduced a more emotional, *intimate* element to your relationship, but it reduced the passion you felt. Is that right?'

'Yes,' I sigh. 'It became about what *we* wanted rather than what I wanted, and I guess I wasn't used to that.' Suddenly, I feel the need to convince her I'm not some heartless bitch who plays around with men's emotions because I can't deal with it all. 'Joe was the first relationship I'd had that'd gone beyond a few weeks. I'd avoided all the messy emotional stuff prior to him, so when our relationship deepened, I think I struggled to keep up.'

'You tried to relate to Joe on a more emotional level?'

'Yes, but after a while it became more difficult. We were barely having sex, and he was often away on business trips.'

'How did you feel about the loss of intimacy, Lucy?'

'Dejected, I suppose. I'd really tried to meet him half-way but felt I wasn't good enough anymore.'

'So, you tried to adapt to a more emotional relationship with Joe, one you've previously described as "how it's supposed to be". But when the opportunities to be intimate with each other started to dry up, it left you feeling dejected.'

I nod.

'And where do you think Rob fitted in to all of this?'

'He was attentive and passionate. I felt wanted again.'

'You felt like you'd rediscovered the passion you'd described earlier?'

'Yes, but I liked being around him too.'

'Like you did at first with Joe?'

Where the hell is she going with this?

But the nerve she hits is well and truly twanged and I struggle to reply, squinting and staring at her while trying to gather my thoughts and make sense of why I now feel so raw. ' I... don't know. Can we talk about something else?'

But is this what I do? Trade intimacy for passion, then run away when I can no longer control it? I shudder at the thought. *No. NO! This can't be right. I loved Joe, didn't I?*

'Lucy, our time is nearly up. Do you want to see me next week?' Marj says, pulling me out of my head.

My voice falters. 'I... I don't know.'

'Do you feel you need to?' Marj asks.

Something has changed. Stirrings within me hint of an answer to the question I never dared ask myself being close to the surface. *Did I really love Joe?*

'I think I'd better.'

I pay Marj her fee; we say our goodbyes and I bolt. By the time I reach my car I am gasping for air, unable to decipher if I'm angry, shocked or just numb, my mind zooming into overdrive as I get in and drive home.

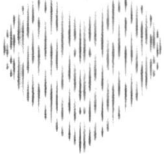

CHAPTER 42

Something is festering within me. My nightmare is back with a vengeance only it's twisted and I'm now dreaming about Rob dying.

I've spent the morning sitting outside smoking, drinking coffee and recounting memories, hoping to ease my conscience. Nothing is helping. The guilt I have felt for so long has yet another strand. The realisation that my commitment to Joe was far less than one hundred percent. Rob lit up an exit sign from a relationship that wasn't working, and truthfully, I now see it was doomed from the get-go. But would the same thing have happened with Rob? It's a bitter pill to swallow, the epiphany lighting up in big bold letters in my psyche: *I don't do intimacy.* Relationships, in my mind, are short term, a seed sown during my fun-loving girl-about-town times. The end always came when the passion wore off, or a line was crossed, and I could no longer control the outcome. *Am I always going to be like this?*

My internal analysis is interrupted by my mobile phone ringing. I don't want to answer it, but reluctantly go inside and pick it up. It's Em ringing me from work, so I answer, hoping she can provide momentary relief from my wayward thoughts.

'How're you doing?' she asks.

'Okay, I guess,' I say, hiding my truth from her yet again.

'Did you ring Rob?'

'No. Why do you ask?'

'Well, you remember Anton from the wedding? He wants to come over at the weekend.'

She sounds excited, but something tells me there's a 'but' coming.

'But?'

'But he's been talking to Rob, and Rob wants to come too... to see you.'

'What?' I gasp. 'No! I don't want to see him.' My defences spring up like a deflector shield.

'Luce, I don't know what's gone on between you two in the past, but Anton says Rob is in a really bad place and needs to see you. Can't you at least talk to the guy?'

She snaps at me like I'm spoiling her carefully constructed plans.

'No, Em. I can't!'

'Don't you think you're being harsh?'

'You don't understand, it's too—' I can hear myself whine as I plead my case.

Em pauses far too long for comfort. Finally, and through sighs, she says, 'Right, that's it. I'm coming over after work and you can tell me what all this is about.'

'Em, please... don't—' But it's no good. I can tell by her tone she means business. I need to concoct a convincing story to cover myself.

I spend the next few hours trying to busy myself with mindless tasks around the house. But every nerve in my body feels like it's being stretched to breaking point as I try to figure out what I'm going to say to Em when she arrives. Even though she's my best friend, my confidante, I haven't been able to tell her the whole truth about how Joe died, or why. Can I do it now and risk losing her?

My head spins in time with the wooden spoon I'm mixing Arrabbiata sauce with when three swift knocks on the front door pull me back to the present. I trudge to door to let Em in, drawing in a deep glug of air as it opens.

'Hey Em,' I say, any attempt at a cheerful greeting falling flat as she hugs me.

'Luce, I'm so sorry for being grumpy with you earlier.'

She pulls away and studies me, frowning.

With tears welling, I reply, 'It's okay, really,' hoping she can't see me trembling, and trying to ignore the knots tightening in my stomach. 'Can we eat before—'

'Good idea,' she says, nodding. 'I'm starving!'

We make our way into the kitchen and Em sits down as I pour us both a glass of wine. It's now or never. Em deserves the truth. Only, I don't know where to start, how to make sense of all that has happened, and where Em fits into it all.

Taking a seat beside Em and releasing the sigh I've been holding since she arrived, I begin my speech. 'Em, you know when Joe went away on a business trip a few months before he died, and I went to Jen's for a break? Well, that's when I met Rob.' My heart thumps as I look for a reaction. She cocks her head to the side, brows furrowed.

'Go on,' she says.

'We kinda hooked up.'

'You did what?' Her eyes widen, her neat brows arching in surprise.

'I... I had an affair with him, only, it went further.'

'What do you mean?'

'Well, you know Joe and I were having problems,' I continue

through staggered breaths, barely able to look her in the eye.

'That's an understatement,' Em scoffs. 'You and Joe were always having issues about something or other, but is that a good enough reason to cheat?'

Her words sting like a slap to the face. 'It wasn't like that!' I protest. 'We had a connection, and Rob said he loved me.'

'After only a few weeks?'

She glares at me, eyes probing.

'And did you think you loved him too?'

'I... I thought I did.'

'You sound like a schoolgirl with a crush,' Em says, tutting.

It cuts me to the core.

'I know it sounds ridiculous, but at the time it felt good; reminded me of my old life.'

Em rolls her eyes, head shaking. 'I get it, Christ knows I do, but Luce... you were married. How could you let it go further?'

'I don't know. It just happened,' I reply sighing. 'Rob and I... well, we kept in touch after I came home. When Joe got back from his trip and things didn't get any better between us, I realised I didn't want to be with him anymore. It just wasn't working.'

Em's frown softens. 'I'm amazed it lasted as long as it did, really. You were like chalk and cheese! But I do remember you telling me things were stale. I just didn't realise they'd got that bad.'

'They were never *bad*, Em, not really. Joe was a good man, a good husband, but it wasn't enough. Rob gave me the excuse I needed to end it.' I can't look Em in the eye as shame creeps out from the box I'd packed it in.

'Luce?' She reaches over and clasps my hand.

'Joe found out, Em. He heard me talking to Rob on the phone, making plans to leave. That's what we were fighting about.' I can no longer contain the festering mass rising from within and slump on the table, burying my face in my arms, the flood gushing out.

'I'm so sorry. I didn't know.'

Em wraps loving and reassuring arms around me as I sob into her shoulder.

Lifting my head up to face her, the words I've been keeping for so long from her finally blurt out, 'I pushed him too far and he... he slapped me, and I just went ballistic. I kept hitting him again and again and told him I hated him.' And I cry like I've never cried before.

We sit for ages, Em hugging me tightly and stroking my hair, providing the sanctuary for my guilt to spill out.

'What am I going to do?' I say between snivels and sobs.

'I don't know, Luce,' she says softly. 'I don't know.'

Em holds me, shushing and rocking me gently until my tears subside. I straighten and look at her through puffy eyes. 'Do you hate me?'

'Why would I hate you?'

'Because now you know what I've done, what an awful person I am.'

'You're not, Luce. Why would you think that?'

'Because I killed him!' I'm five years old again, confessing to a dastardly dead.

'You didn't *kill* Joe. He had a motorbike accident, remember.'

'But if he hadn't found out. If we hadn't argued like we did, he wouldn't have left!'

'It was his choice to do that, Luce. You couldn't have known how it would end.'

It doesn't make me feel better hearing her say it.

'But—'

'There is no "but" Luce. It was truly awful what happened to Joe, but you can't keep blaming yourself! He knew what he was doing when he went off like that.'

'He didn't know he'd be hit by a truck, though, did he?'

'No, he didn't, but neither did you, and you've been slowly dying ever since.'

Her words pierce my flesh like sharpened blades. I am dumbstruck. *Is that what's been happening to me?*

'Luce, you need to forgive yourself. You couldn't have known what would happen, and Joe made his own choices,' Em says, her tone softening, 'but you really need to sort things out with Rob. It's unfinished business.'

'How can I? He's part of the reason Joe is dead!'

'But it's not his fault either, is it? And from what Anton says, the guy's really cut up about it all. You need to let him know where he stands.'

'He'll get the message soon enough,' I reply, cold indifference sweeping over me.

'Lucy! You can't keep running away from this. You're hurting other people *and* you're hurting yourself.'

'I'm not running away!' I fire back. 'Why does everyone accuse me of running away all the time?' As the words leave my lips, Brian's angry face flashes through my mind.

Em hunches and sighs, holding her hands out towards me signalling her desire for a truce.

'Look,' she says, 'I'm sorry if what I'm saying is cutting you deep, but you and I both know that in the past we've avoided getting close to people. We had our little rules that kept things fun, but maybe now it's time to put on our big-girl pants and allow ourselves to get more deeply involved.'

'I tried to do that with Joe and look how that turned out,' I reply, sarcasm tinging my words.

'I know you did, but maybe you just weren't ready for what he wanted from you. Christ knows it's taken me years to reach the point of feeling ready to give it a go with someone.'

She sighs again, a wistful look crossing her face, and for a moment, I think she's going to cry.

'Maybe it's time to put the wild days behind us and, *ugh*, settle down.'

I almost giggle... almost. But again, the words 'running away' and 'not ready' pop into my mind, emphasising what still needs to be addressed.

'You really like Anton, don't you?'

'I think I do. And I want to see what happens next,' she says, grinning. 'But do yourself a favour, Luce. Talk to Rob. If nothing else, to get a bit of closure and let him break free too.'

I nod, sniffling. She's right. I have spent far too long running away, selfish to think Rob could walk away from this unscathed.

We eventually eat our cold dinner, and Em contacts Anton to arrange for the four of us to catch up at the weekend. We decide to meet in Cromer, a quaint and unassuming seaside town. But I still feel uneasy about it, knowing deep down it will take more than talking to Rob to qualm the guilt I still harbour over Joe's death. But Em and Marj have helped me realise I need to do right by everyone.

CHAPTER 43

Rain lashes against the windscreen as Em and I park up and get out of the car, the chilly sea breeze seeping through to my bones turning my insides into ice.

We walk the short distance to Cromer's Pier. The foreshore is deserted save for a few older people shuffling around in long macs and rain hats. Each step I take causes deep down flutters to intensify. Em hasn't said much, except for the odd excited babble regarding what Anton might be wearing, whether he'll be as excited to see her as she is to see him, and if he's brought her any gifts. It all seems so puerile compared with my dark thoughts.

The past few days have been dire. I've spent hour upon hour trying to reconcile my feelings and figure out what in the hell I'll say to Rob to atone for what I've put him through.

Em lets out a squeal, pulling me out of my head. I look up and see them. Anton beams and quick steps towards Em. Rob looks pale and distant, like he's somewhere else. I toss him a wave and a feeble smile, but he looks away in disdain, muttering a stony, 'hello' as he approaches.

After several hugs and kisses between Anton and Em, and a polite, 'hi' from Anton to me, Em thrusts her hand towards Rob. 'Rob, I'm Em, Lucy's best friend. Sorry we haven't met properly before, but

I didn't know you existed until recently.'

Rob shakes Em's hand, managing a courteous, 'nice to meet you,' as I glare at Em.

She rolls her eyes and links arms with Anton.

We make our way along the shoreline path. Em and Anton walk in front holding hands and in animated conversation. Rob and I follow in silence. I guess neither of us know what to say.

After walking for several minutes, and with Em and Anton far enough away to be out of earshot, I finally speak up. 'How have you been?'

Rob doesn't respond at first, but stops dead and faces me, his brow creased, eyes questioning. I follow suit, my pulse quickening, a look of fear no doubt etched across my wind-chilled face.

'How do you think I've been?' he finally says.

'I'm sorry,' I whisper, bowing my head and trying hard to swallow the lump in my throat.

'Are you?'

I look away, not able to face his scorn. 'I didn't mean for that night to happen. I'm so sorry.'

'Of course you didn't,' he cuts in, 'but it's a bit late for that, isn't it?'

I look back into eyes etched with an intangible pain, noticing dark circles underneath and an unshaven chin. Guilt batters me.

'I don't know what to say. I... I'm sorry.'

'Yeah, so you keep saying. But perhaps you can start by telling me why you slept with me that night,' he says, his tone rising.

'I was drunk and got caught in the moment.' But as the words leave my lips, and as truthful as they are, I realise how pathetic and heartless I must sound.

'You used me,' he says, his voice terse, jaw clenched.

'No! It wasn't like that!' I say, bleating. 'I didn't want to talk about the past. I... I *couldn't*, so when you touched me, I guess I found a way out. I'm sorry. I'm so sorry, Rob.' Tears well, threatening to spill.

'Do you think I'm a complete idiot? I'm not falling for that again!' he replies in a tone colder than the offshore wind.

This is torture. Honesty is not my friend.

'I wish I'd known when I met you what a cold-hearted bitch you are!'

His words sting, and it's not the first time I've heard them. I stare up at him, nostrils flaring, fists clenched, line drawn in the sand. 'Well now you know!'

'I'm wasting my time here. I obviously mean nothing to you.'

He turns and walks away leaving me gripped by anger and a sudden sense of foreboding.

'No!' I shout after him, panic rising. 'Please. Not like this!'

He turns his head slightly but continues to stride away from me.

'What's the point, Lucy? What's the fucking point!'

Tears flow like a torrent, and I know I can't let him walk away like this. 'Rob, please. Let's talk now. Rob!' Big fat glugging sobs gush out as pity consumes me.

He halts, turns around and, without a flicker of warmth in his expression, waits for me to catch him up.

'So, talk, Lucy. I am not going to end up in the shithole you left me in last time.'

I snivel and nod. 'But let's just go somewhere more private. Get some lunch, or something.'

I look up and notice Em and Anton heading back towards us.

'You okay, you two?' Em asks, frowning.

'Yeah… um… we need to talk about—'

Em nods. She knows what I need to do.

'We thought we'd go somewhere for lunch and meet up with you guys later.' I'm not sure if I'm asking or telling her.

'No worries. See you at the pier at three pm?' Em says, glancing over at Rob.

She hugs me, whispering out of earshot of the other two.

'Ring me if it gets too much, okay.'

I nod, and she lets me go, leaving me to my fate.

With nerves already frayed, I look up at Rob and he motions for us to leave, his face blank, revealing nothing. My stomach is so unsettled I know eating will be a chore.

Rob and I walk the back streets of Cromer in silence, finally coming across a pub serving lunchtime food. Without even asking if this one will do; he grabs my hand and leads me inside and to a booth at the far end of the dining area. Like an obedient puppy, I sit down opposite and take off my coat.

'Do you want a drink?' Rob says flatly.

'A glass of house red,' I reply without hesitation.

He slopes off to the bar leaving me contemplating what I'm going to say.

After he returns, a waitress who looks all of fourteen swings by our table and asks if we want to order food. I haven't even looked at the menu, so quick as a shot, I pick one up and flick through.

'Burger and chips please,' I tell her, and she scribbles it down on a tatty notepad.

'Same,' Rob says, without even looking at the menu.

She scuttles off, and that ominous festering returns.

'So, start talking,' he says when the waitress is out of earshot.

He's so blunt and cold. So different from the Rob I used to know. It's like I'm with a complete stranger.

'I... I don't know where to begin,' I say, my voice wavering under the pressure.

'You can start by telling me why you didn't talk to me after your husband died. You should have told me what had happened.'

I want to tell him I was so consumed by guilt that everything and everyone fell by the wayside. But it's not true. I *have* to tell him the truth for both of our sakes.

I sit up straight, clearing my throat ready to speak, and look him squarely in the eyes. 'The night Joe died we were fighting. He'd just found out about us, and I told him I was leaving him... for you.' I can't keep my composure and slump, head down, eyes closed before him.

Rob is silent. I sense my answer isn't enough, and when I finally look up, I'm meet with an expectant gaze.

'I blamed myself for his death, I still do, and every time I thought of you, or heard about you, it just made it worse.' His stony silence pains me. I'm running out of truths. 'I didn't mean to hurt you, Rob. I just couldn't handle the guilt of what I'd done. I'm so sorry.'

'I could've helped you, if you'd have just talked to me.'

His expression shifts, hard edges softening, and I glimpse the man who once filled me with passion and excitement, who wasn't afraid to love me. His watery eyes glisten, making the wound in my heart deepen.

'But our affair caused Joe's death. How could I ask you to help me through that?'

'You blame me?' he says, his face hardening again.

'No, I didn't mean it like that. I let it go too far. It's *my* fault. It's all my fault.' Tears tumble down my cheeks as my nightmare reignites.

'What do you mean, you let it go too far?'

'I should never have—' and I stop, cupping my face with trembling hands.

'Should never have what? Slept with me? Led me on?'

'No, NO!' I cry out.

'Did you ever have any feelings for me Lucy?' he asks, his eyes boring into mine.

Oh god, what have I done? 'I think so... sort of.'

'Sort of? What the fuck does that mean?'

'I loved you. It's just... I'm not sure what that is.'

'It was just a fling for you? Just about sex?'

'No!'

'What then, Lucy? I need to understand!' His eyes widen, his voice breaking.

'I don't know. I... I didn't want to be with Joe anymore. Knew I didn't love him like I should. You gave me a reason to end it.'

'I was your escape route out of a bad relationship?' he says through gritted teeth.

'No! At the time I truly felt like I loved you. I wanted to be with you!' I try to reassure him, but even I'm not convinced. This is going rapidly downhill.

Rob freezes, staring out of a window as if trying to make sense of what I've just thrown at him.

'I'm sorry,' I say in a whisper.

He faces me again, eyes burning into me.

'Is that supposed to make me feel better? I LOVED YOU, LUCY, and fuck knows why, but I still do!'

I gasp, taken aback by his confession. 'I... I don't know what to say. I loved you too, Rob. As much as I could love anyone.' I hope my words will placate him and stop me feeling like a scolded child.

After an uncomfortably long pause, he finally breaks the silence. 'So, that's it then. We're done?'

Words escape me.

'Lucy, I need to know. Is there any hope of a future between us?'

His face softens again, but his eyes tell of a longing as yet unfulfilled.

'I don't know,' I reply, dropping my gaze. And I don't know why I said that. I should know. I should tell him there is no hope, that what we had was tarnished when Joe left and never came back because of what I did to him. That there's no recovery from it. Only, I'm too gutless to admit it.

'When will you know?' he says in a growl. 'I can't keep waiting around hoping you'll come back to me.'

I didn't expect this, didn't ask for it, and really don't have a clue when I'll be able to pluck up the courage to truthfully tell him where he stands.

'I need some time,' I say with a sigh. 'This is all—'

'How long, Lucy?'

His reddened eyes plead with me. 'I... I don't know. A few weeks, maybe. I've been seeing a counsellor. Maybe she can help me figure it out.'

He reaches over and pulls my hand up onto the table, cupping it between his, igniting an unwanted spark way down low.

'Please don't take too long. I don't know how much more of this I can take,' he says. 'I never gave up on you, but this waiting around... it's killing me all over again.'

His watery eyes stab at my heart, confusing my thoughts further. Why can't I do the right thing and just let him go? 'Give me two weeks,' I say.

Our food arrives and we eat in silence.

When we leave the pub and head back to the pier, Rob grabs my hand. I don't resist, even though I know I'm giving him the wrong message.

On the drive back home, Em wants the lowdown on me and Rob. I tell her the gist of our conversations, but her lips stay pursed, eyes narrowed as if troubled by what she hears.

'I think you already know if there's a future or not,' she says flatly. 'Why don't you just tell him? Don't you think he's been through enough?'

I feel a sudden pang as it's clear she sympathises with Rob. Ironic really, given it's the first time in a long while she has championed relationship rights from the male perspective. She's right, though, but my head's a mess. I don't want to decide anything, at least not until I've spent some more time with Marj.

On the plus side, Em had a fantastic time with Anton, and they've agreed to see each other again. She's beaming as she tells me about their time together, and I sense she really is smitten with him. It's a side to Em that rarely comes out. My Em, the errant party girl, now looking for a wholesome relationship. The irony is almost laughable.

We reach my place just after 6.00 pm and I'm exhausted, drained by the day's events.

'Oh, I almost forgot!' Em says, taking a slurp of tea. 'Ibiza!'

'What about it?' I ask, jolted.

'Well, remember how I said I'd come and visit you before you came back? I kind of put dibs on the villa, so it's free for a week at the end of the month. Why don't we go? We could use it as a "goodbye to the old ways" kind of holiday!'

'What? Are you *insane*?'

'Come on, Luce! We both need it! I mean, it looks like I might be getting into something with Anton, and you've got a decision to make about Rob, so why not? We can put the past behind us and see it as a new beginning!'

'No! I can't!'

'Why on earth not? Surely a bit of R&R will help at a time like this? It worked for you before!'

'It's complicated,' I reply, gobsmacked by her suggestion. And it is at that precise moment I realise why... *Brian*. I haven't told Em about what happened with him. In truth, I haven't really given him much thought, but I know that he's another loose end.

'Spill, Morris,' she says sternly, tossing me a quizzical glare.

'Okay, okay!' I raise my hands in surrender. 'So, you remember the guy I had a few liaisons with on holiday?'

'Brian?'

'Yes. Brian.'

'What about him?' Her eyes widen with expectation.

'We kind of hooked up again.'

'What? You had a thing with him?'

'No!' I protest, 'It was just, you know, casual.'

'You sly bitch!' she giggles. 'And?'

'Well, it was good for a while, but then he muddied the waters, so I put an end to it before I left.' It's a variation of the truth.

'How did he muddy the waters?' She asks, her jaw dropped lower than the Grand Canyon.

'He wanted more than I could handle.'

'Eh? And you didn't want that?'

'No, but—'

'But what?'

'I liked him. And not just because the sex was good. But it just got too messy, and he didn't know that I left.' I cringe, waiting for her to chastise.

'You did a runner? Lucy Morris, what are you like!' Her mouth curls as she belts out a laugh. 'But why would that stop you going back to Ibiza?'

'He owned the club I worked in. I don't want to risk running into him again. I'm dealing with enough shit as it is!' *Damn fine excuse.*

'Well, that's easily done. We just avoid the club!'

As easy as that?

'When are you proposing we go?' I say knowing I'm already defeated.

'Saturday 22nd October, for one week. That's when the villa's free. I'll book a week off work when I get in on Monday.'

'Fine.' I sigh. 'What have I got to lose?' *Except my sanity, my dignity and possibly my knickers.*

She giggles, and surprisingly, excitement tingles in my gut.

CHAPTER 44

'I've asked Rob to give me a few weeks,' I tell Marj as I sit across from her in our afternoon session. 'I'm going back to Ibiza with Em at the end of the month, so I really need to decide by then.'

'And what will help you make your decision?' she replies, pushing her glasses up her nose.

'I really don't know. Time's running out, and I know I can't keep him dangling for much longer. I owe him that much.'

'You mentioned you told Rob that you didn't know if you knew what love really was. Can you clarify that a little further for me?'

I draw in a long, deep breath, my speech prepared. 'I think my idea of love has always been tied to the notion of it being something mature, something that happens naturally when two people feel secure and settled with each other.'

'And did you feel secure and settled with Rob?'

The answer comes surprisingly quick. 'No. It was more like...' I scratch my head, searching for the right words. 'Fun.'

'In what way?'

'Well, when we were together, I didn't have to think about day-to-day stuff. I was in the moment with him, and he was attentive and passionate towards me. But I guess all relationships are like that at the start.'

'Is that what you believe?'

'Isn't that what everyone *wants* to believe?'

'Perhaps, but it's what you believe that's important here.'

She writes something down and gazes across at me, eyebrows furrowed.

'Lucy, you've talked before about how you've kept past relationships free from emotional ties. But it sounds as though there might've been more to your relationship with Rob than just fun and passion. Something that made you want to leave Joe for him even though you didn't feel secure and settled with him.'

My mouth gapes. 'I... I don't know,' I say. 'It was wrong, I know it was wrong, but I felt... safe.'

'How so?'

'Because I was in control, and it felt good.'

'To be back in control, or being with Rob?'

'Huh? I stare across at Marj as reality bites. 'Oh my G—' Was I in love with Rob, or just trying to break free from the emotional tethers I had to Joe? Was he really just an escape route? It feels like a fireworks display has gone off in my head as thoughts spark and explode in unison. *What the hell?*

'Lucy?' Marj says softly. 'You seem to be elsewhere.'

'Sorry. My head... it's spinning.'

Her eyes dart to the water jug, then she clasps her hands over her notepad as though signalling she'll wait.

Her cue registers and I pour myself a glass and guzzle it down, releasing a sigh as I finish. But I still can't focus. Can't reconcile the idea I might've used Rob to escape being tied to Joe; to loving Joe.

'Marj, do you think I loved either of them? Maybe I'm incapable of loving anyone.' My heart sinks.

'Only you can figure that out, Lucy. It boils down to your beliefs and expectations when it comes to relationships.'

'I'm not sure I understand.'

'Well, you said you feel your relationship with Rob was different from what you had with Joe, that with Rob it was "fun" and with Joe it was "mature". But is it that black and white? Could there be similarities between the two, and with most of the relationships you've had?'

'What similarities?'

'We've talked before about how, at first, you had fun and passion with Joe, but it changed when you realised he wanted a more intimate connection with you, something that could be described as "love". Perhaps you expect relationships to be fun and passionate but pull back when they become more emotionally involved because you feel your control is slipping. Does that sound right?'

'Yes,' I whisper, shuddering.

'And then what happens?'

'I find a way to get out of them,' I say, slumping in my seat.

'The question you need to ask yourself now is are you ready to explore a more mature, intimate connection, and is Rob the person you want to explore it with?'

Am I?

'I just don't know. With all the guilt I feel over Joe's death, and now this...'

'Ah yes... the guilt. Perhaps we need to explore that aspect more.'

'What's there to explore? I killed him. The End.'

'But from what we've just talked about, you were going to lose Joe one way or another. I'm wondering if by hanging on to the guilt, you're protecting yourself from the pain of losing him.'

'Protecting myself?'

'Could there be another reason why you're holding on to that guilt?'

'Because it was my fault he died!' I snap. *Where's she going with this?*

'Okay, let me put it another way. Sometimes when things happen to us that are painful, we subconsciously try to protect ourselves from experiencing it again, creating a safety net, cloaking us whenever we feel threatened. Does that make sense?'

'Like a blanket to wrap ourselves up in so we don't have to feel cold?'

'Exactly. I'm wondering if guilt has become your blanket, preventing you from having to re-experience the loss you felt at Joe's passing.'

'But if the guilt is there because it should be, what then?' It feels like we're going around in circles again.

'You said that you and Joe were fighting because you were going to leave him for Rob. Had Joe survived, would you still feel guilty?'

'Probably... yes. I never meant to hurt him.' The mass in my gut bubbles, reminding me of its continued existence.

'But either way, you were going to lose Joe?'

'I guess so.'

'So, prior to fighting with him, you'd already decided to leave him?'

'Yes.' My frustration builds and I fidget in the seat. *What is she getting at?*

'Would it be fair to say that you considered the feelings that would arise for you both as a result of separating?'

'I suppose so. Deep down, I suspected Joe and I weren't going to last, and I knew it'd hurt him deeply.'

'You felt *guilty*?'

'Yes, I felt guilty.' And the lightbulb finally switches on.

'So even before telling Joe you were leaving him, you felt guilty because you knew what you had done and what was about to happen.'

'Yes,' I say, my voice hushed. 'Even if he hadn't died, I guess I would still feel guilty.'

'And what purpose did that guilt serve?'

I stare at her through narrowed eyes, and then it hits me. 'I would have to take responsibility for hurting him.'

She nods. 'Exactly! When we blame ourselves for something we have done, guilt can be our way of acknowledging our actions and taking responsibility for them.' She straightens, preparing for the next onslaught. 'You were leaving Joe and you realised it would hurt him, so felt guilty about it, and acceptance of that guilt could be seen as taking responsibility for your actions. Did it ever cross your mind to change your decision and stay with Joe?'

'No,' and that truth hurts. No matter how many times I try to make sense of what happened, the truth is, no matter what, I would've left Joe. Our marriage was decaying like a fallen leaf and if I didn't care, I wouldn't have felt so guilty about wanting to leave him.

'It sounds like you considered the impact of your actions and took responsibility for them, but it wasn't enough to prevent what was inevitable in your mind.'

'I see. The guilt was justified.'

'Is that how it feels?'

'I suppose so. I always knew that one day I would hurt him, even though I didn't mean to.'

'Once we accept responsibility for something, we give ourselves the opportunity to move on from it,' she says. 'Can you allow yourself to move on from it now, Lucy?'

'Maybe.' I draw in a deep breath to help fully absorb what has just been said.

After several minutes have passed, Marj asks, 'Lucy, do you feel ready to explore the other strand of guilt, the one where you blame yourself for Joe's death?'

Her question knocks the wind out of my sails, and I gasp, anticipating the fallout. *Am I ready for this?*

'Uh-huh,' I say, mumbling.

'What role do you think guilt plays for you regarding Joe's death?'

'I... I—' and I can't get the words out. My mind races, and I tremble as coherent thoughts evade me.

Marj gives me a reassuring smile. I think she realises this one is the biggy; the major cause of my ills for the past few years.

Finally, words form. 'It reminds me that I'm responsible for Joe's death.'

'You feel responsible for Joe's death?'

'You know I do!'

'Going back to when you accepted that through the choices *you* made, guilt made you take responsibility for them, I'm wondering if the same applies to the choices Joe made on the night of his death.'

'What has that got to do with it?' I stiffen, fists clenching.

'Well, you told me previously you and Joe argued when he found out about the affair with Rob. What happened in between the argument and Joe dying?'

'He stormed out. Went off on his motorbike.'

'Was it your decision for him to do that?'

'No, but it's what he always did when we argued. He said it helped him calm down and clear his head.'

'So on that night, he did what he always did when you fought?'

I nod. 'I suppose so. But that night, it was the worst argument we'd ever had. I tried to stop him, but he was so fired up and he—' I turn away from Marj so she can't see the tears welling and bury my face in my hands.

Marj gives me time to release my pain, eventually pushing over the tissues.

'Lucy, do you want to continue?' she says in a hushed voice.

I turn back to face her and muster a nod between heaves. 'I tried to reach him. I really did, but he told me to fuck off. Those were his last words to me. He slapped me, and I got so mad that I just wanted to kill him, but... but I didn't mean for it to really happen!' I wail, covering my eyes again as the truth gushes out. 'I need to go to the bathroom,' I mutter, bolting for the door.

I reach the bathroom just in time, slumping down in front of the toilet as the mass in my gut erupts and spews out. On and on it goes until there is nothing left but dry retches and stale breath. I rip off toilet tissue and crawl to the sink to clean myself up, every inch of me quaking. My eyes are puffy, my cheeks ruddy from the stain of tears, my soul shattered. *I'm sorry, Joe, I am so sorry.* The words cycle in my mind as tears threaten again.

Once I've gained some semblance of composure, I make my way back to the therapy room and sit back down in a heavy heap, head bowed.

'Are you okay?' Marj asks as she leans towards me.

'I'm sorry... '

'It's okay, Lucy. Take your time.'

'I just can't forgive myself.' I close my eyes.

'Lucy, I really feel like we are getting somewhere with this, but unfortunately we are out of time for today.' She pauses for a moment. 'How would you feel about coming to see me next week?'

'Okay,' I nod, dabbing my eyes with yet another tissue, then fumble in my bag to find my purse.

'Please call me if you're really struggling,' she says as I hand the cash over.

After paying, we say our goodbyes and I head out to my car, once again feeling numb and *empty*.

CHAPTER 45

It's dark, damp and cold as I stand on my patio smoking my third cigarette in a row. Having barely slept, memories of the night before Joe died spin in my head, taunting me, wearing me down, giving no sign of an exit.

I stub out the cigarette and head back indoors. The numbness and emptiness I felt after Marj's session replaced by sobs spewing out erratically. I can barely focus on anything, and everything in my house—the sofa, the kettle, photos of Joe—stab at me, constant reminders that sap away any strength I might have had in reserve.

Sitting down at the kitchen table, I hold my head in my hands, trying to regain some sense of control over these wayward thoughts and emotions. It feels like the whole thing has just happened. I can hear Joe's raised voice in my head calling me every name under the sun as tears tumble over his ravaged cheeks. Chameleon-esque emotions surge through my body as our fighting intensifies. 'Get the fuck out!' I'm yelling, as the smite of his slap stings my cheek.

Why can't I shake this? But then it hits me with the force of a tornado: because it *is* my fault. He needed to get away from me. He needed to distance himself from me to deal with the fallout of what I'd done to him. I'd forced his hand.

But Marj's voice resounds, challenging me, speaking of choices. I was furious after he'd slapped me, spitting like an angry cobra, but I didn't really want him to go, did I? I knew, just like I knew all those other times when we fought, he would need to deal with it somehow. He did what he always did and went out on his bike. It *was* his choice, only, I'd forced him into it. I'd had an affair, and I'd told him to get out. Christ, I even felt like I wanted to kill him in that moment, but only because he slapped me. The reality bites that I was always going to hurt Joe, but the guilt, is it genuine?

Thudding on the front door wakes me from an impromptu slumber, and when I open it, Em is on the doorstep, bottle of wine in hand.

'Em? What are you doing here?'

She thrusts the wine into my hand and barges past.

'Have you switched your phone off? I texted you ages ago to ask if I could come over. We need to get our flights booked.'

'Oh… I think my phone might still be upstairs. Sorry.'

'Have you been asleep?'

She studies my face.

You look rough. You okay?'

'Yeah.' I say, feigning a smile.

'Luce. What's up?'

'Nothing. I'm fine.'

'You don't look fine. Has something happened? Is it Rob?' Her face crunches into a frown.

'Rough session with Marj yesterday,' I say, hoping to put her concern to bed.

'Oh… Do you wanna talk about it?'

'Not really.'

'Well, if you're sure.'

She eyes me up and down.

'Have you eaten?'

'Not yet. Have you?'

'No, and I'm starving. Shall we call for take-out?'

I nod and make my way into the kitchen to find some take-out menus, wiping my face and running my hand through dishevelled hair.

We settle on Chinese and Em phones through our order, then searches through my kitchen cupboards for some clean wine glasses.

We sit at the kitchen table with full glasses of red wine in our hands. I'm not sure if drinking is a good idea, but glug it anyway, twiddling the stem.

Em stares at me, eyes narrowed.

'Luce, you look shocking. I'm worried about you.'

'I'm fine, really,' I lie.

'No, you're not. I can see you're not. Is it Rob? Has he been in contact again?'

'No. I told you, bad session with Marj.'

'I thought all this counselling malarkey was supposed to help! Clearly, it's not!' she says, scoffing.

'Em, I can't deal with this right now. It's just been a bad day, that's all.'

'I wish you'd talk to me about it, Luce. I want to help.'

'I know you do, but there's just some stuff you can't help with,' I sigh, touched by her concern, but eager to move on from it.

'Like what?'

She's really pushing me now.

'Like coming to terms with the fact that I killed Joe!'

'Luce, how many times do you have to hear it? YOU DIDN'T KILL JOE! He had an accident!' Her voice is shrill, tinging on angry.

'Because of me!'

She shakes her head. 'For Christ's sake, Lucy! I've lost count of the number of times you'd called me after Joe had pissed off on his bike because you two'd had a fight! And it wasn't the first time you'd told him you were going to leave, either!'

I glare at her, mouth agape. She doesn't stop.

'Remember that time you'd had a big bust-up because he'd accused you of seeing that work mate who'd sent you a get well card when you had tonsillitis! He went ballistic, and you didn't speak to each other for days. Joe wasn't exactly Mr Forgiveness, was he? But he was definitely Mr Jealous-freak!'

'But he didn't DIE before!' I shout back, my thinking skewed and irrational like that of a child.

'No, but judging by how he'd reacted in the past, he was lucky nothing had happened to him before. You had no control over what happened after he left. A fucking truck hit him! You didn't make that happen!'

Em takes a deep breath and lowers her voice.

'Please Luce, for your sake, and mine, you need to put this into perspective. In all the times he'd stormed off before, this was the unfortunate one when something *did* happen.'

I glare at Em, stunned into silence. Is there any truth in what she's saying? Joe *had* always stormed off on his bike when we'd had fights, and every time my attempts to stop him were futile.

Em gets up and goes to answer a knock at the door. She comes back a few moments later carrying our take-away food. I don't say anything, running on autopilot as she pulls out plates and cutlery.

We eat in silence. Em occasionally glances over, smiling feebly as if to reassure me. Only, I don't know what I feel right now. I've spent so long blaming myself that acknowledging the fault may not be entirely mine is not registering.

We finish eating and Em suggests we get on and book the flights. I clear the boxes away and head to the living room to find my laptop.

'I'm sorry, Luce.' Em's tone is sullen, her eyes lowered.

'Don't be. I needed to hear it,' I say, wiping stray tears from my cheeks. She strides over, flinging her arms around me and weeping into my shoulder. The tears spill out from me too, and we hug each other tightly, taking refuge in each other.

Em eventually pulls away and looks me square in the eye.

'Luce, can I ask you something?'

'Anything,' I reply with a sniffle.

'Well you know I really like Anton, it's just... well, I'm scared.'

'Scared? Of what?'

'The whole commitment thing, I guess. I just don't know if I'm ready for it. It's kinda new territory.' She frowns, eyes darting as if searching for the answer to a question she daren't ask. 'Do you think I'm ready?'

'You're asking me? The person who wouldn't know how to commit if it smacked her in the face!'

'You committed to Joe.'

'And look where that got me!' I grab her hand, shaking my head. 'Only you know if you're ready, and only you know if there's something holding you back.' Oh, the irony.

She twists her hair with her free hand as if contemplating.

'Is there something holding you back?' And the penny drops. 'Damian.'

She nods.

'Em, what really happened?'

She takes a deep breath as if preparing herself. 'You know some of it now. He was a bully, but there's more.' She looks away.

'Em?' Fear engulfs me.

She turns back and lowers her eyes, pulling back her hand.

'He took me to places... clubs. The kinds of places where women serve the men. Where anything goes...'

I gasp.

'I let him do it. I let him let other men use me.'

'My God! Em!' I cover her hands with mine.

'Luce, there's more. I... I got pregnant and... and Damian was furious. He made me—'

'What Em?' Sickness bubbles, anticipating what she might say next.

'I had an abortion.' Em heaves as sobs pour out. 'I killed the baby, Lucy. I killed it.'

I wrap my arms around her, tears tumbling down my cheeks as she buries her face into my shoulder and cries like I've never heard her cry before.

My Em—my beautiful, strong, independent best friend—crumples before me, and in that moment, I realise we have both been wrapping ourselves tightly in blankets.

I hold on to her tightly, acknowledging the common ground we have both trodden is also part of our glue. That somehow, we have and will always be each other's safety nets.

'Em, I'm so sorry. I'm sorry that I wasn't there for you when you needed me.'

She looks up at me through glistening lashes.

'I couldn't tell anyone. I felt so ashamed.'

'I know how that feels,' I say, proffering a sympathetic smile. 'But you've told me now, and I've told you. We are here for each other now, and that's all that matters.'

'It feels good to let it out,' she says sitting up and wiping her face.

I nod, sharing the feeling, stroking her face. 'Fancy some more wine?'

She nods and follows me to the cupboard where more bottles are stashed.

We spend the rest of the evening working through our shared grief until we are empty, then set about sorting flights; a welcome distraction for both of us.

Excitement builds as we go through the process. Memories of Ibiza drift back and I realise I'm looking forward to going back, like I've been ignoring its homing beacon for far too long.

CHAPTER 46

Brushing imaginary sand from the top of Joe's headstone, I then trace my finger across the words:

'Joseph Adrian Morris

Born 12th March 1975 Died 16th May 2009

Beloved son, adored husband

Forever in our hearts'

I am numb, as though reading them has removed all traces of life from me and I can't articulate what I know I need to say.

A chilling breeze wafts through the cemetery and I pull my scarf tightly around my neck, even though it's not the wind making me feel cold.

'Joe—' But I stumble on the words.

Shaking my head, I try to rid myself of the greyness filling every fibre of my being. Why is this so damn hard? Why can I not pour out how sorry I am for everything that happened, how I still hold dear the good times we spent together, and how, in a strange way, I still miss him?

I walk around the graveyard to clear my head. Row upon row of headstones old and new, some neat and with freshly laid bouquets of flowers and posies, others withered and crumbling, neglected, just as Joe's has been by me for several years.

'We're sorry for your loss.' Words spoken in kindness and from shared grief. Sympathetic smiles and warm embraces. The thoughts hang heavy.

I pause at a nearby bench as decrepit as some of those graves and sit, pulling a cigarette packet from my pocket, but an elderly man tending a nearby grave glares across at me. I put them away, shamed.

He carries on tidying the plot as I watch, resting against a spade when he's done. I can't help staring. Is he the husband? Does he come here week after week to keep the memory of his lost love alive? Without warning, he wipes his face from what I imagine are tears tumbling down his cheeks.

My heart cracks open for him, for the grief he is reliving day by day, and stray tears prick the corners of my eyes.

I know what I have to do now and make my way back to Joe's grave.

Later that day, I set about sorting through Joe's belongings: clothes still hanging in his side of the wardrobe and in the tallboy, boxes with CD's and DVD's, papers, mementoes, and his beloved collection of cameras old and new. I stick coloured dots across furniture, knick-knacks, electronics and appliances I know were his, and finally, go to the garage and pull the cover from his project bike. By early evening, Joe's life is boxed and bagged, ready to be carted to Op Shops and recycle centres. All that remains are photos and things I brought into the relationship.

I flick through albums, scanning all the ones with him in, and search thumb drives, carefully selecting photos and moving them to an 'Archive' folder. The only picture I keep on display is one of Joe and I on our wedding day. A happy photo of a day promising a good life. A memory I will now hold and be thankful for.

CHAPTER 47

The weekend has flown by and I am feeling lighter, as though the shell I was wearing has been prised open to reveal healing skin.

Yesterday, Em and I went shopping in the city to buy last-minute holiday essentials. I've pushed all thoughts of Joe and Rob to the back of my mind as I once again find myself caught up in the excitement of going to my second home—Ibiza.

Em and I are at our favourite pub by the river sitting indoors having a drink or two, making last-minute arrangements and chatting about what we'll do when we get there. Errant thoughts occasionally flit through my mind, but I dismiss them all, filing them in the 'to be addressed later' tray.

Em has been keeping Anton updated. She feels like they are getting serious, so much so she's going to visit him for a week after coming back from the holiday. It's refreshing to hear her talk this way, as though our deep and meaningful has removed the blockade preventing her from following her heart.

'Have you made a decision about Rob yet?' she asks unexpectedly.

'Err… no,' I say, knowing it's the truth.

'Time's running out, Luce. You said you'd let him know in a couple of weeks, and that was over a week ago. You can't keep him hanging.'

'I know. I know. I just haven't really thought about it, what with all the other stuff that's been going through my head. I'm going to talk to Marj about it on Tuesday. I'll call him after that.'

'You must have some inkling as to what you'll do,' she says.

I shake my head. 'Marj asked me to think about whether I was ready to be with Rob.'

'In what way?'

'If I can give him the kind of commitment he wants.'

'And do you think you can?'

'I really don't know.'

CHAPTER 48

Something feels different today, but I can't put my finger on what it is.

'So how have you been since I last saw you, Lucy?' Marj says, her mouth crinkled in a smile.

'I've been okay. Wednesday was rough, but things have been better since then.'

I tell her about Em's visit on Wednesday evening, about how she has helped reinforce the new perspective I need on the events leading up to Joe's death.

'I visited Joe's grave on Friday.'

'And how did it make you feel to go?'

'Anxious, I guess. I went to say sorry to him, but it took a while to get into the right headspace and find the right words.'

'What helped?'

'I saw an old man at a graveside and wondered if he was a grieving husband. I saw him cry and it affected me.'

'Affected you?'

'Yeah... I felt so sorry for him, for his loss. It made me realise how much I'd pushed away the people who cared enough about me to feel sorry for my loss.'

Marj smiles and nods.

'I've spent so long blaming myself, and you were right, I haven't really grieved. I haven't allowed myself to grieve. Maybe because I didn't feel like I deserved it.'

'And you feel differently now?'

'To a degree, yes. Don't get me wrong, I still feel responsible, but know there was more to it. I guess I just needed to tell Joe how sorry I was, and work at forgiving myself...'

'And how do you feel now?'

'Lighter, maybe? Like I said, I still feel partly responsible, I probably always will, but think I can accept that not everything that night was my fault.'

'It sounds like you have made some progress with reconciling your feelings around his death,' Marj says.

'Maybe. It's still early days, but the nightmares I was having about it all don't come as often.'

We both pause for thought, digesting the latest revelations in my book of life.

'There's still Rob to deal with, though. I haven't sorted out the situation with him yet.'

'Have you given any more thought as to what you'll say to him?' Marj asks.

'I'm stuck. I don't seem to be getting anywhere with that one.'

'Did you think about the question I left you with?'

'I did, briefly, when I was talking to Em on Sunday.'

'And did anything come to mind?'

'Not really. I just don't know what I want, but I can't keep him hanging either.'

'Perhaps you can consider what love means to you now. Take a few minutes to think about it.'

I do as Marj instructs, closing my eyes hoping some spark of enlightenment will come. *What does love mean to me?*

After a few moments, I open them and look across at her. 'Settling down, I guess. Being comfortable with someone and being content with day-to-day life.'

'You see it as something that is comfortable and offers contentment?'

'I think so.' But another thought springs to mind and I blurt it out. 'Providing I don't have to make too many sacrifices.'

'Sacrifices?'

'You know, changing too much of who you are to make the other person happy.'

'Do you think that as people grow older together there may be an element of change occurring anyway? Growth even?'

'Probably. It's just that sometimes you see people together and know they're not right for each other. One has sacrificed more than the other and ends up full of resentment.' The penny drops with a loud 'ping' as the words leave my lips. 'Like I did with Joe.'

Oh my God!

I've never said the words aloud, even though deep down it's how I felt.

'You felt you changed too much to please Joe?'

'Yes.' My voice is barely a whisper.

'And after a time, you realised you and Joe weren't right for each other?'

I nod. It pains me to acknowledge it, but I know I can no longer bury the truth.

'It's like I'd traded my freedom and all the things that made me tick for a life that became stale and... *boring*.' I gasp as the shock sets in.

'You felt your life with Joe had become stale and lacked the excitement you craved.'

'I guess I always knew I couldn't be what he wanted me to be, as much as I tried. It was just too big of an ask. I started to resent him, and I think he resented me for it towards the end.'

'And when Rob came along, you found someone who could give you the fun and excitement you felt you were missing?'

'Perhaps. We had fun together, and he seemed to accept me for me.'

'You mentioned before that your relationship with Joe started off as fun and exciting too, but soon became *boring*. What would it be like to settle down and do the day-to-day stuff with Rob, perhaps even sacrificing part of who you are to be with him?'

'I honestly don't know. I've spent so long dismissing any feelings I had for Rob because of Joe's death that I haven't even thought about what it would be like to have a full-blown relationship with him. Maybe he was just an escape route when things got steadily worse with Joe.'

'Lucy, do you feel Rob would expect you to change who you are?'

'I don't really know. I guess it would happen anyway, but from my experiences with Joe, I feel kind of exposed, like I could end up being fake again and get hurt.'

'Vulnerable, even?'

'Yes, vulnerable.'

'Lucy, it seems you have some questions to ask yourself.'

'Like what?'

'Well, for example, is what you feel for Rob enough to overcome any sacrifices and changes you'd have to make?'

'But I'm not a fortune-teller, so how can I figure that out?'

'By going on what you feel for him *now*. You decided to leave Joe for him. What was Rob offering that made the prospect worth the hurt and guilt of losing Joe? Is it still on offer, and is it enough?'

She's right. I need to think carefully about my feelings for Rob, for what I want in life to see if it's worth taking the risk and being vulnerable for.

'I will think about it,' I say, my head filled with more questions than answers.

'Our time's nearly up today, Lucy. Is there anything else you want to talk about before we finish?' she asks.

'I don't think so. I know what I need to do now.'

'Okay,' she says, smiling warmly and nodding.

'Umm... Marj, do you think I need to come and see you again?' I say with trepidation.

'That's entirely up to you, Lucy. I feel we've made real progress in these past few sessions, but only you can decide what you do next. If you do stop coming to see me, just know my door is always open if you want to come back at any time.'

'Thanks, Marj. I really appreciate what you've done for me.'

'You've done the work, Lucy. I've just been the paper for your pen,' she says, still smiling.

I reach for my bag to pay her the final amount.

We say our goodbyes, and as I leave, sadness seeps over me knowing I may not see her again. She has been a big help, and part of me doesn't want to cut her loose.

Driving home, I'm deep in thought sifting through my memories of Rob, looking for clues. Does he truly accept me as I am, or was what we had just a holiday fling? Does he want us to settle down and become a regular Mr and Mrs? And can I risk opening myself up to him?

CHAPTER 49

My suitcase is overflowing as I cram in last-minute essentials.

I've busied myself over the past few days making changes to the house: rearranging the remaining furniture, taking down pictures, and packing away knick-knacks I no longer like. My wedding photo sits above the fireplace, acting as the happy memory I need it to be. It takes my mind back to the day, a wonderful day for us both. Our faces brimming with excitement, expectation and love for each other. I *did* love him then. That picture proves it, and I loved him for a good while after, too. A fitting memory of the happier times we shared, in the days before expectations were unreachable and my stubbornness was impenetrable. Before our marriage fell apart.

I need a fresh start, and in some ways, changing the house we bought together is helping me get it. I'm able to have what I want where I want, and with no compromises. It's cathartic.

I've also spent a lot of time mulling over what I'll say to Rob. At Marj's suggestion, I've thought about what I value in life, what I want from it. I've questioned how I feel about him now. Does he expect more than I am willing to give?

Part of me will always be a party girl, someone who enjoys going out, drinking and dancing. I'm not yet ready to give that up. But I've realised what I want from any relationship is to be myself, and not have to worry about pleasing someone else all the time. Compromise will always be part of the equation, but my experience with Joe has taught me there is a line I am unwilling to cross. The one where my own enjoyment, values, and core being is sacrificed too much. Is that what maturing really is? I have a better sense of who I am and what makes me tick now, and maybe one day the idea of a relationship that goes beyond physical desire could blip on my radar.

Even though logic tells me I'm not to blame for the mechanics of Joe's death, guilt still lingers, and Rob may always be a stark reminder of all that happened. *Can I ever make peace with it?* The thoughts linger as I tug the zipper on my case shut and lug it downstairs.

I hover by the table staring at my phone, psyching myself for the call I'm dreading making. After many false starts, and with my pulse zooming, I give it one last shot and pick up the mobile and dial Rob's number.

'Lucy?' Rob says.

'Rob, hi,' I say through rasping breaths.

'How are you?' His voice is soft yet shaky, hesitant perhaps.

'I'm okay. You?' My hands tremble as I hold the phone to a now clammy ear.

'Truthfully, I've been better. These past few weeks have seemed like an eternity.'

'I'm really sorry. I... I just needed time. You understand, don't you?'

'I know, I know. It's just, well... I've been going out of my mind waiting for you to contact me. *Please*, put me out of my misery.'

I'm rendered dumbstruck. My heartbeat zooms as an adrenaline surge hits. But, as quickly as they gathered, the clouds disperse revealing a clearer path.

'I'm sorry, Rob. I just don't think it can work between us,' I say in a whisper, acutely aware of the pain I'm inflicting on him.

'But why?'

'I don't feel what you feel anymore, and I just can't see us together now. Too much has happened.' I gulp back the brevity of my words.

'But how would you know unless you gave it a go? Can't we just see where it leads? You might feel the same again,' he says, his voice faltering.

I mustn't waver. There is no happy comeback from this. 'I... I'm sorry. I just can't.'

'But Lucy, I love you. I never stopped loving you. Does that mean anything to you?'

'I know you do, and it does, but it's just not going to work. Being with you will always remind me of Joe and of what I did to him.'

He goes quiet. The phone crackles, an unbearable silence now hanging between us.

'I *am* sorry, Rob. I really wish it could be different, but truthfully, that's how I feel,' I say, wiping away stray tears.

I hear him sigh, then he hangs up, leaving me listening to the monotonous sound of the dial tone.

I feel so *guilty*, but rather than keep it buried deep inside, festering, I let it pour out, acknowledging my loss.

When my tears finally subside, I head outside for a much-needed cigarette.

CHAPTER 50

Em and I are sitting outside on the balcony of her parents' villa in Ibiza sipping wine and chatting.

Em has already phoned Anton to let him know we arrived safely. I eavesdropped on her conversation, smiling to myself at the mushy-ness of it all. She's really falling for him, and I can't help feeling a pang of envy for her newfound happiness.

We have decided to ease ourselves gently into the island way as Em is very much seeing it as saying goodbye to the old times only, I'm not sure if I'm fully signed up. The past few weeks have produced many epiphanies, least surprising being that I'm not yet ready to give up some of my old ways just yet.

Em lets out a huge yawn and tells me she's going to bed, but I'm not tired yet and feel like sitting here for a while longer soaking up the heady seaside smells and listening to the distant sounds of busy tourists drifting up from Santa Eulalia.

I follow her inside, say goodnight, grab a blanket and another glass of wine and head back outdoors. Many thoughts flit through my mind. Letting go of Rob, releasing some guilt, and being back here. It feels like I've been on a mammoth journey, and I'm exhausted by it all. But this is a fresh start. I've spent the past few years hiding and know my previous visits here have very much been about escaping; running away from emotions I couldn't face. This time feels different.

I feel like I'm home.

CHAPTER 51

Em and I are drinking Sangrias outside a beach shack, warming up for the rest of the evening. We've really taken it steady so far with last night being the first time we ventured out to Ibiza Town to go clubbing, careful to remain inconspicuous. As usual, we attracted plenty of attention, but Em no longer wants to end up in some random guy's bed, even if the sex is good. It's remarkable to see Em turn down a gorgeous guy in favour of dancing with yours truly!

I, on the other hand, am yearning for more. As each day goes by my gut is telling me something is not right, that something is still missing or unresolved.

Em interrupts my thoughts. 'So Anton tells me that Rob is having a tough time of it.'

She stares into me, her face brimming with expectation. I have barely spoken of the phone call since it happened.

'I guessed he might be.'

'Luce, why couldn't you give it a go with him? There was definitely something between you.'

Sighing, I resign to telling her the truth. 'He wasn't enough.'

'What do you mean?'

'What I felt for him wasn't enough for me to get involved with him again. He was a constant reminder of Joe's death, of the guilt I

298

felt... still feel.'

'And you couldn't get past that?'

I look her square in the eyes. 'No. I couldn't.'

'You know you've hurt him, right?'

'I know. I wish I hadn't, but it couldn't be helped,' I say, my voice hushed as sadness twinges.

'So, what is enough, Luce?'

'That I don't know.' My cheeks flush in anticipation for what I'm about to say. 'Maybe I need to stay here so I can find out.'

'What?' Her eyes widen. 'You can't be serious! I thought you were done with all that running away stuff!' she says, barking her displeasure.

'I am. But there's something about this place... I like it here. It suits me.'

She's lost for words.

Unperturbed, I break the silence. 'I thought we could go to the club I worked at tonight. I wouldn't mind catching up with some people there.'

She shakes her head and sighs.

Later that evening, Em and I venture out and I finally convince her to go to the club I previously worked at.

As we enter, I can see it's not as busy as it was during the summer season, but there's still a pumping beat coming from the dance floor and a buzz of people milling around.

Tara is behind the bar and squeals when she sees us.

'Lucy!' she says, a beaming smile on her face. And I realise I've missed her.

'How're you doing?' I ask as we hug awkwardly across the bar top.

'Good, good. So, what brings you back? Are you coming back to work?'

'We're on holiday again,' I say, tilting my head towards Em, and lower my voice. 'I'm not sure if I'm staying yet. We'll have to see.'

'Well, the room's still free if you need it.'

'Does Juan have enough staff?'

'Not at the moment,' Tara replies. Roca's reopened, so the staff we temporarily had have gone back there. We're two people down.'

Em seems to guess what we're talking about and scrunches her face.

'Why don't you have a word with Juan? He's not in tonight, but he'll be here on Thursday night if you're still around,' Tara continues.

'I'll think about it.' I wink and toss her a grin.

Tara leans over the bar, beckoning me closer.

'Brian was spitting feathers when he found out you'd gone.' She whispers loudly, raising her eyebrows.

'What's that got to do with me?' I say, pulling away far too quickly.

'Do you want a drink?' I say, turning to Em to avoid Tara seeing my ruby-red cheeks.

'Sure. G&T please.'

She's glum even though I haven't decided anything yet. Déjà vu. We still drink and dance the night away, though, like two best friends content in each other's company. Earlier grumpiness forgotten, but a lingering thought mulling around in my head.

CHAPTER 52

The autumnal nip in the air seeps through to my bones, and I shiver as I sit and ponder on the concrete step in front of the Ermita de 'Sa Creu d'en Ribes'. The pines waft in the breeze as if to welcome me back, and I feel at peace being amongst these familiar friends.

Em was still fast asleep when I left the villa at sunrise affording me the chance to mull a few things over in my mind in my adopted Ibizan thinking spot.

Going to the bar and seeing Tara has stirred something within me. An ache for the release I felt living in this bohemian place where no one really knows me, or cares.

It's as though every fibre of my being can reach out and mould with these surrounds, as if this place wants me to become a part of its chameleon-like landscape. But my mind whirrs with uncomfortable truths like *you're just wanting to run away again,* and, *you haven't finished what you started.* As much as I want to ignore them, I know there is still much to do on my journey where guilt and grief have twisted paths. And yet, being here now offers the opportunity for gentle steps, the hard ones having already been trod. But what about Em? What about my life back in Norwich? Can I just walk away indefinitely and start afresh here even though there are still loose strings on both sides?

A gust of wind rustles the branches of a nearby carob tree standing solitary and proud in amongst the pines. A gnarled brown pod slips from a branch and, transfixed, I watch it whirl and twist as it drops to the ground, abandoned to the air currents as if trusting it will fall exactly where it needs to, where it's supposed to.

And just as before, it's as though the question I daren't articulate has been answered. It is time to give myself up to this place and see where it helps me land.

I belong here.

Em is up and about when I return to the villa, having spent several hours mulling over my decision.

'Where'd you go?' she asks as we sit outside with our morning coffees.

'Just for a walk up the hill,' I say, not ready to tell her where my head's at.

She wrinkles her nose. 'You wouldn't catch me willingly walking up hills,' she says, tucking into a bowl of muesli. 'I get enough exercise dancing.'

She tosses me a wink.

These moments spent together are more precious now, more poignant. The past few years of my life seem to be coming full circle and I'm so thankful to have had Em at my side through it all. But what happens now?

CHAPTER 53

Em and I are almost ready to go out. We've partied hard over the past few days, but Em has been bugging me constantly to find out if I'm going to stay or not. Today is the day I've resolved to find out and finally tell her.

We head off into town. Our plan is to get something to eat then go to one of the beachfront bars for a few hours, followed by a taxi to the club. I've got butterflies performing backflips in my stomach in anticipation of what I'm going to do tonight and how I'll tell Em, all riding on if I can get my job back.

As we're sitting in a seafood bar munching on some calamari, Em pipes up.

'So, have you decided what you're doing yet?'

This is it. I nod my head.

'So?' Her tone is low, almost demanding.

'I'm going to see Juan tonight to see if I can get my job back,' I say, my nerves fluttering into life.

'So, you're staying,' she says frowning.

I reach across the table and clasp her hand. 'You know that I love you and I will miss you dearly, but I *have* to do this. I *want* to do this. This place... it took me in when I needed it and made me feel alive again. It feels like home,' I tell her, hoping she'll be convinced enough to be happy for me.

'But what about home? Your house, your family, me?' she says, wistful and teary eyed.

'I know, but for the first time in ages I feel like I know what I want... and it's being here for however long I want it.' I squeeze her hand and try to give her a reassuring smile, but it's not working. She starts to cry. 'Besides, you and Anton might have a future together, so I won't be as big a part of your life anymore.'

'You'll always be a big part of my life. You're my best friend, and I love you too,' she says.

She turns her head away from me. I well up too.

'Look at it this way, you'll have an excuse to keep coming here for a holiday to visit me. Besides, I might not even be able to get my job back.' I get up and stride over, hugging her tightly.

'You're right, I suppose. We are both doing what we need to do. I just wish you didn't have to be so far away.'

I squeeze her, not wanting to let her go as we both cry. 'But it hasn't happened yet, and it shouldn't stop us from enjoying the rest of this holiday.'

'I know,' she says, pulling away and wiping her face with a napkin. 'And if my inner party girl ever needs to come out to play again, I guess I can come here.'

I giggle at the thought.

We finish eating and make our way through Santa Eulalia's bustling main strip to a bar for some drinks. I tell Em I want to go to the club just after 9.00 pm to see Juan.

Her expression hardens. 'Luce, I'm gonna go back to the villa after we've finished here so I can phone Anton before it gets late. I'm tired and could do with an early night.'

Words I never thought would leave Em's lips. All this gooey romance stuff is really affecting her!

'Okay,' I say, downing a gin and tonic needing Dutch courage. Not just to prepare me for my chat with Juan, but also because there's something more I need to talk to Em about, something that's been lingering inside.

Em heads off to the bar to get more drinks, so I steal the chance to organise my thoughts. When she returns, I resolve to start slowly. 'Things are changing a bit, aren't they?'

'Guess so,' she says, taking a big swig of beer.

'I feel like we're both changing a heck of a lot, don't you?'

Her brow furrows. 'Where's this going?'

'It's just... well, it's something Marj touched upon in one of my sessions... and it's bugging me.'

'What is it?'

'We were talking about Rob. Why I slept with him even though I knew we needed to talk about the past and lay the cards on the table.'

'And what did Marj say?'

'She wondered if I used sex to avoid talking, I mean... really talking about my feelings. It struck a chord.'

'How'd do you mean?' Em's eyes narrow.

'I guess she was trying to help me see that I might be avoiding emotional intimacy by changing the situation to a physical act.'

Em's mouth circles and her jaw drops.

'Em?'

'I know,' she says, gasping. 'I think I've been doing the same thing.' She covers her mouth with her hands.

We stare at each other for several moments as if acknowledging each other's realisation.

'How did we get like that?'

'I dunno,' she says, dropping her hands and folding them across her chest, but then the lightbulb comes on. 'Damian,' she breathes. 'I only started seriously doing the one-nighters after Damian was out of the picture.'

I nod, recognising the point in history when our nights out took a more contrived turn. When they stopped being about dancing and fun and became about being the hunters in a game of cat and mouse, all the while feigning being the mouse. Control. It was all about control. 'It may have started then, but why did we carry it on for so long?'

'Maybe over time it became what we were comfortable with.'

'Perhaps, but it was reckless, stupid even.'

Em nods repeatedly, her hands now clasping her cheeks. 'Probably why it's taken me so damn long to find someone I want to have a relationship with.' She gulps down her drink as if to bury the distaste of it all.

It strikes me that Em had a good reason to keep her emotions buried. But what was my excuse? I followed Em's lead but must've chosen to carry it on. Habit seems to be the only reasonable answer. Joe, and Rob, broke through the barriers I had constructed, but only for a while. Where does that leave me now?

My head spins.

'Hey Luce, the way we were then isn't how we are now y'know,' Em says.

Her words pull me back.

'And I'm not going to keep beating myself up about what I used to be like. I need to stay hopeful about what's to come.'

'You're right,' I say after pondering over it. 'If we're both making fresh starts, there's no point in dwelling on the past. Onwards and upwards, I say.'

'I'll drink to that,' she says, clinking my glass with hers.

We drink and chat for a while longer before parting ways; me searching for a cab to take me to Ibiza Town, and Em heading back to the villa.

The taxi drops me on a street near the club, and as I make my way to the entrance, the butterflies begin their finale. *Why am I so nervous?*

As I enter the bar area, I spy Juan filling a shot glass from the optics and stride over to greet him, calling his name as I approach.

'Lucy!' he says, turning and grinning from ear to ear. 'It is nice to see you again.'

'You too, Juan,' I reply. 'Has Tara told you I might be interested in coming back?'

'Yes, yes. Come down to my office and we can talk about it.'

He finishes serving a customer then walks to the side of the bar, opens the hatch and beckons me through.

A buzz sparks through me as I walk the familiar path to his office, plonking myself in the seat at the desk opposite his.

'So how have you been?' he says, rifling through a stack of unkempt papers, searching for something.

'Good,' I reply, nodding and smiling. 'You?'

'Oh, much better now that rubbish with the other club has been sorted out. Brian has been, *how you say it...* a pain in arse, but better now.'

'That's good to hear,' I say, my pulse quickening as he pulls out a form. 'Do you think it might be possible for me to come back?'

'Yes, of course. We need more staff right now and I know you do a good job.'

He pushes the form over to me, the same one I filled in what seemed like an age ago.

'That's so great. Thank you,' I say, sighing with relief. 'Do you want to interview me again?'

'No, we don't need to do that. I just need you to fill out the form again and tell me when you can start,' he says, winking, clearly delighted we're both on the same page.

'I fly back to England on Saturday and will need to sort a few things out again, but maybe in a few weeks? Would that be okay?'

'Yes, fine. I'll put you down to start on the 14th November. Okay?'

'Absolutely! I'll let you know if there's any change to that, but hopefully it's a done deal.' I struggle to contain the urge to squeal.

'Gracias, Lucy. And welcome back!' he says, beaming.

'Thanks, Juan. I'll let you get on.' I lean forward to hug him, and I'm giddy with excitement as I prance up the stairs and out towards the bar, hoping to see Tara to tell her I'll take the room again.

With a massive idiotic grin, I walk towards the side hatch to let myself out, but as I close the hatch and turn around towards the main bar area, I'm stopped dead in my tracks. Brian, looking as sexy as ever, is standing a few metres away with a leggy brunette in close proximity. I gasp involuntarily as I spy his hand pressed lightly into her back. *Shit!* Panic grips and I bolt for the door, head down, praying he hasn't spotted me.

Once outside, I gasp to fill my lungs, realising I've been holding my breath since fleeing. Searching around for a taxi, I stand at the roadside, panting, my mind whirling with erratic and unwanted thoughts. And Sod's Law says the minute you really need a taxi there are none there, so I hurry towards the main promenade, hoping for better luck.

My pace quickens to a jog as the desire to flee strengthens, but just as I feel I'm at a safe distance a hand clamps my shoulder, jolting me to a halt. I scream and swivel around to see who has stopped me. Brian.

'Running away again, Lucy?' he says in a silky-smooth voice that electrifies my core.

'No!' I say, yelping, panic turning to anger. 'Get off me!' I thrust my hands against his chest to push him away.

'Oh no you don't,' he says, grabbing my wrists and pinning them against my sides.

'LET ME GO!'

'Not until you and I have had a little chat,' he says, his face and tone stern.

'About what?' I try to wriggle free, making no attempt to hide my annoyance.

'Your leaving. Us,' he says.

'There is no us! There never was.' I can't believe I'm hearing this. 'Besides, you seem to have a new playmate, so fuck off and leave me alone!'

'What? What the hell are you on about?'

'The girl in the club,' I reply, flatly.

'Kelly?' He smirks.

'If that's her name. She'll be wondering where you are, I'm sure.'

'She's the new manager at Roca. I was showing her the ropes. Not that it's any of your business.'

'Nothing you do is any of my business,' I say, hissing. 'Now leave me alone.'

Brian eases his grip around my wrists and titters. 'Are you *jealous*?'

'No! Why would I be jealous?' Deep down I know it's not really the truth.

'I don't know, Lucy. You tell me. You seem to be the one who's constantly running away from me!'

'I'M NOT RUNNING!' I yell, thrashing my hands and freeing my wrists.

'STOP!' he says, grabbing my wrists again. And like an obedient dog, I stop thrashing about and stand stock-still, glaring at him.

He lets out a huge sigh, releasing me, but before I can step away, his hands cup the sides of my head pulling me towards him. His lips, belying any sense of rage, lightly brush mine and a groan seeps out of him.

'Brian!' I protest, my lips pursed, wavering as I try to focus. But it's useless. His tongue infiltrates my mouth and I submit to the lust building rapidly within me.

Encircling his neck with my freed arms, I press myself into him, fuelled by his moans as our kiss deepens, desire leaping within me.

He pulls away, leaving me wobbly and panting, my arms still around his neck.

'Now that wasn't so bad, was it?' he says, brushing his lips against my nose.

No. No, it wasn't.

'Lucy, we really need to talk. Come to my place?' His tone is more commanding.

I nod, knowing it's needed.

'I need to make a call before we go,' he says, so I release him and step away to give him space. It is then I realise that, in all likelihood,

I'll end up in Brian's bed tonight and know I won't resist.

'Kelly? Yep, it's Brian. Listen, something's come up and I won't be able to finish showing you around tonight. Juan's in his office so tell him I said he could finish off in the club with you. Okay? ... Yep. I'll see you tomorrow evening. Bye.'

He puts his phone away and walks over to me, grabbing hold of my hand.

'Come on, let's get a taxi,' and well, there's one now waiting by the roadside!

We get in and buckle up as Brian instructs the driver. I've thrown caution to the wind yet again, knowing full well where this'll lead. Why do I keep doing this, and with *him*?

Once in the back of the taxi, Brian turns to me. 'So, where have you been for the past month or so?'

'I went home for my cousin's wedding,' I say, trying to give the impression his presence is not filling me with an overwhelming desire to jump his bones, although suspecting I'm failing miserably.

'I see. And are you back for good now?'

'That's none of your business.'

'Stop being such a bitch, will you?' he says, scolding.

I want to tell him to fuck off, but pause to think and digest, finally replying, 'Sorry. Yes, I'm back for good. At least, I will be in a few weeks.'

'Good,' he says smiling, leaning over to plant a kiss on my forehead.

We reach Brian's place and pull up outside. He pays the driver and we both get out and head up to the door. I quiver only, not out of fear as I follow him up the stairs. This place is so familiar it almost feels *welcoming*?

We enter the kitchen. Brian drops his keys down on the countertop, gets some wine and glasses out and pours us both a drink.

He hands me a glass and I look up at him, noticing how incredibly blue his eyes are. A tingle builds.

'Thanks,' I say taking a glug. 'Can we go out for a smoke?'

He nods, motioning me towards the patio doors in his bedroom. We both sit down at the table. I put my glass down and fumble around in my bag for my cigarettes and lighter, nerves rearing. Brian watches my every move.

As I light up and take a long drag, he says, 'Are you ready to talk to me now?'

'I guess so,' I reply, gazing out towards the skyline.

'You ran away from me. Why did you do that?'

'Because you broke our arrangement.'

'And how did I do that?' His voice stays constant.

'I told you I didn't want to get involved, and you seemed to change your mind about that.'

'Maybe I did, but you knew from the start that I wanted to get to know you.'

'But I told you I didn't do relationships!' Annoyance bubbles under my skin.

'And why is that, Lucy?'

'Because they get too... messy.'

'And that's a good enough reason not to have one?'

'Yes.' God, if he only knew how messy my relationships have been in the past.

'I see. So, it *was* just about the sex for you.'

'I suppose so.'

'Then I guess there's no reason to go any further.'

A pang jolts me. *What?*

These feelings are confusing the hell out of me. First jealousy and now... *what is this?*

'Wait, Brian... maybe not,' I say, not really sure of where I'm going with this, then shake my head. 'No. I should go.'

'Do you want to go, Lucy?'

His voice is molten. It sends a thrill right through me, permeating every inch of my already magnetised body. I stare at him, trying to figure out what I should do.

'I... I don't know.'

'I don't want you to go. I'd much rather you stay with me tonight. But—'

'But what?'

'But only if it's because you want to. Because you want to see where this goes and won't run again if it gets... heavy.'

'What do you mean?'

'I mean that I really do want to get to know you, Lucy, and I definitely want to fuck you, but it might result in us getting involved... emotionally.'

I can feel panic welling. My head tells me to bolt out of the door, but I don't. I just sit there, gawping at him.

I take another drag on my cigarette.

'You're shaking, Lucy. Are you okay?'

'I... I think so,' I say, not even convincing myself.

He stubs out his cigarette, stands up and holds out his hand. Without thinking, I take it and he pulls me close, wrapping firm arms around me so my face nestles into a lightly stubbled neck. My head is spinning. This is such new territory.

What am I doing? Why am I still here?

He pulls away and gazing down at me with eyes drowsy with lust, says those magic words. 'Come to bed with me?'

I nod, making not effort to resist, allowing Brian to lead me inside and towards the bedroom.

He switches on the side light, grabs a condom from his side table drawer and turns to me, clasping my hands and pulling me towards him.

His hands move up to my face as he leans down, planting soft kisses on my lips. There's a tenderness to his seduction, a warmth, a surety that tonight, we are more than just casual lovers. I willingly respond, opening my mouth so our tongues can entwine as warm hands drift from my face to the zip on the back of my dress. He pulls the zip down slowly, as though relishing every inch of the touch of my skin, moaning.

Urgency takes hold and I grab his trouser button, swiftly undoing, then tugging and pulling his shirt free. Our clothing quickly falls by the wayside, laboured breaths and widened pupils signalling our desire for each other.

I feel strangely self-conscious as Brian gazes down at me, raising a hand to caress my breast, but it dissipates as soon as deft fingers tug lightly at my nipple. He takes my hand and leads me over to the bed, lying first and pulling me slowly down on top of him.

I curl myself over him, circling his neck with my arms as I lean in to kiss his open mouth. His chest hair brushes delightfully against my breasts, his hands gently massaging up and down my back.

I gasp as his hand reaches around to my pubis and a lithe finger teases my now pulsating clitoris. His fingers circle me, causing my arousal to increase exponentially. His erection is hard against my buttocks, ready for me, as I am for him, and I throw myself against him as the delicious sensations take over, biting down on his shoulder, swaying in rhythm with his finger. *Oh God, this is heaven!*

'Lucy, I want you,' he says, rasping, and removes his finger from me. I shuffle backwards so he can put the condom on and lift myself up so he can position himself under me. Slowly sinking down onto him, I throw my head back and rock back and forth, moans freely seeping out. He falls backwards onto the bed, closing his eyes and absorbing the sensations, then drunkenly opens them and watches me writhe on top of him.

I can feel him pushing up into me, so match his rhythm as I move up and down him. With each slide his panting increases and I build up the speed, responding to the desire deep within my groin.

Brian's hands hold my hips, pushing them up and down in time. I'm close to coming.

'Lucy, you feel so good,' he groans, and the sound of his voice is enough to tip me over the edge. My orgasm explodes within me, and I stiffen, reaching out to greet it.

Brian's groans become louder and he comes, yelling out as he does so, and I collapse onto him.

We lie there for a while, catching our breaths, revelling in the sensations that have just swept through our bodies. How does he do that? How does he rip through my defences and ravage me in a way that is so damn irresistible?

Eventually, I clamber off him and roll onto the bed. He gets up and heads to the bathroom.

A few moments later and he's lying beside me in bed, smiling.

'I've missed you,' he says, leaning over to plant a kiss on my lips.

'It's the sex you've missed.'

'That and other things,' he says, smirking.

My eyelids feel heavy, and I snuggle up next to him, lying my head on chest. It's not long before I close my eyes and drift off.

CHAPTER 54 – AFTER SUNRISE

I pull the blanket more tightly around me as I sit on the balcony and have a smoke. The air is chilly. Even in this Mediterranean paradise, winter is on its way and the once azure-blue sea is a darker, a more intense shade of turquoise.

The events of last night replay in my head over and over. I'm again trying to make sense of what has happened, shaking my head at times when it all seems too hard to figure out.

A clattering inside interrupts my thoughts, then the patio door swings open, creaking as it does so.

'There you are.'

I turn in my seat. 'Yes,' I say, 'I didn't mean to wake you.' A tingle of nerves hit my belly.

Strong arms wrap around me from behind as Brian plants a kiss on the side of my neck.

'When I woke up and you weren't there, I thought you'd gone again,' his relief evident.

I turn, smiling up at him.

'What time did you get up?'

'Sunrise. I guess some habits are hard to break.'

'I guess they are. I'm going to get a coffee. Want one?'

'That'd be good. Thanks.' My nerves quell.

This might be all right after all.

'How do you have it?'

'Black, one sugar,' I say, smiling.

THE END

ACKNOWLEDGMENTS

A huge shout-out to my family and friends for all their support and love, without which I wouldn't have dared to pursue this writing lark.

I'd also like to acknowledge the Katharine Susannah Prichard (KSP) Writers' Centre in Greenmount, WA where I found my tribe, my passion, my purpose and my Yayas.

Author Bio

 Lisa is a mum, wife and author who heads up a publishing company in the Perth Hills, Western Australia.

She was previously co-director of Footprints Publishing and prior to that, ran Wild Weeds Press.

Lisa served on the Board of Management for the Katharine Susannah Prichard (KSP) Writers' Centre for five years, has facilitated a writing group there, and hosted several publishing-related workshops.

Lisa is drawn to penning stories about life and loss with a dash of love thrown in for good measure.

The Sunrise Girl is Lisa's debut contemporary women's fiction novel. *The Sunset Girl* telling Em's story, is still being written.

In 2020, Lisa released a contemporary fiction novella, The Wash, which is also available online through all major global book retailers.

Lisa's novelette, *For the Love of Dogs* was published in September 2021 by Gumnut Press. She also has stories in *Paw Prints of Love*, a romance anthology published by Gumnut Press in 2020, *Destination Romance* and *Passages* romance anthologies published by Serenity Press in 2018, and *When Love Breaks Down*, a novelette published by Serenity Press in 2019.

When not writing or loitering around the hills, Lisa enjoys reading, travelling, music and more wine than is good for her.

All Lisa's titles are available globally through all major online book retailers.

LISA
WOLSTENHOLME
writer
dreamer

Connect with Lisa at:

www.lisawolstenholme.com

Follow Lisa on:

Facebook: www.facebook.com/WolstenWriter

Instagram: www.instagram.com/lisa-writes

If you enjoyed reading *The Sunrise Girl*, please consider leaving an online review. Reviews help authors gain much-needed exposure.

Thank you for reading.